SOMEONE SPECIAL

EVA MOORE

Someone Special

A GIRLS' NIGHT OUT NOVEL
BOOK ONE

EVA MOORE

To Rachel—
Hope you had fun at #BLC19.
♡ Eva Moore

Cover design and Book Interior by Lee Hyat Designs

For my husband.
You bring laughter, adventure, and love into my life.
Thanks for being my someone special.

ONE

"THIS IS BETTER THAN CABLE!" remarked Mrs. Grady, from her habitual perch by the window. Dani looked up from the stove. Something good must be happening two stories below on their normally quiet street. Dani briefly turned her attention back to the bubbling pots on the stove. Confident that her three meals were coming along nicely, she tucked unruly curls behind her ear and turned from the kitchen to join her neighbor at the window.

Below, two very muscular men with shirts removed, in deference to the fierce sun and brutal heat weltering up from the pavement, were wrestling an ugly sofa in through the double front doors of the building. Their lean muscles and trim waists twisted and flexed with effort. Dani's face flushed with heat, a welcome change from her recent numbness.

"They can move my furniture anytime! Then again, I'm not sure my blood pressure could handle it!" Mrs. Grady cackled. Dani continued to observe the scene below. While the slick and straining bodies held her gaze, the implications flooded her thoughts.

"I bet they're moving in the new tenant across the hall from us." An empty ache spread through her chest as Dani was hit by the grief that she managed to keep just below the surface. "Well, across from me. It will be strange having someone else living there in my old place." Her throat tightened at the reminder that she was living alone in Helen's apartment now.

She returned to the kitchen, grasping for calm, trying to avoid sinking into her grief. She drained the pasta, mixed in the homemade marinara sauce along with some freshly grated Parmesan, and reduced the chicken soup to a simmer. At least managing to create three large meals at once required her attention. She spun too quickly and knocked a wooden spoon to the floor. With a huff of frustration, she threw the offending utensil into the sink.

"Are you OK, Sunny?"

"Yeah, sometimes it just hits me that she's gone. That she won't sit at your Wednesday night dinner again. That she won't ever tell another crazy story about her service or her travels. That no one will be there when I open the door. It's just hard." Dani's voice cracked and her shoulders drooped under the weight of her sadness.

"I know, sweetheart. I miss her too. She was my best friend." Dani let herself be bundled into a hug, even though it was a poor substitute for the hug she missed.

"Mine, too. Now that she's gone, I feel lost."

"That's normal, dear. After all, you practically gave up your life to take care of her these last six months."

"What did I give up? A lackluster career in accounting and a dead end social life down in Houston? You know as well as I do, I didn't belong there." Dani shook her head. "No. I gained so much more, moving up here to help out. I met all of you, and got to spend more time with Aunt Helen. And with how quickly her health failed...well, I wouldn't have wanted to be anywhere else."

The pancreatic cancer had snuck in under the radar, and when they found it, it was too late. It hit vicious and fast. She'd been home for Christmas when Aunt Helen broke the news. Now, it was June and she was alone again.

"I know she loved having you with her. You were the grandchild of her heart."

Her grandfather's sister, Aunt Helen, had never married. She had no children of her own, and had spoiled Dani and her sister like crazy as a result. Summer trips wherever Aunt Helen happened to be living that year, fantastic surprises from abroad, and boxes of massive navel oranges every New Year's were her trademarks. And her stories! Dani had vivid memories of curling up at the foot of her chair and listening to her tell stories of her time in the Navy in her irreverent and slightly salty way. Dani let the fond memories roll through her mind.

"Remember how pissed she was when Dad brought up the idea of a nursing home?"

"Oh my goodness! I thought she'd have a stroke then and there, and save us another trip back to the hospital. She was not a woman to tolerate limits on her independence."

That independent spirit was her trademark, and Dani hadn't been able to stomach the idea of Helen losing that. When she had refused chemo and radiation, and begun to look at hospice care, Dani had offered to move into the vacant apartment across the hall and help take care of her. The move set her family at ease, and Dani felt blessed that she could help her surrogate grandmother wring every last drop of joy from her remaining days. They had visited favorite haunts and dear friends until leaving the apartment had become too difficult. Hospice nurses had come to handle Aunt Helen's medical needs, and given Dani a few much-needed breaks. Just handling her personal care had become around the clock job near the end. So Dani had given up her month-to-month lease on the apartment across the hall and moved to Helen's couch. Given the moving crew downstairs, she assumed her old apartment wouldn't be empty anymore.

Aunt Helen was gone, and Dani was as lost as ever. Everything she owned was in boxes and shoved into corners. She was surrounded by the remnants of her aunt's life, and it was difficult to see how hers could share the space.

She'd always had trouble figuring out where she fit in. She'd been raised to believe she could be whatever she wanted. But what if she couldn't figure out what that was? She'd bumped along okay until now, but she hadn't really pursued anything with passion. After going to college in Houston, she'd accepted a job working as an accountant at a multi-national energy firm. It had been lucrative, but it hadn't been satisfying, and her asshole ex-boyfriend even less so. She'd been sprinting on the hamster wheel and going nowhere. She had zero desire to hop back on. Coming home hadn't been a hardship, but what now?

"Moving in was the best thing for both of us. She kept her freedom, and I gained my own. But now I have too much freedom. I have no job, no friends, and no idea what to do about any of it. And I've got all of her estate to handle...I keep losing hours at a time just holding an afghan she knit or rearranging the framed postcards from her travels." The tears she'd been fighting to hold back ran silently down her cheeks.

"It's a big job. Don't rush it. You've got a lot to deal with. Losing Helen was hard on us all. Just keep putting one foot in front of the other. Come to our dinners. Talk to your friends. Bake her favorite desserts. Share stories of her that make you laugh instead of cry. It will get easier with time."

The timer ding pulled Dani from her maudlin thoughts, and she bent to remove the shepherd's pie from the oven. She set it aside to cool and quickly packed everything else into the fridge. At least her neighbors would benefit from her lack of a plan.

Dani turned back from the fridge, wiping the tears of frustration and grief from her cheeks. She had to shake things up and move on with her life. It's what Aunt Helen had wanted, and she knew she had to live up to her end of the bargain. When Helen had agreed to let her come help, it was always with the understanding that when she was gone, Dani would take up the reins to her life and do something spectacular. *Now if I could just figure out what that is...*

"Well, Mrs. Grady, you're all set. You've got the shepherd's pie for Monday night, the spaghetti and meatballs for Wednesday, and chicken soup for Thursday. Make sure you nuke a vegetable to go with. I stocked your freezer today, so you should have plenty to choose from. Also, let Joe know that I left the fennel out of the soup this time, just for him. Tell everyone I said hi." She gathered her things and moved toward the door.

"Are you sure you won't join us, Sunny? I worry about you eating alone so much."

The use of her aunt's favorite nickname for her sparked a brief smile, but Dani shook her head. "I just...can't yet. Maybe next week." To be honest, she couldn't stand to see the sadness in her heart reflected back in the eyes of her aunt's friends. It was bad enough to feel it herself. "I'm going to go bake some cookies to welcome our new neighbor to the building. I'll extend an invite to your dinner party on Wednesday, if you'd like."

"The more, the merrier, I always say. And if he turns out to be a bachelor, send him over on Tuesday!" Still chuckling, Mrs. Grady closed the door behind her, and Dani waited to hear the bolt snick in the lock. She'd fallen into the habit of checking up on her neighbors when Aunt Helen had gotten too weak to do it herself. Making meals, listening for locks, dropping off mail, it didn't take long and helped a lot. Sometimes it felt like those were the only things she accomplished in a day.

"I really need to change that," she muttered.

Dani walked down the hallway, skirting past a pile of boxes left outside the door across the hall from hers. One of the moving men came out of the apartment for another load, and sent her an appreciative glance and smile. Dani ducked her head with a blush and quickly headed inside. Why hadn't she said hi? Why on Earth had she blushed? She had to get out more, preferably with a male of the species. Shaking her head over her reaction and the dismal prospect of that happening any time soon, she pushed aside her worries in the kitchen, baking her famous dark chocolate chunk cookies for her mystery neighbor.

"I DON'T KNOW how you managed it, man."

"Managed what?"

"You pick an apartment in what is practically an assisted living home, and end up with a bombshell across the hall. I got a place in the new high rise downtown, and my neighbor is the cat lady. Some guys have all the luck!" Seth plopped down on the couch that had just recently been shoved through the narrow doorway and into place. He stretched his arms up high over his head and groaned as his shoulders released their tension. "How many more trips do we have to make?"

"Two more trips with boxes, the TV, and then the mattresses," Nick replied. He slicked his sweat soaked hair back from his forehead and flopped on the couch next to his buddy. "Tell me more about the bombshell."

"5'7", blonde, stacked, but shy, ducked into the apartment across the way."

"Maybe she just isn't used to seeing bare chested men roaming the halls. Like you said, this building doesn't exactly cater to the younger crowd."

"I still don't know why you picked this place. There are openings in my building. We could've been kings."

"Now you get to be king all by yourself. You won't have to worry about any unfair competition from this quarter." Nick deflected his friend's concern into the competitive insults that defined their friendship.

"Unfair, my ass! You know you'd be hiding in my shadow," Seth replied, and it was on. Break time over, Nick and Seth heaved themselves up off the couch and headed back down to the truck for the last few loads. Carrying the conversation back out into the hallway, they continued hauling Nick's few possessions into his new place. Thankfully the apartment was small enough that it didn't feel empty with his lack of stuff. The small bedroom was now filled with a bed and dresser, and the living room/kitchen open space was just big enough for his hand-me-down couch and a kitchen table. Furniture shopping was not high on his to-do list.

"What does your mom think of your new place?"

"I could move into a dump, and she'd still be ecstatic that I came back home. Dad is already pressuring me to take over the business. That is much easier to accomplish with me close at hand. I think she wants to send my cousins over to renovate the place. Tile counter tops offend her. I keep reminding her it's just a rental."

"Are you going to do it?"

"What, get new counter tops?"

"No. Take over the business from your dad." Nick hefted a box up on his shoulder, wondering what it would feel like to have a family that cared as much as Seth's.

"Not right away. I want a little freedom first. I just got back and already they want me to jump right back into all that responsibility. No way. But eventually, yeah, that was always the plan, now that my days of 'seeing the world' are over."

"No one said you had to leave the sandbox."

"If I never see sand again, it'll be too soon."

"So instead you'll join your cousins in the general contracting business."

"They promised I could start helping with demolitions."

"That fits. You've always been good at breaking shit. Do they expect the house to still be standing when you're done?"

"Shut up. Have I broken anything today?"

"Not much to break."

The stacks of boxes and the few pieces of furniture Nick had kept barely filled the small truck they'd rented to move everything from his storage locker. After six years in the service, four of those deployed, first in Afghanistan and then in Iraq, Nick had left the Army when it came time to re-up. Years deployed hadn't left him much time to accumulate stuff. It made moving again pretty straightforward, if a little depressing.

Since Seth had gotten out at the same time and decided to move back closer to his family, Nick had opted to tag along. It wasn't like he had anyone waiting for him to come home. He wanted to be near his buddy, but he also recognized his need for some private space to decompress. He knew the signs, the symptoms. Lord knew he'd been coached in how to recognize it in his men. He wasn't fine, far from it, but with a little down time he could put things right. He'd been able to keep his military mask in place, so no one suspected anything. He wouldn't be able to keep it hidden from Seth if they were roommates though. So, when he had seen the opening in a smaller building a bit further from downtown, he jumped on it.

"So, what are you going to do?"

"I've earned a little R&R. I've got enough in the bank to give me a few months to fat ass and figure that out."

"Lucky bastard. Got anything in mind?"

"Nothing firm yet. A few hobbies. Anything that doesn't

involve PT at dawn or barking orders sounds good right about now."

"Well, if you get desperate I can get you on a construction crew, but early starts and barked orders come with the territory."

"Thanks. I'll think about it."

"Open offer. Just let me know. My dad would love to have a new face to harass."

"Yeah, it sounds great." Sarcasm dripped from his lips. "You just want someone else to be his whipping boy."

He was looking forward to having some peace and quiet for a while. He had enough saved to buy himself a month or two of freedom before jumping back into the working world. He vowed to use it wisely.

They brought the mattress and box spring up last, which were of course the hardest to get through the doors and into the apartment. Nick cursed as he caught his knuckle on the outer door. The apartment building, built in the late 70's, lacked charm, but it did boast a swimming pool and a functional elevator. He was also grateful it had an available rent-controlled veteran housing unit. With a few muttered curses and forceful shoves, it was done. He was officially moved in. Nick popped them each a celebratory beer before collapsing back on the couch.

"You're really gonna live all the way over here, all by yourself?" Seth asked.

"Dude, let it go." Nick's frustration colored his tone. "I know it's hard for you to believe, but I really do just want a little peace and quiet."

A firm knock on the door interrupted his statement, and he

grimaced. Really? People? Already? Probably someone complaining about the moving truck. Annoyed, he got up to answer the door, and swung it open before he realized he was still half dressed. His heart jumped to his throat, pulsing madly, choking any words of greeting that might've made their way out of his mouth. There stood the woman who had to be the bombshell, blond and brightly smiling. Her long, loose curls teased the face of an angel. Startling blue eyes, framed by long brown lashes looked at him curiously.

"Hi, I'm Dani Carmichael. I was looking for the new tenant. Is he or she here?"

Stunned by that smile, Nick didn't immediately reply. His fingers twitched with a barely contained desire to reach out and touch. His heart thudded thickly in his chest, and his mouth disengaged from his brain, leaving him mute and gaping.

"I'm sorry, I just assumed when I saw you moving the furniture in. Do you know when they'll be here?" Dani shifted, waiting for a response he couldn't quite muster. Now he knew the meaning of dumbstruck. He watched a blush creep up her neck, and she looked past him, clearly hoping to find someone capable of speech.

"Nope, he's here alright," chimed in Seth. He came forward to shake Dani's hand. "I'm Seth Valenti, and this is Nick. He'll be your new neighbor, so if you ever need any help with your pipes or pickle jars, feel free to call." Nick shoved him back and shot him a fulminating glare.

"Ignore him. He's an idiot most of the time, including right now."

"That's alright," Dani met his gaze again, and he just wanted to bask in her gaze. "*Are* you my new neighbor?"

He finally got his brain to sync up with his tongue.

"Yes, I'm Nick Gantry. Nice to meet you." He finally remembered his manners and stuck his hand out to reach for hers, when he noticed the plate she was carrying. "Are those for me?"

She pulled her gaze down over his bare torso on the way to the plate of cookies in question. Each pause made his pulse leap.

"What? Oh! Yes, I made you some cookies to welcome you to my apartment. Um, that is, your apartment. Which used to be mine. So." She handed him the plate quickly and shoved her hands in her pockets, and he couldn't help but notice the way it highlighted the generous curve of her chest beneath her thin t-shirt.

"The shower can be a little wonky. If you don't jiggle it right, you'll end up with a cold shower. If you need anything or have questions about the building, just knock on my door. I'm home most days now. We're a pretty close group of residents around here. Anyone would be glad to help if I'm not around." God, she was cute when she was flustered and rambling. If she kept talking and he kept staring much longer, he was going to need that shower to run cold. Maybe he should ask her to come in with him and demonstrate the jiggle. He struggled to follow the words coming out of her mouth while that image completely derailed his concentration. "Mrs. Grady in 212 wants to invite you to a dinner party she's throwing Wednesday night at six."

"Huh? What? A dinner party? She doesn't even know me?"

"She will after an hour at her table," Dani grinned, clearly knowing more about this Mrs. Grady than she was letting on.

Dammit, that was a killer smile. Nick found himself nodding and agreeing to go, while under the influence of that grin. It shouldn't be legal to ask questions wielding that kind of power. Here he'd been looking for a retreat, and he was already getting sucked out into the company of strangers. Dammit!

"Well, I'll let you get back to unpacking. It was nice to meet you Seth, Nick."

"Thanks for the cookies."

Dani turned and quickly walked back into her apartment, setting her blond curls bouncing. Nick couldn't look away, until she and that lethal smile of hers had made it all the way inside.

Seth commented from the couch, "Now I get it. You chose to live here to brush up your social skills before upgrading to a place like mine. That was tough to listen to, man. You didn't even invite her past the door."

"I didn't want her to have look at your mug any longer than necessary. And I thought your building was full of cat ladies..."

As Nick razzed his buddy mercilessly and washed down the cookies with beer, his mind couldn't fully focus on the conversation. Blond hair, blue eyes, and that genuine smile danced through his mind, and he wondered when he'd get to see them again.

TWO

MONDAY MORNING, dressed in one of her "accountant suits," as Aunt Helen had called them, Dani made her way downtown to see her aunt's lawyer. She walked through the doors of Daly, Robertson, & White and was immediately engulfed in grey and beige modern monotony. The somber décor matched her mood, but then a memory cracked her stony façade with a smile. Her aunt had walked the same corridor in her most outlandish outfits, chosen specifically to liven the place up.

"It's a public service. These poor folks have forgotten what color is." Aunt Helen did everything with a purpose, down to choosing what scarf to wear. Dani rethought her wardrobe choice with a wistful smile. She shifted the homemade coffee cake in her hands. She had her own way to brighten the day.

When she'd left Houston, Aunt Helen had managed to get her part time work for her law firm's accounting department, reasoning that a job was a must. But Aunt Helen's condition had deteriorated so quickly, she'd had to leave after only a few weeks. Thankfully, they had been Aunt Helen's attorneys for years, and had been more than flexible. Dani had agreed to be executor of her aunt's estate. It had come as no surprise that

Helen had left very specific instructions for how her possessions should be dispersed. She made her way to Michael Robertson's office, double checking the file under her arm and fidgeting with her purse strap. Why was she so nervous? When she entered his office area, a familiar face greeted her with a smile, the kind that offered comfort without pity, and Dani returned it, some of her anxiety fading. She handed the coffee cake to Olivia Stone, senior paralegal and former lunch buddy, who pulled her into a hug.

"Dani, how are you? No, scratch that. Stupid question. It's good to see you. Lunchtime isn't the same without you."

"We'll have to get together soon and compare notes. I've been trying a few new recipes."

"I'd love to taste them. Does he know you're here?"

"No, I just got here."

"I'll let him know. I wanted to say, Dani, your aunt was a special lady. She always made sure to stop and catch up with me, every time she came in."

"I don't imagine you'd be surprised at how many similar stories I heard at her wake." The number of people who had packed the small viewing room had surprised even Dani, each with a story of a small kindness gifted by Aunt Helen.

"Like I said, a very special lady. I'm so sorry for your loss."

"Thank you for sharing your memory of her."

Olivia turned and peeked through the door, half closed behind her.

"He's ready. You can go on in."

Mr. Robertson, the younger, was indeed ready, and rose from his chair to greet her with an outstretched hand as she passed through the door into his office. She crossed to the supple leather arm chair situated in front of an antique mahogany desk.

"Good morning, Ms. Carmichael. How are you?" His strained smile put Dani on alert.

"I'm fine. As well as can be expected." Dani wondered why he was nervous. He'd called this meeting after all.

"Would you like anything before we begin? Tea, coffee?" Was he stalling?

"No, thank you. I'd rather just get down to business. Now, I understand you wanted to check in with me about my progress with my aunt's estate?"

"Among other things..."

"Well, I've taken care of all the specific item bequests to her friends and our relatives. I've been in touch with her two chosen charities regarding the gifts she left them. The Silicon Valley Humane Society has chosen to set up a trust to help pay for the care of animals who cannot be adopted to keep them from being euthanized. They will also be putting a plaque on a special kennel for older dogs that will benefit. I told them I'd pass along the information to you so you can look over the proposal and see if they've missed anything. The public library will use the funds to add a half-circle padded bookshelf bench in the children's section with a plaque in her honor. They will use the balance to increase investments in children's literature, once you've released the funds. Libraries were her favorite place. After so many years running libraries on Naval bases at home and abroad, she got such a kick out of the read-alouds with the littles. So much more fun than reading to the sailors, she said." Memories of her own childhood mornings spent listening to her aunt tell stories made Dani heartsick again. She blinked back the tears that began to well, and paused to re-group her thoughts.

"I'm still sorting through her storage unit and deciding what to keep and what to liquidate or donate. I rented the locker across the way, and I'm sorting it into three piles as I move out the boxes and go through them. All the receipts should be in order in this file." She pulled out the folder she'd tucked into her purse and laid it precisely on his immaculate desk.

"That's fine, excellent, really. I'm impressed with your efficiency. Most of my clients take a bit more time to tackle some of the larger tasks. How are you holding up? Is it too much?"

"No, actually it's been good to have a project. After spending so much time helping Aunt Helen, my days are rather empty. Tackling her estate gives me a project to work on. Going through her personal things has been harder, more draining. If I get through one box in an afternoon it feels like a major accomplishment. So often I get caught up in the memories... I know she's in a better place, and not in any more pain. That's a blessing...but I can't help mourning the hole that's left in my life. How selfish is that!"

"Not selfish at all, I think. Normal perhaps, healthy certainly. You do need to mourn for your loss. Which leads me to my other reason for arranging this meeting today. The will that was read to you after your aunt's passing had another envelope which she specified should be delivered into your hands 30 days after her death. It is my understanding that she wished for you to have a bit of distance from that difficult event before she entrusted you with this next task. I'd best let her explain her wishes in her own words. I'll leave you to read it in private. I am happy to go over any details you'd like clarified when you're done. Just knock at the door, and Ms. Stone will find me." He handed her a greeting card envelope and quietly closed the door behind him.

Under her breath, Dani muttered, "Oh, Aunt Helen, what are you up to now?" Sliding her finger gently beneath the flap, she carefully opened the envelope and the first spontaneous smile in weeks bloomed across her face. A greeting card with a sexy, muscled, nearly naked man wearing a short apron and holding a birthday cake emerged. Across the bottom of the card, the caption read, "Happy birthday!" Opening the card, Dani felt a folded piece of stationery drop into her lap. Ignoring it for the moment, she read the punch line, "You can have your cake and eat me, too!" Dani chuckled, appreciating her aunt's sense of humor one more time. Helen had always managed to find the best cards. Refocusing her attention on her aunt's folded letter, she read the handwritten note, and the laughter mingled with the tears she let roll freely down her cheeks.

My Dearest Danielle,
I hope that made you laugh! I bet you could use one or two right now. You know I never miss a birthday. I thought I'd use this opportunity to give you the perfect card, which of course I found months ago and have been dying to show you ever since—pun completely intended.
Dear girl, I hope that taking care of my passing has not been too stressful for you. I love you, and I don't want you wasting anymore time taking care of the details of a life well lived instead of picking up your own life that's been on hold too long. You sacrificed for me and helped me spend the end of my life exactly how I wanted to. Now let me give you the best re-start to yours.
I know goals and deadlines inspire you so I'll give you one of each. As a goal, I'd like you to find your passion. Yes, you're a good accountant, but it's not your life's work. I found my passion in books and devoted my life to sharing them with others. It fulfilled me in a way that I cherished throughout my life. I want that for you, dear. Fulfillment. Passion. With that goal in mind, I am setting you a deadline. Six months from today, I want you to be doing something you love. Try new things, reconnect with old friends, and make some new ones. Find a man who sets off all your bells and whistles. You are special, Sunny, and you deserve a man who knows it. Rediscover who you are. I'm sure you'll see the same intelligent, sassy, and loving young lady I do.
Now don't get mad at me. I didn't want you worrying about this

or trying to change my mind, so I've hidden some things until now. And damn it, it's my money, and I'll do what I want with it! To give you some of the time you so generously gave to me, I've put aside some money. The first account should cover your costs of living over the next six months, so you don't have to worry about working. Your "job" is to figure this all out! I have also paid a full year's rent on our apartment, so you'll have a stable base for at least that long. If you decide you want to move before then, by all means do. This is just some security if you need it. The second account is much larger. Use it as seed money to start something. Dream big. Do great things. Let your special light shine. I'll be watching, hopefully from above. I know you won't disappoint. If the seed money remains untouched after six months, it will revert to my other charities. You don't have to spend it all at once, but it will be there when you need it.

Sunny, you were the granddaughter I never had, and I love you fiercely, even now. Perhaps now more than ever...Don't shake your head at me. Take this gift as it was meant, a symbol of my love and greatest hope that you will know the same love and fulfillment in your life that I found in mine. Build a life full of passion. Don't let the sadness keep you down. It's time to let in the sun.

All my love,
Aunt Helen

Dani sat there, gripping the letter and the card tightly in her trembling fingers. This was so much more than she had ever anticipated! She had power of attorney for Aunt Helen's finances, so her aunt had to have been very crafty to hide this so completely. Why had her aunt kept this a secret? Because she knew Dani would have argued. Aunt Helen was right. Dani had a lot of trouble making time for herself, so her aunt had made it a priority, no worries and no guilt. Aunt Helen always had a purpose. What could Dani's purpose be? She'd gotten so side-tracked saying yes. She ended up helping everyone but herself. Time for that to change. She had no idea how it would change, but she wasn't going to let this chance pass her by.

"I love you, too." Dani closed her eyes and let her aunt's voice flow through her whirling thoughts and wash away some of the grief that had been keeping her so low. She let her aunt's words take root in her mind. She was someone special, and it was time to let the world know it. Let the sun shine, indeed.

DANI DOVE into the cool chlorinated water and let it wash away her day. Her mind had been whirling ever since she'd left the law offices. Even lunch with Olivia hadn't smoothed things out. The jagged, sticky questions remained unanswered in her brain, waiting to snag her if she wandered too close. Where did she want to be? What if she wasn't good enough once she got there? Why was she facing this alone?

She knew the answer to that last one. She'd trusted too easily and gotten burned for her troubles. The trouble with being an eternal optimist was that the rest of the world tended to take advantage.

She kicked over and began a freestyle crawl from one end of the pool to the other. The late summer sunset was fading, bringing relief from the heat. If only it could relieve her troubled mind as well. A perfect example of an opportunistic bastard was her ex-boyfriend, Matthew Sparks, rising junior executive in operations at her old energy firm in Houston.

Since she'd been firmly in the accounting department and secure in her career, there was no conflict of interest, and she'd spent a year of her life investing in him. They'd met at the annual holiday party, and had quickly become inseparable. She stayed late willingly, to help him out with his files. If those nights often turned into make-out sessions on his desk, well, what people didn't know couldn't hurt her. Long lunches, quickie coffee breaks, and long romantic weekends tacked on to business trips, Dani had believed that she was building a future. She'd been happily content with her office romance, until he'd announced his engagement. To someone else.

With one question, one ring, he made her the other woman. She didn't know what was worse, that she'd been oblivious or that he'd been able to dent her belief that she was a good person. And for a little while she'd beat herself up with, "Why didn't he pick me? Why wasn't I enough?"

In hindsight, she was well rid of him. She counted her lucky stars that she hadn't ended up married to a man she couldn't trust. When she'd come home for Christmas to lick her wounds, and Aunt Helen's condition came to light, it had seemed the perfect escape, so she'd run away.

Running away was easy. Figuring out what she was running towards was a lot harder.

Reaching the wall, and no closure, she flipped over into a lazy backstroke and nearly drowned. Her new neighbor was standing just outside the pool fence, empty boxes in hand, watching her swim. She'd wanted to empty her mind, and the instant heat she felt in the wake of his intense stare accomplished that far better than the icy water had.

She kicked for the edge of the pool, needing to get a grip, while she convinced her lungs to behave themselves.

"Are you OK?" He dropped the boxes and was up and over the locked gate in a heartbeat.

"Fine. I'm fine." She managed the mortified denial around the wet coughs still wracking her body.

"Here, let me help you out of the water." Dani reached up a hand, expecting a boost. While she marveled at the way his strong sinewed hand engulfed her own, she missed that he reached under her other arm and before she knew it, she was flying. She landed limply against his strong chest, and marveled at the lovely feeling of being pressed up against him even briefly. He brusquely stepped back and urged her to sit on the lounge chair. He reached behind her, and Dani expected to feel his warm strong hand slide along her back to pull her closer into his embrace. The solid thumping thwacks chased that idea and her remaining coughs right out of her.

"Wrong tube." She gasped when she could finally speak, embarrassed by her reaction.

"Yeah, it happens."

"Thanks for the assist. Sorry I got you all wet."

Dani watched as his whole body went taut and tense. He didn't say a word and the silence grew awkward. Was he angry about a wet t-shirt? It would dry quickly in the lingering mid-summer heat. *Maybe you should suggest stripping it off so it would dry faster.* The naughty voice in her head needed to get a grip. Dani leapt into the breach, changing the subject.

"So, you're getting unpacked?"

"Yeah."

"Do you know where the recycling is?"

"Yeah. I found it."

The awkward silence returned. Nick Gantry was a man of few words, it seemed. Since he wasn't speaking or even looking at her, she let her eyes roam, from his intensely masculine hands, to the powerful muscular arms that had hauled her effortlessly from the water. From there it was a short step to admiring his shoulders that seemed to carry the weight of the world beneath the wet t-shirt that molded lovingly to them. Her prim and proper eyes logically followed the path of the water, wanting to confirm the extent of the damage she'd caused, as it dripped down the front of what she remembered were truly impressive abs to disappear into his jeans. Her mind helpfully provided the image it had tucked away from moving day, since the white cotton was blocking her view. Her eyes drifted lower. *I wonder if his other attributes are as impressive as the rest of him.*

She could give all the excuses she wanted, but she was ogling a stranger. And she liked it. Though her perusal had only taken seconds, she knew he'd noticed, and she blushed. She couldn't remember the last time she'd had this instantaneous reaction. Why not take the next step?

"Well, you should take a break, enjoy the pool. Come on in. The water's fine."

THE WATER WASN'T the only thing fine at the pool. There she sat with her mermaid hair and barely-there bikini, tempting him to madness. It had taken all of his strength to step back and let her leave his arms. And then, while he was still reeling from the feel of her body pressed against his, she'd gone and apologized for getting him wet. He'd immediately catalogued all the ways he'd like to return the favor. All of the blood in his brain immediately decamped to his jeans, leaving his logic ill equipped to protect him. When he caught her checking him out, he'd had to clamp his lips shut to keep from offering her a better view.

As tempting as she was, he was in no condition to start things up with a woman. Horny as hell, images of all the ways he'd like to take her flashed through his mind. But he'd keep those thoughts to himself. He knew she wasn't the kind of girl up for a hot fling. No, she was keeper material. Too bad he'd never been one for keeping anything in his life for too long.

No, Dani Carmichael was firmly off limits. He had enough to do, getting his own heart put back together, without worrying about eventually breaking hers. He'd do the right thing and go back up to his ruthlessly organized and freshly cleaned apartment. He'd been restless, unable to settle after finishing the task of unpacking, but he could not take her up on her offer of distraction. Maybe there was a ball game on TV. Maybe he'd just have to make use of the cold shower again, instead of the pool as he'd planned.

"Actually, if you're done drowning, I should get back to it. See you around."

He knew he was being rude, but his self-control was nearly at an end. He needed some distance before he did something they'd both enjoy and then regret.

Dani watched her surly neighbor turn tail and retreat. What was he running from? What was he hiding? More importantly, why did she care? Yes, his hot body and distant demeanor intrigued her, but hadn't she learned her lesson? She needed a man she could read and trust. More importantly, she needed the next six months to be completely about herself. She had a lot of work to do to live up to Aunt Helen's legacy. The last thing she needed was a distraction like Nick Gantry. She dove back into the cool water searching for resolve, but the wanting was slow to fade.

THREE

NICK CHECKED THE CLOCK, again. 5:47...5:48. Should he stay or should he go? The song ran on loop through his head as he debated. Although the fact that he'd unpacked both his good dress shirt and his iron would suggest that he had, indeed, made up his mind, he sat perched on the arm of his couch watching the minutes tick by on the clock, anxiety building in his chest. He'd holed up in the new apartment, unpacking, getting phone & Internet installed, organizing his rather sparse belongings into military efficiency. But most importantly, he'd been alone, blissfully alone.

"I'm good at alone." He got up and paced towards the door and back again.

He was hiding, but he also hadn't had a panic attack in three days. He'd still had flashbacks and woken in a cold sweat each night. Still, the solitude had helped during the daylight hours.

He couldn't hide forever, but was a dinner party with complete strangers really the best way for him to re-enter the outside world? What if he spaced out in a memory, or got angry, or worse because of something they inadvertently said or did? What if he ruined his chance at building a home in this building because he wasn't ready? What if he ruined his chance of befriending his neighbors because he turned down their first overture? Damn! Nick took a few calming breaths, trying to force the panic licking at the back of his throat back into submission.

"I'm just going to go. It's just dinner. I can do this. I will do this. I can always leave." Checking the clock one last time, 5:56, he pushed away from the couch and yanked open the door and strode into the hallway.

"Aaaaaaa!" Dani screamed, bobbling the coconut cream cake she held precariously on a glass pedestal. Nick flattened himself back against the wall, and struggled to breathe. She looked at him, wide-eyed and expectant. Words. He needed to use them, and fast, or she'd think he was some kind of idiot who liked scaring people.

"Sorry! Didn't want to be late. You OK? Can I carry that?"

"No, thanks. I've got it now. Are you heading to Mrs. Grady's, too?"

"Yeah. I figured it wouldn't do to say no to my first official invite."

"You mean summons? Don't worry. It's better to get it over with. She'd just have hounded you until you gave in. She's got thick skin."

They continued in silence down the hallway, Nick aware that Dani kept sneaking glances his way.

Nick turned to meet her gaze, raising his eyebrow when he caught her.

"Do I have something on my shirt?"

Dani blushed and flashed him a sunny smile. He was coming to enjoy seeing the rosy tinge brighten her face, and that smile still made him feel tongue-tied. He was in serious trouble. Thankfully, she angled past him to knock on Mrs. Grady's door, saving him from doing something rash.

"Hi, Mrs. Grady! Look who I ran into on the way over."

"Hello, hello! Come on in. You must be Nick. I'm Patricia Grady, but call me Patty please. And Sunny! I'm so glad you were able to come! It's about time you started calling me Patty, too, young lady," she added with a pointed glance in Dani's direction. "I'm so glad you changed your mind."

Pulling the younger woman into a tight one-armed hug, she murmured, "I can see why!" Nick overheard her not-so-muffled comment and was manfully trying not to smirk, as Patty turned back to him. "Well, young man. Welcome to the building! We hope you'll enjoy your time with us. We're a rather close group, more of family really, so if you need anything, anything at all, you've only to ask."

"Thank you, ma'am. I appreciate the offer and the invitation."

"Well, I have a feeling you'll soon be a regular. In fact, I predict all it'll take is one slice of Dani's coconut cream cake! Come on in." Reaching over, she plucked the cake from Dani's hands and placed it on the counter. "Did she bring you cookies to welcome you to the building?"

"That she did, ma'am."

"Are there any left?"

"No, ma'am."

"I rest my case." With a chuckle, she led him over to the dining room table around which several elderly people were already seated. "Also, you don't need to keep ma'am-ing me left and right. I got enough of that to last a lifetime in the service. I sure don't need it now! Let me get you settled in. Everyone, this is Nick Gantry. Go around, and introduce yourselves."

"Hi. Jack Delano. We met briefly when you moved in. Down on the first floor, apartment 111. Been in the building for nearly 40 years, and the super for most of it. You need something fixed? You give me a call. I know my way around these old rooms, and I'd rather do the fixing than have someone give it a go himself. Glad to have you here!" The heavy shouldered, heavy paunched handyman stood and shook his hand. From the carefully maintained buzz cut, Nick guessed this man had also served his country at some point. He was built like an ox, but the friendly smile immediately helped Nick begin to feel at ease in this crowd.

"I'm Kathleen Betancourt," chimed the small bird like woman next to Jack. Nick had placed Jack in his mid-sixties, but this woman had to be pushing 90. Her soft southern accent soothed his nerves. Her short white hair was curled and teased to form a halo around her finely featured face. She was exactly how he'd always pictured a grandmother. Not that he'd know. She also sent a warm smile his way as he leaned over to carefully shake her hand. The underlying steel in her grip as she returned the courtesy surprised him. "I moved around the country quite a bit, base to base, while my Dean was still alive, but now that it's just me I've settled here to be near my grandchildren. Been here the last 15 years or so. It's a great building. I'm sure you'll love it as much as we do." The next guest cleared his throat, and Nick shifted his gaze to the right.

"Lt. Colonel William Jones, retired, but everyone calls me Colonel. Pleased to meet you." The short, wiry gentleman stood and extended his hand. He looked ancient but still had the firm grip of a man used to asserting command. His hair, gone completely white, was cut tight to his head and contrasted boldly with his brown skin. His frame was small but not stooped, and Nick could see him leading scores of men into battle with confidence and ease.

Nick turned to the last occupied seat. Another man was seated there, likely in his mid-sixties, but the years had not been kind. His weather-beaten face, all cracks and crags with the texture and color of leather, transformed with a smile as he stood to shake Nick's hand. "Joe Coleman. Good to have you!"

Nick settled himself in next to Patty Grady, and assessed his opponent carefully. The older woman, mid to late-seventies by his estimation, wore her hair carefully coifed in a French twist and a string of pearls at her neck. If the hard gleam in her eye and amused quirk in her lips were anything to judge by, this interview would be harder than facing his CO after that little incident on leave in Tennessee his first year in. Steeling himself for interrogation, he went on the offensive and fired the opening shot.

"So, how often do you all get together like this?"

"I host dinners here three nights a week, but different people come on different nights. This is my regular Wednesday crew."

"You do this three times every week?" He looked at the spread of garlic bread, tossed salad, antipasto plates, and what he would swear was homemade spaghetti and meatballs loaded onto the table. How did she manage to pull it all together?

"We've done a bit more than usual tonight, since we hoped you'd come join us and bring a healthy appetite. Everyone gets some leftovers to take home this way. Helen and Dani...well, Dani helps me do the brunt of the cooking in advance, so it's no trouble at all. How else would I be able to see all of my friends, and keep up with the building gossip? Which leads me to what we're all dying to know. Nick Gantry, who are you and what on earth possessed you to move into this building?"

"Now, Patty, let the poor boy get some food on his plate before you start in on him! Here, honey, have some garlic bread." Kathleen handed him the breadbasket. He focused on the garlic bread, happy for the distraction.

Wow. This lady meant business. No coy insinuations, no subtle prompts for information, just blunt questions that demanded straight answers. Debating how much to go into, he filled his plate as the dishes were passed around the table.

"Well, ma'am, I mean Patty, what you see is what you get. I left the army after multiple tours at both of our current fronts. I thought the army might've been a career for me, but it just doesn't feel right anymore. My buddy, Seth, was getting out, too, and I decided to relocate near him, since we might end up back in business together at some point. His family is here." He filled his mouth quickly with a bite of spaghetti and meatball to avoid revealing any other details just yet, and his tongue sent up a silent prayer of gratitude. Years of institutional cuisine and fast food had deadened his palate. It was forcefully awakened by the rich tomato, savory oregano, and pungent garlic exploding in his mouth. A quiet moan escaped as he closed his eyes and chewed slowly, enjoying the slight bite to the noodles and the soft braised meaty goodness of the meatball.

Dani turned toward him, and he locked eyes with her. Had he moaned out loud over the spaghetti? Joe dropped the salad tongs, and the resulting clatter startled Dani from her inspection. Nick continued to watch her as she fidgeted in her seat, crossing her legs, and looking anywhere but at him. Was that another blush? What was she thinking? Was she imagining him moaning over something else? That thought brought its reverse image immediately to the forefront of his mind. Imagining Dani, naked and moaning in his arms, did little to help him keep his composure. Nick struggled to push the tempting thought away, before his attention was pulled back to Patty Grady. She resumed her line of questioning, now that everyone had full plates.

"You neglected to mention how you found out about our building. I know there's a very nice new high rise across town that would be perfect for a young man like you."

"Actually, that's where Seth lives. I've lived in barracks and base housing for the last 6 years. I wanted some peace and quiet. This place is smaller, offered rent-control for vets, and had an immediate opening." He didn't mention that he was desperately hoping that this building would be a hideout and a haven, not a bustling community with demands on his time.

The table went awkwardly quiet for a moment, and he froze. Where had he blundered? He looked to the one familiar face around the table, hoping for a lifeline. Dani couldn't meet his gaze as she explained.

"I mentioned that the apartment you moved into was briefly mine. It was available, because I moved in with my Aunt Helen to care for her at the end of her life. She was a Wednesday dinner regular. Her death has been hard on us all."

He was such a shit. Here she was, reeling from a death in the family, moving out of her own apartment, and still doing kind and neighborly things to help him settle in. And he couldn't quit picturing her naked. She deserved so much better, even if she never knew it. Shame washed over him, and he fell silent.

"Don't you have family of your own you'd like to live closer to?" The soft question from Mrs. Betancourt startled him.

"No, ma'am. I don't." He bit his tongue, before he said something he'd regret. The quick and firm denial pushed another awkward pause into the conversation. Thankfully, Patty pushed them past it.

"I know what you mean about communal living." She put down her fork and reached for her wine glass. She grinned at her guests as a memory came to mind. "I was a nurse in Korea. We all bunked in together in the nurses' tents. Imagine twenty women packed in like sardines. Hundred degree heat in the summers. You couldn't turn without bumping into someone. I'll never forget the time..."

Nick surveyed the table while Patty spun out her tale. It

seemed like everyone had decided to overlook his abrupt response. Everyone except Dani. She was staring at him, like she could see into his soul and was steadily dissecting everything she found. Heaven help her if that was true. Nick deliberately turned away from her, and tried to pull himself together while he pretended to pay attention to Patty's story. This had been a bad idea. He'd spent the meal lusting after one fellow diner and being rude to the rest. Clearly, he wasn't ready to be unleashed on polite society. He should have stayed locked up in his room where he could only hurt himself.

The table erupted in laughter at whatever antics Patty and her nurse friends got up to and he did his best to join in so no one would notice he had missed the story. "I still can't believe she dumped that bucket over his head, but it sure cooled him down! Living with my girls in a war zone forged tight bonds, for better or worse, and you got used to living as a group real quick." Patty said as she wiped the tears of laughter from her cheeks.

"I came back here to the States, and boy, was it a huge adjustment. I wasn't married, so I got an apartment on my own and started to work at the local hospital in their trauma unit." She shook her head at the memory. The smile left her face and her eyes looked a little sad. "The quiet almost killed me," she said sadly.

"Working at the hospital was good because it made me feel useful, like I could still use what I'd learned in the army. But now and then something I'd see would send me back to the front, and I chafed at the limitations on what I was allowed to do. And then to head home to that empty apartment, no one to talk to, no one to distract me from my own thoughts and memories...it was brutal." She looked lost in her own memories, then straightened suddenly. Her warm smile appeared and the spark came back in to her eyes. She looked directly into Nick's eyes.

"Don't fall into that trap." A tiny glimmer of hope sparked

in his chest. Maybe coming tonight wasn't the disaster he'd thought. Maybe he'd found the people who could understand.

"You were an army nurse. That explains everything." Nick latched on to the one detail that didn't hit too close to home.

"What do you mean by that?"

"Your home is immaculate. This meal is delicious, nutritious, and was served exactly on time with everything hot. You take care of your friends regularly and enjoy a little bit of chaos getting it all ready. And you keep tabs on everyone and everything in your 'ward,' so you can help if it's needed. How'm I doing?"

Everyone at the table laughed. "He's got you pegged, Patty. Now give the boy a rest and let him eat his meal." Jack passed him the bowl of spaghetti for a refill and shot Nick a quick wink. "There's time enough for you to ferret out all of his dark secrets."

"If this is how you eat every Wednesday, you can tie me up and interrogate me so long as I get dessert! My compliments to the chef." He turned to Dani, raising his glass of water to toast her. He took in her heated gaze, and when he realized what he'd said, he went mute all over again. He'd meant to toss off some joke about coconuts, but the electrical sizzle shorted his circuits as their gazes met and held. He'd never been possessed by such a primal urge to take, to have, to hold. Her blue eyes ablaze, unwilling to break the contact, he tried to rein in his thoughts. He clenched his other hand beneath the table, digging his nails into his palm, hoping the pain would distract him from his rising desire. Thankfully, he had the dessert course to get himself back under control before he had to stand up again. He managed a sip of his water, without spilling, trying to wet his throat which had suddenly gone bone dry.

Dani dropped her gaze and quickly stood up from the table. "Thank you. I'm glad you enjoyed it. Who wants cake? Coffee?"

She hurried back to the counter and returned to the table armed with the creamy white confection. Nick took a full breath while her back was turned. He had to get himself under control. The conversation turned to everyday updates on doctor's visits and grandchildren, as she served up generous slices of cake and Patty poured the coffee. She handed Nick his plate of cake just as he turned to reach for it, causing the slice to tip precariously on its perch.

"I think I am destined to knock this cake over tonight." Nick attempted a chuckle that stuck in his throat as he watched, transfixed, as she licked the dollop of frosting that had dislodged from the cake off of her thumb. His entire being focused on her little pink tongue removing the sweet white smear from her perfect skin. Just that quickly he was back at the edge of his control.

"If you do, you'll have a lot of disappointed neighbors."

"Wouldn't want that," he murmured, imagining how he'd like to please one of his neighbors very much.

"So, Nick, what kind of action did you see in Iraq?" Joe asked, his deep voice rumbling into the gap. "I've heard that it was brutal in some areas, what with all the insurgent action. Stories from the boys over at the hospital reminded me a lot of Viet Nam, where you were never really sure who was the enemy."

Jarred by the sudden change in topic, Nick's mind flashed to the raw angry images he usually shied away from. The heat, the sun, the chaos...Samarra, Iraq was suddenly vividly present in his mind. The panic was coming. The tingling in his arms. The churning in his belly. He tried to will it away with a few cleansing breaths. In the space of a few seconds, overwhelming desire evaporated and was replaced by howling pain.

"Oh, you know, we saw a bit of everything." Quick shallow breaths refused to obey his command to slow down. If he didn't make his escape soon, he'd lose it in front of these people. He stood abruptly. "Mrs. Grady, I'm sorry to eat and run, but I've just remembered something I need to do back home. Thank you for having me."

He stumbled towards the door and the minute it closed behind him, he sprinted for the safety of his own four walls.

In the awkward silence after his abrupt departure, glances were exchanged around the table. Joe was the first to speak.

"Aw, hell, Patty. I'm sorry to bust up your nice dinner." He hunched his shoulders and was wringing his hands, as if he was afraid he'd get punished for disobedience.

"Not your fault, Joe. Relax. You asked a question we were all wanting to. I think his reaction answered another question he evaded earlier."

"He's got the shakes," chimed in the Colonel. "I saw it when he put down his fork. In my day, we called it shell shock. Not sure what they're calling it these days, some bunch of letters."

"PTSD," Patty supplied. "It would explain his hiding in that apartment, and wanting a quiet building close to the VA. I can't think of any other reason he'd choose this place over living with his friend. That or some other injury we can't see..."

"How do you know he's been hiding?" asked Dani.

"He hasn't left this building but once since he moved in, and that was a short trip to the grocery store. My network assures me I didn't miss anything while I was at the salon this afternoon."

"How could I have doubted your intel?" Dani smiled knowing full well not to doubt her neighbor's skill.

"Well, we'll just keep an eye on our new friend, make sure he knows he's got ears and shoulders ready and waiting if he needs them. Gentlemen, Kath, I trust you know how to offer your support and encouragement firmly but subtly?"

A chorus of "yes, ma'am's" echoed around the table. There was no question of who was in charge of this campaign.

"Well, now that that's settled, I have some news to share." Eyes swung expectantly towards Dani. "Aunt Helen had one last trick up her sleeve when I went to visit her lawyer on Monday." She proceeded to tell her aunt's closest friends of the plan to help Dani find her passion. There was a decided lack of surprise around the table.

"You knew?" Guilty faces avoided eye contact.

"Well, I'm glad you know now. I was bursting to tell you, Sunny!" Kathleen offered her a bright smile from across the table. "I didn't know how she'd planned to pull it off, but I supported the idea from the beginning. I hope we did right to keep the surprise. You doing all right with it?"

"Surprisingly, I am. The shock was a big one, let me tell you, but I get it. She knew I'd never get on board with the financials, unless I couldn't do anything about it. She knew me well. I just hope I can make her proud. For the time being I'm going to reconnect with old friends and enjoy my new hometown. Then I'll start tackling the bigger question of what to do when I grow up."

She chuckled, and then added, "I want you all to know how much I appreciate your love and support right now. I don't want you to worry about me. I'm not going anywhere right away. I'm sure you'll all have opinions about what I should do. I'd love to hear them, soon. I promise. For now, I'm going to say goodnight and start on my plan first thing tomorrow."

"Sunny, you'll take some of the leftover cake to Nick, won't you?" asked Patty. "After all, he did promise to come back if he had dessert!"

Trapped by manners, Dani agreed and fixed him a plate

before leaving. All the way back down the hall, she ran through what she'd say when he opened the door. "Hi. Why did you run away? Here's some cake." No. "I'm here for dessert. Oh, and there's cake too." *Tempting, but no Ms. Horny-pants. Stay focused. Polite, neighborly concern, no I-want-to-jump-you vibes. I won't get involved with the mysterious man next door. Clearly, he has some work to do, if Patty and the others are right. No, the next few months are going to be all about me. The last thing I need in my life is a man.*

When she reached his apartment, she knocked with firm resolve on the heavy outer door, and it swung open under her hand. The latch must not have engaged when he closed it behind him. She would tell him to listen for the click. Not wanting to intrude, she called out from the doorway. "Nick? Are you here? Mrs. Grady sent me with some cake for you."

Silence greeted her, and she wavered. Should she go in and leave the cake on the table, or just step back and close the door and try again tomorrow? She didn't want to intrude on his privacy. She had really only wanted to make sure he was OK. But coming back tomorrow would only prolong her having to think about him and all the swirling emotions he'd set loose at dinner. As she pondered her options, a car backfired out on the street. She heard a muffled groan from the couch.

"Nick? Are you here? Are you OK?"

Setting aside her concerns, she entered the darkened apartment, trying to make out the shapes of the furniture. As she neared what she assumed was the couch, she heard labored breathing and shivering. Turning on a lamp, Dani quickly found the source of the noises. Nick was curled up in a ball on the couch, his arms wrapped tightly around himself as if trying to hold himself together. She reached out to touch his shoulder, "Nick?"

He jerked in surprise, startling her and sending the cake she carried in her hand flying. As it plopped on the floor, she half smiled that his prediction had indeed come true. But her smile quickly faded, as she took in the raw fear and panic on his face.

"What's wrong? Are you hurt?"

He stared at her, through her really, his chocolate brown eyes unseeing in terror. She immediately lowered to her knees and switched to a calming and quiet voice, even though her own stomach was fluttering with panic at finding him like this.

"Nick, it's me, Dani." She slowly reached a hand out to his shoulder again. He still flinched when she touched him, but not quite so violently. "I'm here. You're safe here. I'm here. I'm going to stay here for a while, to make sure you're safe. You can trust me."

He nodded tersely, before he burrowed back into his ball. She shifted onto the couch and lifted his head onto her lap. She stroked her fingers from his sweat-dampened forehead, over his short caramel tipped hair, and down his back as she spoke quietly to him to soothe and distract. Dani kept up her ramble, telling him her life story and how she came to be living in the apartment across the hall. She shared her favorite memories of Aunt Helen and her fears about someone new living in her home. Slowly, Dani felt the tension drain from his body, and he fell asleep curled up next to her, his head still resting in her lap.

"What happened to you?" she wondered aloud. The adrenaline that flowed through her system began to seep away, and she felt limp. She moved a pillow from the armrest to the back of the couch for her head, and reached over to turn off the lamp. "I promised to keep you safe, and I am damn well going to. I just need a quick nap. We can talk it all out in the morning."

FOUR

Nick woke slowly from a delicious dream. He was on a warm beach, relaxing on the sand. He could smell the coconut oil from the lovely ladies sunning themselves nearby. He turned his head and felt a firm toned thigh under his cheek. Now this was some R&R he could get into. Sliding his hand under his cheek, the sleek muscles tensed beneath his touch. The sea breeze ruffled his hair, soothing his overheated cheek. Then he realized it wasn't the breeze, but a soft hand caressing the back of his neck and shoulders as well. Feeling relaxed and unspeakably aroused at the same time, he turned his head and began nuzzling and kissing his way higher and higher.

Pushing himself up on one hand, he continued his quest for bare skin. Strangely well dressed, this beach bunny of his. He turned his gaze to her face and saw the blond hair and angelic face of his new neighbor. She was sitting reclined on a beach chair with her eyes closed. His own sleeping beauty. He leaned closer and gently took the lips that had been tempting him all evening. The first taste shocked him in its power and simplicity. This was need, raw and undeniable. The primal urge to take roared up and nearly snapped its tether. Pulling back from the kiss, he looked at her again, stunned by his reaction. She was no longer sitting on a beach chaise, but on his couch, and her beautiful blue eyes were wide open, and filled with desire.

DANI HALF WOKE from her nap to the unmistakable sensation of lips being pressed to her own. Such a soft kiss should have been a sweet prelude to more. The lightning bolt of passion it unleashed was completely unexpected. It had been months since she'd been kissed, but she didn't think the drought had anything to do with how quickly she caught fire. She'd never felt a reaction like this. To have it happen in a dream was disheartening. Why couldn't she find this level of passion in real life? Stunned into immobility, Dani received the kiss passively for a moment, until her dream lover hesitated and began to pull away. She bit back a moan of protest. Heat and desire pulsed through her body now. Stopping was unthinkable.

He did pull back from the kiss. When she opened her eyes to persuade him to resume his attentions, she found herself looking at her new neighbor, in a dark and cold room. She was sitting on an ugly, lumpy couch with a very large, very aroused, near stranger in her lap. She could only stare at him as her brain worked furiously to tally what she saw with what she felt. He stared at her lips, delicately cupping her face with one of his large calloused hands, as if studying them to unlock their secrets. None of this made any sense.

Giving up on logic seemed the most rational choice in light of the undeniable need still buffeting her system. Dani leaned in to take his lips with hers again, desperate for that connection again. The moment their lips touched, she was thrown right back into the inferno their desire had created. More. All she could think was more. Passion burned through her system as she struggled to get closer. She tugged him up to sitting, and climbed into his lap, no longer content to be a passive participant. She leaned in, changing the angle of the kiss and pressed her breasts into his chest as she took his mouth.

His arms wrapped around her, and she found herself pulled into his strong embrace. She cradled his head with both hands, deepening their kiss and ratcheting their passion even higher. His hands roamed down the length of her torso, and up again, this time underneath the layer of her shirt. He moaned as his rough hands came in contact with silky skin encased in a thin layer of lace. It was the same moan of gratitude and delight that had turned her on at dinner. It worked even better now. Pulling back to look at her, Nick's ragged breathing filled the room as he reached for the hem of her t-shirt and tugged it over her head. He pulled her to his chest and rolled her into the back of the couch, bringing his weight down beside her. Dani reveled in his strength. She wrapped one leg around his waist, anchoring him on the couch and more importantly bringing his hard heat into intimate contact where she needed it most.

The sizzling contact rocked through her core, and she pulled back overwhelmed. She needed to breathe and get back a little control. Unfortunately, along with a full breath, Dani found some clarity. Her earlier reservations came flooding back to her. What was she doing? For goodness sake, she was half naked and clinging to a man she'd only just met. Men in general didn't figure into the plan right now. Sure, this felt good. OK, amazing really. More phenomenal than any other man she'd ever been with and they were only kissing...but that was beside the point. This wasn't right, and she knew it. Before Nick could resume their kiss and steal her wits with his lips and his very talented hands currently reaching for her bra hooks, Dani put up her hands in front of her. She laid them on his chest, and fighting the urge to flex them and feel the glorious muscles she'd seen on display on moving day, she pushed him back.

He eased back to focus on her face. She didn't know what he saw in her eyes, but he took a deep breath and dropped his hands. Dani pulled a pillow between them to cover herself. Hugging the scant coverage to her chest she rolled as far back against the back of the couch as she could. She had to minimize their contact, or she was going to forget her own resolve. She firmly ignored the twinge of regret at leaving his embrace. Nick leaned back to help put some space between them, and rolled right off the couch, landing on the forgotten coconut cream cake.

A startled bark of laughter escaped from Dani's lips, and she began shaking silently as she tried to suppress the giggles that threatened to break free. The absurdity of the whole situation was too much to contain. Nick looked up at her from the ground, still visibly aroused with a self-deprecating smile lightening his face, and laughed along with her. *Damn, he is sexy when he laughs.* No. Stop. Big belly laughs turned into tears, and finally wound down into shared smiles as the sexual tension in the room dissipated.

Dani tugged her shirt back on and moved from the couch to the armchair. Distance was going to be critical to her success. Nick got up and tugged his dress shirt off over his head to inspect the damage the cake had inflicted. Determined not to get distracted by his naked shoulders or chiseled back or golden skin sliding over flexing muscles, Dani quickly shifted her gaze on the floor until he returned from his bedroom with a plain white t-shirt on.

"Never did get to try that cake." He scooped the mess off the floor with a paper towel.

"I'll make you another one. Are we going to talk about what just happened?"

"Do we have to?" he asked in the petulant tones of a ten year old boy, grinning ear to ear.

"Yes, we have to. What happened at dinner?"

"After everything that's happened in the last 30 minutes, that's what you're going to ask me?"

"Yes, and don't think I'll be as easily diverted as your hostess was tonight."

"She wasn't diverted. She simply chose to pursue it another time. I have no illusions about who was in control of that exchange."

"Well?" Nick's silence stretched, and Dani grew impatient. "Listen, I walked in here tonight to deliver some stupid cake and found you completely incapacitated. Aside from my initial nerves, I think I handled it pretty well. I also think I deserve to know what's going on."

"Look, about the kiss. I'm sorry I frightened you. I honestly..." Dani raised a hand to cut him off.

"The kiss didn't scare me, you idiot. It may have sizzled every last nerve ending in my body, but it didn't scare me. What scared me was this big strong man curled into a very little ball looking like the slightest movement would cause him to shatter into a million pieces."

"Damn it. Why did you come here, Dani? Did Patty send you to check up on me? Can't a guy have a little privacy?" He whirled on her, his voice angry and harsh. But beneath the anger, she heard embarrassment and fear. She couldn't back down.

"She did send me down with a piece of cake, to apologize for whatever set you off. When I saw you curled up in pain, I just couldn't walk back out. Are you having nightmares? Panic attacks?"

"I don't need your help, or your pity, or any goddamn cake!" He stormed off to the kitchen, and chucked the messy remnants of said cake in the trash with undue force. "I just need everyone to stay the hell out of my space! I am fine." She wasn't sure who he was trying to convince with this tantrum, but it wasn't working on her.

"Sure, you're fine. Uh-huh. Clearly. Listen, everyone at that table could see it and relate. You don't have to do this alone." Her temper rose in response to his aggressive tone, but she ruthlessly reined it in.

"I just need to get back on my feet. I'll get over it. I don't need anyone poking and prodding me, feeding me cake, kissing me senseless, trying to get me to talk." He dropped back onto the sofa in defeat.

The pain and frustration in his voice tore Dani apart. She wanted to wrap this man in a hug and soothe his battered mind and soul. But she knew better than to let any of that show. Sympathy and care could easily be mistaken for pity by the hard-headed males of the species, so she opted for a matter of fact tone as she responded.

"Well, it's 3 am and your defenses are low. Tell yourself whatever you need to, but I didn't kiss you to pry out your secrets, and I give my cakes to everyone, whether I need intel or not. You don't have to do this alone. There are people who can help. Not everyone needs to know, but at least the people close to you..."

"So they can walk on eggshells around me? Wonder when I'm going to snap and lose my mind? Avoid talking to me because they are worried they'll set me off? Or just pat me on the back and say 'thank you for your service' because they can't think of anything else to say?" His defeat was painful to hear. He'd given up before he'd begun. "No, thank you. I'll just hole up here for a while until I'm stronger. No one needs to know. You won't tell." It was an order, not a request, but Dani decided to give him a pass.

"Who would I tell?"

"Mrs. Grady, the fastest gossip in the west. You won't."

"No, I won't. On one condition. Since I already know, you have to let me help. I promise no nagging, no blabbing, just someone to help."

"Why would you want to help me? I'm no one special to you." He rested his head in his hands, elbows propped on his knees, as if the weight of the problems inside was too heavy to hold upright.

No one special. Just the only man who'd ever flipped every switch in her body simultaneously. With a kiss. "It's what I do. I can't stand by while someone is hurting. You left before I made my little announcement, but my aunt left me some money to figure out what I want to do with my life. I'm going to take advantage of my free time and have some fun before I buckle down and get back to work. You might like to join me. Or I could just be an ear when you need to vent... I have skills, and I am willing to put them to use for you."

"This isn't because I kissed you senseless ten minutes ago?" He tilted his head on one hand and attempted a half-hearted grin.

"Of course not!"

"Because regardless of what my subconscious thinks, I'm not really up for more of that right now."

"Oh, so that was your subconscious I felt a minute ago," Dani's inner voice slipped past her filter.

Nick barked out a laugh. "It's nothing personal. I just can't dive back into the dating pool yet. I understand if you want to change your mind. I won't hold it against you."

Even if I asked really nicely? She really ought to do something about that naughty voice in her head. *Like listen to it.* Forcing herself to hush that voice, she firmly answered, "I'm positive. I don't need anyone in my life either right now. I've got six months to figure out who I am and who I want to be. Having a man in my life would just muddy the water. Honestly, I'm offering to help because it's what I do, what any of us here would do. I just happen to be the only one who knows." She neglected to mention that the other dinner guests had hit pretty close to the mark with their own hypotheses. The more people he had on his team, the better, even if he didn't know it. She let her reassurance echo in the dark room, while he mulled his options.

"OK, then. I know I can't hide out here forever. I just keep hoping it'll get better."

"Well, your first step has to be going to the VA and talking to someone. That makes it real. That's scary." She reached across the space between them and gripped his hand in hers. In the quiet and the dark, she needed to touch him, to reassure him.

"I get not wanting to face it if you think it's going to get better on its own. But here's the thing, Nick. You don't know what this is because you haven't asked. You don't know how to fix it because you haven't talked to someone who can tell you. You're not the only soldier to come home with trouble like this. Have you looked into it at all?"

"No, not really. I mean, I know enough to recognize it for what it is. They drilled me about watching for it my men. But going to talk to somebody? I just...can't." His voice shook on that last admission, and Dani deemed they'd made enough progress for one night. She deliberately switched her tone to one of calm confidence.

"I'll do some research for you, let you know what your options are. I'm good with lists." She rose from the chair and crossed towards the door. His words stopped her.

"You're going to make me another project, aren't you?"

"I don't know what you mean."

"Like dinners for Patty and the gang, and care taking for

your aunt. I'm another charity case for you, aren't I?" He rose to pace, frustration in his weakness evident in every stride.

"My aunt was not a charity case. She was someone I cared about that needed my help. You're not a charity case, either. You are a friend, and I help my friends when I can."

"Is that what we are, Dani? Friends?" He stopped in front of her, challenging her to acknowledge the energy still sparking between them. He didn't touch her, but he came close enough that she wanted him to. Could she do this? Could she handle being this turned on by someone who had to remain just a friend? She tested her fortitude, letting the powerful emotions he unleashed wreak havoc on the inside. Could she behave? When the temptation to touch became too great, she forced herself to step back before he scrambled her wits again. He was hanging on by a thread, and he needed her help. Of course, that came before the pulsing need he inspired. She had to. For him.

"We will be. We should go to bed." His eyebrows shot up to the ceiling, and she realized what she'd said. "I meant I should go to bed in my bed, and you should go to bed in yours. Geez, get your mind out of the gutter, Gantry. I'll talk to you tomorrow."

"OK, sleep tight." *Oh, I'll sleep tight, all right.* With all of this unfulfilled sexual tension, she was wound up like a rubber band and ready to snap! She really had to leave before she did something foolish. The quiet vulnerability in his words stopped her yet again.

"Hey, are we good with earlier? You know, the kiss?"

"Kiss? What kiss? All I remember is a very enjoyable dream. Good night, Nick." With a false cheeky grin, she patted him on the shoulder and escaped, certain that sleep would be elusive.

THE NEXT MORNING, Dani, exhausted, set up her laptop on Aunt Helen's cozy kitchen table with her favorite mug at her elbow full of steaming hot coffee. She was going to need the back-up after a fitful night full of distracting dreams. She took stock while waiting for the screen to wake up and connect to the Wi-Fi. Her apartment was currently a hodge-podge of different styles, an eclectic mix of her favorite things and Aunt Helen's, but it suited her. It already felt more like home than her modern apartment in Houston ever had. She felt comfortable and prepared to tackle her latest project. Turning to look at the picture of Aunt Helen that she'd taken in front of the castle up in Napa, she murmured, "OK, here we go."

The comforts of home soothed her as she delved into the difficult task of researching Post Traumatic Stress Disorder. The support sites for vets all said the same thing. Talk to counselors. Get help. You may not be acting "normally." You are not alone.

The sites for spouses and family members were more disconcerting. "How can you be supportive and understanding, while second guessing your spouse?" Dani wondered aloud. On one hand, the sites encouraged spouses to try to help their partner avoid trigger situations or cope with the aftermath.

On the other hand, they also gave "practical" suggestions of setting up a safe room for any children, and setting up a private savings account as an emergency fund if bills went unpaid or it should become necessary to take the kids and leave for safety. Heavy thoughts, indeed. She really didn't need to step into that role no matter how hot his kisses were.

Dani copied and pasted links for several support groups and a site that shared video clips of veterans talking about their experiences. If anything, she could show him he wasn't alone in this. She took copious notes on both the possible treatments as well as the symptoms. She wanted to ask him more specifically about what he'd been experiencing. Nightmares, flashbacks, anxiety, avoiding people, depression, difficulty sleeping, outbursts of anger or irritability, the list went on and on. The more she read, the more it became clear that what he needed was just a friend. She would just help out, no matter how many of her buttons he pushed. She turned to her favorite picture and poured out her concerns.

"Aunt Helen, this poor guy! How could he think he'd get over all this by himself? I know, Army Strong, and all that, but seriously. I hope I can help him. Hell, I hope I can keep my hands off him." She let the memory of those hands invade for just moment, and her body immediately reacted.

"You should see him, Aunt Helen. Big, strong, and sexy as hell, with a wounded streak. You'd love him. Jesus, can I pick them or what?" She shook her head to dispel the haze of desire fogging her brain. She was not going there ever again. Somehow, she had to resist. She made herself repeat what she'd read online about the warning signs of PTSD. She looked up at her aunt's picture, wishing that it would answer back. She needed a smart ass, no nonsense, nugget of wisdom to keep her on the straight and narrow with this guy.

"I can't let this happen. Last night was just an anomaly, a stellar kiss that will fade to a funny memory. He is really in no place to get involved, and neither am I. I've got my own stuff to work on. If I'm not vigilant against letting it happen, our chemistry is going to explode." *It has been way too long since the last explosion.* Ugh, her inner vixen really needed to get on board with the whole friends-only plan.

"I want to help him, but the next six months need to be about me. I am not going to let your gift go to waste, Aunt Helen. I'm going to build a new life, without any distractions." *But oh, what a lovely distraction he'd be.* "No! I can do this. I am a powerful woman in control of my future...And I'm talking to a photograph..." she sighed, missing her aunt for the millionth time that morning. Some days she could totally function on her own, but other days the grief crept in and she ended up talking to a memory. It was doubly hard to be surrounded by all of her aunt's favorite things. She knew she should start packing them up, but she'd miss every story, every memory attached, and she couldn't bear to lose another point of connection. Enough of this. She had work to do. And if she kept herself busy working on everyone else's problems, maybe she could avoid thinking about her own. She crossed the kitchen to refill her coffee for round two on the Internet, and was interrupted when her cell phone buzzed incessantly from its charging station. She raced to get it, and was glad she made the effort when she saw Jamie Donovan's face on the display.

She and Jamie had been co-captains of the cheerleading squad in high school. When Dani had moved back to town in January, she had looked up which old friends were still in town, and Jamie had popped up. She was a life coach based in San Jose, and she'd recently done a series of segments on a morning talk show that had gone viral. They'd managed to meet up for coffee once, but between Jamie's suddenly crazy schedule and Dani's increasing level of care for Aunt Helen, they had settled for phone calls and texts to stay connected. Dani needed to fix that now that her days and nights stretched empty before her.

"Hey, Jamie. What's up?"

"Just calling to check in. How are you holding up?"

As Dani filled her in on Aunt Helen's surprise and her push to sort out her life, she realized what a blessing it was to have a friend to lean on. She shared her grief and frustrations. She was sitting in a canoe without a paddle, but here was a friend who wanted to help her carve the paddle she needed. As she shared her emotions, she felt them begin to fade. Jamie had such a gift for active listening. She resolved to pay that same gift forward to Nick.

"I'm going to make a suggestion. Feel free to say no, if it would be uncomfortable, but I'd like to help you with your project. I had a participant drop out of my retreat in Santa Cruz this weekend. It's an intensive session designed to clarify purpose and set goals. It sounds like you could use this right now. The spot is yours if you want it."

Dani's jaw dropped. She knew how coveted those spots were, and how far in advance people booked to talk to Jamie. She looked back at Aunt Helen's smiling picture on the wall, and grinned. *Nuggets of wisdom, here I come.* "I'll be there."

FIVE

Nick was caught off guard by the knock on his door the next morning. His hair was still wet. He was still tugging a on his t-shirt, as he opened the door on the second knock. There was Dani, clutching a notebook to her chest. Ten minutes earlier and she'd have caught him in the shower. He grinned at that visual, thankful she couldn't read his mind and gestured her inside.

"Good morning. Can I offer you some coffee, a doughnut, maybe an apology?" He watched her carefully, measuring her reaction to his words as he walked into the kitchen.

"Coffee would be great. No thanks, on the doughnut. And no apology necessary. I thought we covered that last night."

"We did. But things can look different in the morning. How do you take your coffee?"

"Fake sugar?"

"Nope, sorry. I've got the real thing, and some milk that I don't think has spoiled yet."

"In that case, black is fine. Thanks." She crossed the room and sat down in his brown leather armchair, the only other piece of furniture in the living room aside from the hideous, orange, lumpy couch. He wondered if the choice was deliberate.

His own memories of their time on that couch were a little too close for comfort. Did she feel the same charge looking at the spot where she'd climbed all over him last night? Regardless, he had to set that aside. He knew *that* wasn't why she'd come.

"So, if you're not here for an apology, what can I do for you?" Nick handed her a steaming mug of coffee.

"It's more along the lines of what I can do for you. I did some research this morning, and I just wanted to drop it off so you could look at it while I'm gone. I'll be busy through the weekend, so I won't be back to bug you until Monday." Damn, she was efficient. Or pushy. He couldn't decide which. He certainly hadn't expected her to be this quick.

"Wow. That was fast. Um, OK. What've you got?" His shoulders tensed, and his grip on his coffee mug began to shake ever so slightly.

"So, first things first. Ground rules. I'm going to ask some hard questions today. If there's anything you don't want to tell me, that's fine. But think about the answers even if you can't share them yet. Then I'll give you some resources to check out at your own pace and some privacy. Cool?"

"OK. That sounds reasonable." He was far from calm about what she was proposing, leg twitching and eyes darting around the room. This was going to be torture.

"Do you want to sit down? Get comfortable?"

"I don't think sitting on that couch with you in the room is going to help me relax."

"Right. Good point. Kitchen chair then? Take a deep breath and try to relax your shoulders. We're just friends talking. So how long have you been back in the States?"

Nick dropped on to the shaker style kitchen chair backwards, keeping the high ladder back as a barrier between them. He shrugged his shoulders a few times and cracked his neck. "About four months. I spent some time back in Virginia debriefing and returning to stateside duty before my discharge came through. Started looking at where I wanted to be. Seth had been talking up California for months while we were overseas. His family has a solid construction business out here. It sounded good. I searched online for apartments and found this place the day it was listed. Signed the lease without even looking at the place."

As he wound down, she gently asked the next question on her list.

"How long have you been having troubles?"

"Since before I got back."

"Can I ask? What does it feel like?"

Nick took another deep breath.

"Well, right now, my shoulders are tense and my stomach feels like it's trying to tie itself in a knot."

"OK, we'll back off for a bit."

"No, no...you need to know, I guess. Just give me a minute." He got up and started pacing a circuit around the living room, shaking his arms out. "I don't ever really feel 'at ease', you know? I'm always on my guard, waiting for something to happen. It doesn't take much to trigger it, a sound, a smell. If I'm not careful and let my mind travel back to the front, the memories creep in, and then all of a sudden it's like I'm back there, in the thick of it. Going to the grocery store the other day, I almost passed out before I got through the checkout line. The panic nearly took me under right there."

"What made you panic?"

"That time? I couldn't see around the corners at the end of the aisle. I couldn't see what was coming or lurking. Somebody dropped a can and it sounded like a shell casing hitting the ground. A woman with two kids hanging off her cart came whipping around the frozen foods aisle and I nearly deliberately rammed her cart with mine. I left with whatever I had in my cart before I fell apart. I've been eating cereal and salsa for three days."

"What does it feel like when you have an attack?"

"Sometimes it's a slow build up. Other times, like last night, it hits me fast. My arms go all tingly like I've got a pinched nerve or something. My stomach cramps up, and my vision starts to blur around the edges. Then the shakes start. Sometimes my head just shuts down. Those are the good attacks, where I just blackout. Other times, I'm back in Iraq..."

He trailed off, stopped pacing, and stared off into the mid-distance. He'd never told anyone about this. He couldn't quite believe Dani had gotten it out of him so quickly. Her patient eyes and killer smile were a lethal combination. He didn't really want to turn around and see her reaction. He didn't want to see pity or worse on her face.

"I know that as an officer, you've been trained on how to detect PTSD in your men. I know it's harder to see these things in yourself, but I found this checklist of symptoms. You've got them across the board." She shuffled through the papers in the journal, not meeting his eyes when he turned to look over her shoulder.

"I know. I've been trying not to think it, but I know."

"This other page is a list of sites you might want to surf through this weekend. I read through a lot of them. They all outline symptoms and treatment options, but there's one that helps make a connection with other vets through video clips. It might help you feel less isolated here, without having to leave your apartment. Slow and steady wins the race, right?" She was rambling again. She did that when she was nervous. Was he making her nervous? He had a good idea of what she'd read on those sites. Was she afraid of him? Was she right to be?

"The last one on there is the link to the local VA branch and the regional hub. It's just about two blocks from here. It looks like they have both inpatient and outpatient programs depending on what you feel you need. Just take a look over the next few days. I'll check back in on Monday, and we'll see where we are and what you want to do." She stood quickly and turned to face him, like she was uncomfortable with him standing behind her. She handed him the notebook without meeting his eyes. Damn it. It had been a long time since someone had cared enough to go to bat for him. He couldn't let her walk away scared. Change the subject. Keep it light.

"Where are you going? You mentioned you'd be away?"

"Well, my friend Jamie called this morning and invited me to her retreat in Santa Cruz. She had someone drop out at the last minute. With the stress of the funeral and the will, she felt I might need couple of days to recharge at the beach. I'm going to trust that the universe has something in store for me, so I'm heading to the coast."

"I hope you have a good time. And thanks, for getting on this so quickly, and for not letting what you read scare you away."

"I'll admit, it put me a little on edge, but what did GI Joe say? Knowing is half the battle? I know now what to watch out for and how I can help and how I can't. Anyhow, I should get going. I've still got to pack and wrap up a few errands before I drive over the mountain tonight."

"OK. I guess I'll see you Monday." He didn't understand the sadness that swept through him. He tried to force a smile and followed her as she began walking to the door.

At the threshold, Dani hesitated. She turned back to him and gave him a tight hug. Shocked by the sudden contact, Nick's body seized and pulled her even closer. Dani whispered, "We'll beat this. We'll find a way. I'm in it with you, and we will beat this." She pulled away before the hug could stray from friendly support into dangerous territory, and disappeared into her own apartment.

Nick, after carefully closing and locking his own door, gave himself a firm mental shake. He'd had to actively suppress the desire to lean in and give her a kiss goodbye.

"Get your head in the game, Nicky boy," he chastised himself. "She could be just the thing you need to get you through this. Don't screw it up!"

DANI WALKED through the aisles of the local grocery store, picking up what she deemed essentials: lunch meat, bread, a few condiments, milk, eggs, cereal, and pasta. If he couldn't go to the grocery store, she'd bring the grocery store to him. She called Mrs. Grady from her cell phone and got the answering machine. Knowing that she screened her calls, Dani was not surprised. She'd keep her message short.

"Hi, Mrs. Grady. It's me. Listen, I can't tell you much, because I don't want to break a confidence, but I think our new friend could use a little company this weekend. I'm going to be out of town for a few days, and I just don't want him to be stuck there all alone. Be subtle! Talk to you soon." She hung up quickly before the older woman could get to the phone and grill her for details if she was indeed listening. After checking out with the groceries, she swung by the dry cleaners to pick up clothes she had dropped off a while ago, and returned a bag of library books that were due soon. Satisfied that she had her errands done enough to leave town, she headed home to pack.

She added her perishable produce that wouldn't last the weekend to the grocery bags and set them outside Nick's door. She debated with herself for a solid minute about whether or not she should knock or just leave the bags. In the end the idea of milk sitting out in the hallway for hours made her decision for her. She compromised on her middle school impulse to ding dong ditch.

After ringing the doorbell, she hightailed it back into her own apartment, shutting the door before he could open his. There, done. She started to put away the dry cleaning, and as she was removing the plastic wrap, she saw Aunt Helen's winter coat. She'd had it cleaned to give to charity and forgotten that it was in this load. She brushed her fingers over the bouclé cashmere lapel and triggered all sorts of memories.

Aunt Helen, walking through the dormant San Jose Rose Gardens, arguing over the expense of having spent good money on a coat she would only have to wear ten days a year. Aunt Helen, clutching it tighter around her neck, happily warm on a wintery weekend in February visiting her friends in Chicago, during some of her last strong days. Aunt Helen, too tired to get up from her bed, instructing Dani on what to do with her coat and other clothes when she had passed.

Dani sat heavily on the edge of her bed, holding the coat tightly as if she could still hug the woman who wore it, and let the tears fall. Sometimes grief hit so hard and so fast that all she could do was cry until the storm had passed. She felt like she was stuck in a boxing ring with a champion. Just when she thought she could stand up again, grief punched her in the gut and knocked her to her knees. She had lost her great-aunt, but she had also lost her best friend and confidant. Aunt Helen had been gone a whole month now, and Dani still thought of something she needed to tell her at least ten times a day. She'd started a journal as a way to continue sharing with her aunt. That helped her process a lot of her thoughts on grief and loneliness. But when something this visceral hit her, the journal just wasn't enough.

A loud knock on her door jolted her and had her moving

back into the living room, still clutching the coat to her chest. She opened the door, and there was Nick. His jovial smile quickly faded to a look of concern.

"Hey, are you alright? Are you hurt? What's wrong?" His words mirrored her own from the night before. She retreated into her apartment, and he followed shutting the door with a snap.

"I'm alright. Or I will be in a little while." The tears were still tracking their way down her face with every blink of her lashes. "Have you ever lost someone close to you?"

He nodded guardedly.

"Then you know. Sometimes the smallest thing can make you miss them like it just happened. This was Aunt Helen's coat. It came home with my dry cleaning." Dani hated explaining her feelings to a man. It always made her feel like her tears were silly.

Without a word, Nick stepped closer and pulled her into a hug, pressing his lips to her forehead. He didn't beg her to stop crying. He didn't tell her to get over it. He didn't try to fix it. She took the strength and comfort as it was offered and within moments began to feel the pressing sadness in her chest recede. Pulling back, she looked him square in the eyes.

"Thank you. I guess I needed that."

"Anytime. I just came by to thank you for the groceries. You didn't need to do that."

"No, I didn't need to, but I wanted to. I was going out anyhow."

"I'll pay you for them, at least. What do I owe you?"

"Consider it a gift from Aunt Helen. A welcome to the building. She was never a big baker, so instead of showing up with cookies or cakes, she'd bring by a simple bag of essentials to stock the fridge the first night. She'd appreciate me carrying on the tradition."

"OK, well, thank you. You gonna be OK now?"

"Yeah, I'm OK. Thanks."

"Well, I'll let you get back to packing. Have a good trip. I'll see you when you get back." He tucked his hands into his pockets and shrugged up his shoulders.

"Bye, Nick. Thanks again." She followed him to the door, ready to close it behind him. He paused a moment on the threshold, looked her in the eye, and then without another word turned and went into his apartment. Perplexed by what that last look had meant, Dani shrugged and closed her own door, a bit surprised to find that she did indeed feel OK. For the first time in weeks, the platitude hadn't been a lie.

SIX

DAWN CAME SLOWLY on a Saturday morning on the coast. Dani savored her first coffee of the day on the back patio of the bed and breakfast, watching the sunshine begin to clear the Santa Cruz Mountains. Tucked back in the mountains, the B&B was a peaceful oasis, surrounded by redwood giants. Breathing in the crisp woodsy air, she sat with her warm mug, and let her thoughts run free. This was just the sort of place Aunt Helen would have loved hiking around for a weekend. Dani got lost in old memories of trips and adventures. Even as the sun began to warm her shoulders, the gaping hole in the center of her chest felt so cold.

Dani sat with the weight on her heart, wishing that she could change things. But change them to what? What the hell do I want to do? Then she realized that was exactly what she was here to figure out. She took a few deep breaths to clear her mind and start fresh, letting hope creep in around the edges of her grief. Picking up her now empty mug, she headed into the sitting room where Jamie was getting the conference set up. Her friend's sleek auburn ponytail hung straight as a nail down the middle of her back as she fussed with the breakfast trays, reminding Dani of their cheerleading days. Her All-American girl look had changed little in the ten years since high school. Jamie had always been a sweetheart, but when she was on the court performing, she had been driven, all business. No wonder she'd been elected captain three years running. It looked like she had turned that determination on her career with amazing results.

"What can I do to help?" Dani asked, moving to take one of the scone and fruit plates Jamie had carried in from the kitchen.

"Just put these over on the table. That'd be great! Thanks!" Jamie pulled her in for a real hug, before turning to arrange the furniture into a loose circle. "I'm so glad you came, Dani. I hope we get a chance to catch up a bit, outside of the sessions."

"I'd really like that, Jamie. I feel like I've lost track of everyone."

The other attendees began trickling in slowly, introducing themselves and getting their coffee or tea and a little snack. The group was small, only six people, so that everyone paired off nicely and had the benefit of some quality time working alone with Jamie, as well as group reflection sessions. Demand for Jamie's time was rising, and Dani felt lucky that she'd been able to snag some of it.

Once everyone was settled, Jamie turned a smile on everyone, rubbing her hands together.

"OK, everyone! Let's get down to business!"

Butterflies danced in Dani's belly. *Here we go.*

Back at his apartment, Nick spent Saturday morning cleaning. Again. He scrubbed the kitchen, swept and mopped the floors, and even detailed the bathroom grout with a toothbrush. He was avoiding looking at his computer. Every time he saw the silver rectangle with the slowly pulsing light on the edge, a tremor shook his belly, and he found something else to clean. Looking at the websites Dani had recommended would likely trigger something. Hell, it was already triggering a low-level panic in his gut, and he hadn't looked at anything but a scrub brush!

He was sorting his minuscule amount of laundry into loads when he heard a knock on the door. His heart kicked up, and a smile crossed his face as he hustled to the door. It must be Dani on the other side of the door. But wait. She was on the other side of a mountain range this morning. Just how disappointing that was shook him a little bit, but he pushed that thought away and opened the door to find Jack Delano waiting with a smile.

"Hi there, neighbor! I was hoping you'd be home. Got a minute?" Jack's bluff and jovial greeting banished the last of Nick's disappointment, and he welcomed the man into his new home. He wasn't sure he was fit for company, but Jack was already inside striding to the small kitchen.

"Come on in. I was just cleaning up a little bit."

"A little bit, nothing! This place is shining like a barracks five minutes before inspection. But don't worry. You'll get out of that habit soon enough. I just thought I'd give you a tour of the place and introduce you to her quirks. She has a few but hopefully they won't be too much of a pain."

"Thank you, sir. I'd appreciate it."

"Here now, none of that 'sir' business. Yeah, I served, Viet Nam, but that's long behind me."

Nick glanced pointedly at the buzz cut still featured prominently on his balding pate.

"Oh, that? Ha ha ha! Son, it's the only haircut that manages to make me look like I still have a bit of hair! Plus, it's easy for my barber to handle. He's a vet, too. You'll find a lot of us in the area. The first round moved out here after WWII, building up suburbs in the warm California sun. Then a lot of guys from my era ended up settling here because of all the bases between Monterey and Alameda. Some of us got out and started families. Others who had more trouble readjusting to 'normal' ended up on the streets. Lots of homeless around here have some level of military service behind them. If you're going to live off the grid, sunny California is a beautiful place to do it."

Nick thought of Seth, and how his family had followed a similar path, migrating to California for the work after World War II. He also wondered how far off from "normal" he was. Was he going to be a statistic? What if he couldn't beat this? What if he went off the rails and ended up on the streets? The thought was sobering, and it took Nick a moment to realize that Jack was giving him the tour.

"Now, take a look here under your sink. See that funky looking knob? That's your water shut-off valve. If you ever have a leak under the sink, I want you to turn that full stop *before* you call me. We've had to replace a few ceilings over the years, and it's no fun. Also, the dishwasher works better if you pre-wash. It's a workhorse, and it rarely breaks, but it does clog. And you'll want to wait to run it until you've finished your shower & shave. It will pull the entire hot water load to the apartment, and I don't think you'd enjoy a cold shower surprise when it hits the rinse cycle! Since you haven't called me complaining, I'm assuming Dani told you about the jiggle in the shower. I've replaced that damn water mixer more times, but still it needs a little knock now and again. Now, let me show you how the wall heaters work."

A cold shower might not be a bad idea. Just that quickly Dani and their incendiary kiss heated his thoughts. Nick tried to focus on what the super was telling him. The wall hung heaters were definitely a new experience, having been raised in the Midwest, where a home without central heating and air was unheard of. He paid attention to the instructions on how to turn it on and off and the warnings about how hot "high" really got. He thought about cranking it the next time she came over, just to see her get hot and bothered. Maybe she'd lose some layers. He needed help if he was plotting to use a heater in July to get a woman to take off her clothes. Pathetic. What he really needed was to get Dani out of his head. He reran Jack's comments through his head, turning his thoughts to all the vets from Viet Nam who came back with problems.

"Well, that should just about do it. If you need anything, my cell number is on the magnet on the fridge. Call anytime day or night!"

"Thanks, again. Can I offer you a coffee break before you run off to take care of your next leaky pipe?"

"I wouldn't say no. Got sugar and cream?"

"Thanks to my neighbor across the hall, I do."

"She's pretty fantastic, isn't she...Listen, I know you're just back from a deployment, and probably feeling your oats, but she's handling a lot right now...."

Nick cut him off, feeling the man's embarrassment but determination to warn him off. "You don't need to worry on that score. Dani and I agree that neither of us are in the position to offer anything but friendship right now."

"I understand why Dani's not open, but why are you putting yourself in that same boat?"

He'd opened the door on the question. He might as well see what advice the older man had to share.

"You mentioned your buddies from Nam," Nick paused, grasping for the right words, "how some of them struggled to find 'normal'?" He glanced toward Jack but couldn't bring himself to make eye contact. His chest felt tight and the tingles raced down his arms.

"Oh man, I'm sorry." Jack placed his hand on Nick's shoulder. Nick jumped at the contact, but he made himself breathe and look Jack in the eye. He was afraid of the pity that would be on the older man's face but instead found understanding. Jack took a seat at the table and stared into his coffee.

"I remember my first year back. I jumped at every sudden noise. Took me a long time to get used to sleeping in the quiet." Nick lowered himself into the chair across from Jack. "And I was really angry for a long time, and I could never pin down why. I still have some bad moments from time to time."

"What did you do about it?"

"At first I let it control me. I'd get angry at home and not know what to do with myself. So, I'd bluster around, bitching about whatever set me off, and storm out of the house. I'd meet up with buddies to blow off steam, usually in a bar. I drank too much, trying to black out the images I couldn't bear to see again. I ruined a good marriage in the process. I hit rock bottom. I was a drunk. I'd lost my home and my wife.

"I lived in a state park for awhile, camping out. Then I met a preacher at one of the shelters I'd hit up for meals. He slipped me a card for AA. I got in and got sober. I got the counseling I needed. I got my wife to fall in love with me again and had 20 more years to show her that love everyday, before cancer took her away from me. That woman was a saint."

The older man's eyes took on a shine, the love for his wife still clearly written all over his face. He got quiet, clearing his throat before continuing. He looked Nick square in the eye.

"I let it control me, and it almost ruined me. If you are feeling any of that crap, don't let it eat at you. You've got to get it out in the light where it can't hurt anymore. It's hard and it's scary. I won't lie. You'll want to quit more than once, but you are Army Strong. You can do it."

Nick broke the eye contact and stared into his coffee for a long while. He gathered his courage to share his deepest thoughts and fears. When he finally spoke, his voice came out cracked and rusty.

"I've never been this scared in my life. I didn't feel this scared on patrols or during fire fights. Sometimes it makes me as weak as a baby. And I hate that feeling. Why the hell am I scared now?"

"Because your brain shoved all that scared shitless deep down inside, so you could survive and do what you needed to do during those patrols and fire fights. It shoved it deep, but not out. Now that you're home and not under immediate threat, your brain wants to do some spring-cleaning and force that shit out. Talk to someone, man. Get it out of your brain so you can move on. I know a bunch of vets from my AA group, if you ever want to just have a solid group of guys to talk to. Lots of vets who'll know just what you're going through. I can ask them if they'd be willing to come over some night just to talk."

"I don't know if I'm there yet, but I'll think about it. Thanks for letting me throw this at you. I've done more talking to complete strangers this week..."

"Glad to help."

"Would you mind keeping this between you and me for awhile? I'm not sure I'm ready for Patty to get this bit between her teeth."

"Son, she's had your number since you moved in! I'm convinced she's got these rooms bugged, not that I've ever found any evidence of course..." He chuckled. "All the same, she won't get the details from me. I'll warn you though, she's persistent."

"Thanks."

"Well, I'd better go. 202 called early this morning with a stuck window."

"See you soon. And thanks again for the tour, and the talk."

"Anytime."

And with that Nick was left alone with his thoughts again. He mulled over Jack's story and advice, thinking everything through again and again. He still avoided his laptop like the plague, but at least he was able to sit still for a while.

SEVEN

DANI WALKED along the beach after the first session of the retreat. It wasn't warm enough for swimming, and the brisk breeze whipped her long hair back from her face as she followed the wave line. Waves crept close to her sneaker clad toes and then rushed back to join the swirling mass of ocean beyond, mirroring the motion of her thoughts. So many ideas were swirling in her mind. As soon as one would surface, she would ponder it a moment before it receded and another took its place.

I feel lost. What do I want to be when I grow up? What am I qualified to do? Do I want just another job or do I want to do something I'm passionate about? What else do I want in my life besides work? A man? A family? Something else? What would that be? Where do I begin? Get a life. Build a life. I'm certainly going to try.

Overwhelmed, she climbed the short cliff carved by waves and time and found a dry spot to sit among the tide pools. She closed her eyes and tried to slow her mind, breathing deeply, pushing any stray thoughts away until her pulse calmed and anxiety flowed away. She carefully reviewed the morning session, looking for clues.

Jamie had paired her up with Angela, a stay at home mom who was trying to find a path now that her children were away at college. Their task was to listen to each other explain their frustrations and help mirror it back to clarify what was making them unhappy.

"So, you're an empty nester, huh?" Dani asked.

"Emphasis on empty. I gave up working when baby number two came along. My whole life revolved around taking care of the kids and the house and my husband. I know we're supposed to be all liberated, but honestly, I loved that life. That was my choice. I loved being the driving force for our family life. Now that's gone, and I just feel empty."

"I can't say that I know how it feels to have children and see them move out, but I can definitely relate. I was the primary caretaker for my Aunt Helen. I left my job in Houston to move up here and help her out. She passed away from cancer a few weeks ago, and I feel empty without someone to take care of. It's like I'm treading water in the pool, just waiting for a reason to swim."

"Well, it seems like we have that in common. I hate feeling useless. I keep thinking I should do something that I enjoy, but it's been so long since I got to do something just for me that I have no idea what I like any more."

"I hear you saying that you want to do something you love and something useful, but that you haven't had time to find your passions outside of raising your family."

"That about sums it up. If I'm hearing you right, you enjoy being helpful, too. And that you are looking for a new avenue to utilize your care-taking talents."

Figuring out what she wanted to change was the easy part. The next step was more difficult. By being clear about what things she was searching for, she could set detailed plans to attain it.

"Your homework," Jamie had said over the chatter, "is to describe your ideal outcomes. Now that you know the need you are trying to fill, think about what it might take to fill it. Instead of immediately focusing on, 'What do I want to do?' visualize how you feel, what drives you, fulfills you. How would you feel ideally at work? What do you want to get from your work, aside from a paycheck? When you picture yourself happy, what is making you feel that way? Take notes in your journals and we will share when I see you tomorrow."

Dani opened her eyes and studied the tide pool nearest to her. She saw barnacles, small seaweeds, an anemone, and a tiny crab in the small pool of seawater trapped up on the rock. This miniature habitat, trapped by circumstance and the caprice of a wave, would have to survive together until the next high tide released them from their confinement. For the mobile animals, this was a chance to eat in a calm environment before heading back out into the buffeting waves. The fixed elements depended on the nutrients washed into the puddle on the tide, replenished daily. It amazed her to see how this odd fusion of creatures, came together in endless combinations, and managed to coexist and meet their needs for life, day after day. But wasn't that what life was about? Finding a way to work and live together with the people fate threw your way? Building relationships that fulfilled your needs until the next wave came along and shook things up? She mourned the wave that took Aunt Helen away, but still found herself oddly optimistic about what the next wave had brought in.

Feeling a little shaken herself, Dani turned her gaze out to the ocean and picked up her phone. Before she registered her intent, her fingers had dialed. Nick answered on the second ring.

"Hi. Have you got a minute?"

"Sure, Dani. What's up?"

"I need help with my homework."

"Oh, God. It's not calculus, is it?"

"No, just deep life questions."

"Fire away. I'll do my best."

"I'm supposed to figure out what will fulfill me in a new career? What about it would make me happy?"

"And what was your old career?"

"Accounting. I was good with numbers and fell into it, but I can't say I had a driving passion for it."

"Does anyone have a driving passion for accounting?" Nick quipped, pulling a laugh from her.

"You'd be surprised. There's a lot of satisfaction in a balanced spreadsheet for some people. But not enough for me to go back. If I get to start over, I want to do something else."

"OK, well, what did you like about it?"

"I loved the challenge of constantly learning new things, new rules, new procedures, and making the numbers behave."

"OK, so new challenges and following the rules. Are you sure? I totally had you pegged as a rebel."

"Ha ha. Very funny."

"The problem I see is that you are a bright and well educated woman. You have too many options to choose from if you look at this as a career search. What is going to make this a calling? What will make it special to you?"

"The satisfaction of doing something well, an opportunity to learn new things and try new skills, avoiding boredom..." she twirled her pen above the doodles framing her notes.

"You can get all of that from a crossword puzzle."

"I just want to be useful, helpful. I want to make difference in someone's life." Saying the words aloud was powerful. That was a valid motivation. She found tremendous satisfaction in helping her aunt and their community in the building. Helping others, while challenging herself to continue to learn and grow and succeed, was a worthwhile reason to work.

"I can't think of any better reason to go to work in the morning than to make someone's life better. And after all, helping people seems to be firmly in your wheelhouse. You've helped everyone in this building at one time or other. As they've made sure to tell me when they casually dropped by. All of them. Some, twice."

"Oh goodness. Inundated, are you? They mean well. So, I am going to be a helper. Now if I can just figure out what I can do, and who I can do it for, I'll be all set." Dani groaned over the Herculean task.

"Hey, have a little faith. Just look how much better my life is, and I've only known you a few days."

"You think I've made your life better?" she shyly probed.

The other end of the line went quiet for a moment, before Nick finally replied. "You have no idea."

The silence on the line returned, and Dani wanted nothing more than for him to keep talking. She enjoyed the deep rumble of his voice melding with the rich sound of the ocean waves breaking, soothing her jittery nerves. She definitely wanted to know more about how she'd made him feel better. But she remembered their friendship vow, and she let the comment pass, even though it went against every instinct.

"That must have been a really excellent batch of chocolate chip cookies," she teased. Nick's laughter rolled over the line.

"They were OK. Something was a little off. I think you should try another batch when you get home, just to make sure your recipe is right."

"Nice try. You only get one plate of welcome cookies per move."

"Damn. Well, it was worth a shot. Did you get what you needed for your homework?"

"Yeah, I think I did. Thanks, Nick. Talking it all out really helped."

"I accept payment for homework help in the form of brownies or pies..."

"Fair enough. I'll hook you up when I get home. Have a good night."

"You too, Dani. Feel free to call back if you need any more homework help. I'm happy to work for food."

She hung up the phone laughing. Grateful for the mood boost and his help in clarifying her goals, she stood and brushed the sand from her seat. The tide was coming in, and soon her tide pool friends would be submerged for the night. She gathered herself and began the hike back to the retreat. At peace with her recent revelation, she let her mind rest and simply enjoyed the beauty of the redwoods surrounding her.

Saturday evening, Nick was settled on his couch watching the latest comedy special on cable, when a knock on his door interrupted his solitude. He peered through the peephole and saw Lt. Colonel Jones and Mrs. Betancourt standing outside in the hallway. He shut off the television and opened the door.

"Good evening, Nick. We saw your car parked outside and took a guess that you were home. If you don't have any prior engagements, we'd love you to join us for dinner tonight." Mrs. Betancourt looked up at him, eyes full of hope.

"Nothing fancy, son. Just a walk down to the local Chinese restaurant," the retired army man added.

Nick was wary for a moment. This invitation would require leaving his apartment, walking down the street, sitting exposed in a restaurant for upwards of an hour. So many potential triggers. The hair on the back of his neck stood up with tension. He took a deep breath. He reminded himself that he'd been feeling pretty good all day, especially after unloading to Jack that morning. He could consider this a test. He wouldn't be going that far from home if he needed to get back quickly. He told himself he didn't want this pair walking anywhere on their own and a man needed to eat after all, but the truth was he'd been feeling lonely and isolated cooped up in his too-quiet apartment. Here was a perfect opportunity to get out for a bit. He'd need to know the local Chinese take-out place at any rate. Evaluating his options, Nick decided that the show was worth missing.

As he struggled with his decision, his cell phone rang in his pocket. "Excuse me a moment." He glanced at the display and answered it when he saw Seth's crazy mug shot smiling up at him.

"Hey man, how's it going?"

"Great! I met a couple of my neighbors, and we're going out for drinks tonight. You game?"

Just the thought of hitting a bar and trying to do small talk with women had the butterflies he'd suppressed begin fluttering in his stomach again. All of the potential triggers in that situation sent a shudder down his spine. Given his options, he'd take the elderly couple and Chinese cuisine in a heartbeat.

"Actually, I met some of my neighbors, too. We're on our way out to dinner now. Maybe another time?"

"You lucky shit! You hooked up with the hottie across the hall didn't you? Well, that didn't take long! Alright, I won't hound you tonight, but we should hang out soon."

"Sure, man. Soon. Gotta run." Nick didn't bother to correct his friend's assumption. After all he had met the hottie across the hall, and though he wasn't going out to dinner with her tonight, he had eaten with her before. Explaining would only muddy the water and end up with Seth pushing him harder to come out. His justifications didn't ease the feeling that he'd just lied to his best friend, but he'd rather not explain that he preferred spending time with a couple of 90 year olds than with fun single people his own age. He disconnected the call and dropped the phone into the pocket of his shorts. He turned back towards the door and the two beaming seniors waiting for him who had clearly overheard his conversation.

"I'm starving. Shall we?" he asked locking his door behind him.

The Golden Dragon was a five-block walk, and Nick kept a careful watch on his companions. The older couple seemed to manage it fine, though at a snail's pace. They clearly weren't letting anything stop them from getting out and about. Nick took advantage of the slower pace to continuously scan his perimeters and avoid being surprised at corners and alleyways. Rooftops, windows shaded by blinds, dumpsters, every potential threat seemed magnified, and he jumped at any unexpected movement. He'd thought he was hiding it well, walking behind them. But Mrs. B. and the Colonel pulled him up between them after two blocks, and pointed out various local landmarks and shops along the way. They greeted several other pedestrians as they made their way to the restaurant, and pulled Nick into the conversation.

"We are right here with you, Nick. You are safe." Mrs. B. patted his arm with her tiny hand and he felt remarkably comforted. Comfort was not something Nick usually felt in the company of strangers, and yet with this unlikely duo he felt as if he were walking down the street with grandparents he'd known his entire life. The fact that he hadn't known his own grandparents at all made the feeling all the more unique.

Even the hostess at the Golden Dragon greeted them warmly.

"Colonel! Mrs. B.! It is so good to see you." A small Asian woman came from behind the hostess stand.

"Mrs. Lin, this is our new friend, Nick."

"A friend of yours is a friend of mine. It is a pleasure to meet you. You know, these two kept us in business when we first opened this location. We have been friends a long time. Come, I have your table for you."

Nick followed to a square table in the back of the room. With the hairs on the back of his neck standing at attention, his eyes flicked to every corner of the restaurant, and he could feel his shoulders creeping up towards his ears. Mrs. B. sat on one side of the square table for four facing the kitchens on an angle, and William sat on the other. Nick chose the seat facing the door, next to the Colonel.

Mrs. B. smiled at him. "My Charlie had a thing about that, too. I thought he would give himself whiplash whenever we'd enter a room. He'd always request a seat in a back corner of the restaurant. At first I thought he was being romantic, until he panicked one night in a packed restaurant, and we had to leave. I asked him what the problem was, and he explained all the back booths were taken and he couldn't sit for an hour exposed in the middle of the floor. So much for my budding romantic. We went for fast food all dressed up that night." She smiled, clearly at peace with the memories left by her late husband.

"I still need to sit where I can see the exits, too," said the Colonel with a smile. "I get the creepy crawlies on the back of my neck when I can't see the door." Nick grimaced as he realized that he wasn't hiding his anxiety as well as he thought.

Just then, their waiter came to take their order. He introduced himself as Ben Chu, and shook Nick's hand. He chatted casually with the older couple and updated them on the basketball career of his sixth grade daughter, before asking, "The usual or something different tonight for your guest?"

"Let's go all out tonight and eat like kings! I'm sure Nick here will be able to put a dent in whatever Chef Lin feels like making for us. We'll leave it up to him. Unless you have any favorites?"

"Well, what is your usual?"

"One order of combination fried rice, and two egg rolls." Kathleen said with a smile. "It's just enough for the two of us, but I think we'll need something more substantial tonight."

"Let's build on that, and see what else Chef Lin has in store for us!" Game for an adventure, Nick hoped that he wouldn't later regret the impulse. As the waiter left them, Nick asked the question that had been turning in the back of his mind since he'd opened his door.

"Did Dani ask you to talk to me?"

"No, dear, she didn't. We have eyes and experience. We put two and two together on our own. How bad is it?" Mrs. B.'s gentle voice invited confidences, and promised discretion.

Grimacing, Nick pondered how much to tell them. He didn't feel like he could evade the question completely, since they had already guessed and were looking him with such knowing eyes. Given that those eyes also showed compassion without a hint of pity, he opted for the truth.

"Not great. Panic attacks, nightmares, anxiety. It's not anything special."

"Now that's where you're wrong, son." The Colonel cut him off. "It is special, and it's important, because it's happening to you. Just because it's a common reaction for soldiers just back from the front doesn't lessen the impact in your life or the importance in getting some help. Back in my day, we called it shell shock and a lot of good men suffered for a long time because they didn't know what was wrong or how to fix it." The Colonel's matter of fact tone brooked no argument.

"We hope that you're able to get the help you need, for your sake. I was able to help my Charlie through it by sheer luck, but professionals are so much more knowledgeable these days. Oh look! He did the Peking duck! You're in for a treat, Nick. Chef Lin only does the duck a few times a year."

Ben began bringing dishes laden with the house specialties to the table. Nick discreetly slid him a credit card. He would eat for the week off these leftovers. His new neighbors had adopted him and were determined to help him out. He appreciated the effort but he could better afford the meal than they could. He was smiling at their banter, and that surprised him. By all rights, he should be annoyed at their interference. Whenever any of his army buddies tried to give him advice on any subject, he either snapped at them or clammed up. What was different?

"So, Nick, tell us about your family." Mrs. B. broke into his musings.

Caught off guard, he flippantly replied, "There's not much to tell."

An expectant pause followed as the couple waited for an explanation. Maybe that was it, that steady quiet patience that made him spill his guts. Nick sighed and decided, in for a penny, in for a pound.

"My parents were both only children, and my grandparents passed away before I was born."

"Are your parents close?"

"No. I never knew my dad. He knocked her up and never looked back. It was just me and Mom growing up. And then she died of breast cancer when I was sixteen."

"Oh, you poor boy! What did you do?"

"I survived. I'd been the man of the house for a long time, so I knew how to take care of myself. My buddy, Chuck's family let me crash on their couch, applied to be my foster parents so I could stay and finish high school."

He trailed off, remembering those bittersweet days. Chuck's dad did home remodeling and custom carpentry built-ins. Nick had pitched in with the family business to help earn his keep.

He'd sanded and stained until his hands were permanently maple toned. He'd even gotten a chance to learn to use the power tools in the workshop tucked away in the basement near his bedroom. He'd had access to wood whenever he needed to clear his head. It had been an unexpected gift at a time in his life when gifts were scarce. He'd had peace and stability in his grasp, but then high school had ended and real life had reared its ugly head.

"What brought you into the army, son?"

"I joined ROTC out of high school, so I could afford to go to college. I learned how to trust my instincts and how to be a leader. I graduated with degrees in political science and military history. Once I started my career in the army, I finally felt like I belonged somewhere. My unit became my family."

His heart sank to the pit of his stomach as he remembered the pain of losing yet another member of his "family."

"When I let my unit down, I knew it was time to get out."

The older couple listened to every word, offering silent support without pity. He was grateful. He didn't think he could stand it if they felt sorry for him. Was this what extended family felt like? He had imagined grandparents at Christmas as a kid, bringing cookies and presents. He shifted the image to include Chinese food and kind smiles. It still fit.

Mrs. B. reached over to rest her slim wrinkled hand atop his larger brown and weathered one. "Nick, I am glad that you decided to share your story with us. I know tough times can be hard to talk about. We have been there, and we are here to remember. You've got us now, if you want us."

Although Nick had picked the unassuming building by Google search, he suspected that fate had played a hand in landing him smack dab in the middle of his very own vet support group. Instead of feeling smothered and overwhelmed by their interest though, he was strangely comforted.

The conversation turned to favorite meals abroad. As the older couple reminisced about their culinary adventures in the other countries they'd lived in or visited, Nick processed their well-meaning nudges while eating some of the best Peking duck he'd ever had.

He'd gone to one dinner and walked away with so much more than a full belly. A concerned uncle, caring grandparents, a bossy mother hen...and all because of Dani. She was the thread that held this web together. A warm flood of...gratitude swept through him. Did she know her impact? Did she do this for everyone in the building? Leave it up to Fate to hand him everything he'd ever wanted, wrapped up in a bow, and then tell him he could look but not touch. Fate could be a real bitch sometimes.

Nick rejoined the conversation, sharing his memory of his first meal in Germany on the way home from his first tour in Afghanistan. The good food and easy conversation helped him regain some balance and enjoy the evening. He decided that as soon as he got up in the morning, he'd check out the sites Dani had left for him. She had taken her offer to help him seriously. He should do the same. Obviously it was time, if perfect strangers were able to see he needed help. With the surprising support system he'd fallen into, he grasped a flicker of hope that he might actually beat this. Remembering Dani's sunny smile and calm support, Nick felt a bit of the sadness pull back. He realized it was because he believed her. For the first time in a long time, he believed he'd get better. He believed he could beat this.

As he walked back to the apartment, flush with his new sense of optimism, he heard a child crying. He looked around trying to locate the source of the sound. Mrs. B. and the Colonel paused as well, casting him a curious glance.

"Can't you hear it?"

"Hear what, Nick?"

"The kid crying." He took a few deep breaths to try and steady his nerves. His heart wanted to race out of his chest. He reminded himself that he wasn't in Iraq any more and that he was not going to walk into an IED attack on a street corner in Menlo Park. With his eyes closed, he was able to better focus on the sound and turned towards the alley. He could do this. He willed the tingling in his arms to go away. "Wait for me a minute. Please?"

"Sure, son. We'll be right here."

Nick followed the sound down the alley to a trash bin behind a restaurant. Cautiously peeking around the edge of the bin, his mind flashed to gruesome images of war, filling in horrible reasons that a child might be crying. He reached for his sidearm, and found the space at his hip empty. Nick blinked rapidly to clear his thoughts and focused on the tiny wiggling body making that pitiful noise. Not a child, a dog with his head stuck inside an old cardboard delivery box. Thank God.

He approached the pup carefully, speaking softly and letting the pup know everything he was doing. He lifted the dog into his lap and pulled the cardboard aside so he could wriggle his head back out.

"Well, what's your name, little guy?"

The only response Nick got was a frenzied attempt to lick his face.

"Nope! Not until we've gotten you cleaned up. No collar, huh? You seem pretty comfortable with humans. I bet someone is missing you."

Picking up the small dog, Nick carried him back to the sidewalk where his new friends were waiting.

"This little guy had his head stuck in some trash. I'm going to take him home and get him cleaned up. Maybe you guys know a vet where I could check and see if he's chipped?"

"Sure. There's one I use for my cats not too far from here. You can take him by in the morning."

"Looks like we're having a sleepover, Taco." Nick took stock of his reaction, and was proud that he'd held it together. He'd been close to a meltdown, but he'd pulled himself through it and rescued this dog. Maybe he wasn't as bad off as he'd thought.

"Taco?"

"Well, he's small and likely part Chihuahua mix. We found him behind a Mexican restaurant. It seems to fit. We'll find out your real name in the morning." Nick cradled the tiny dog in his strong arms as carefully as baby, but as firmly as a football, since the little guy really wanted to show his appreciation with chin kisses that smelled like rotten meat.

"Ugh. Come on, let's get you cleaned up."

EIGHT

SUNDAY MORNING FEATURED a one-on-one session with Jamie. Armed with her notebook full of her reflections from the beach, Dani grabbed a cup of coffee and a scone, then settled into a comfy armchair in the parlor of the B&B. Jamie was already seated across from her with her signature espresso steaming at her elbow.

"So, how did your homework go yesterday? Any breakthrough conclusions?"

"Well, it took me awhile to get past all the easy answers, but I know that what I really want to do is be helpful or useful to someone else. In what capacity, I have no idea, but that's what I came up with."

"No surprise there. You always were the mother hen back in high school." Jamie teased.

"Pardon me?" Dani let mock outrage color her tone.

"Please, everyone knew who to go to if they forgot their cheer socks or needed help in algebra. You've always been a helper, Dani. It's not a bad thing. Just interesting to see how that's working out in adulthood. It's an excellent place to start. That innate motivation to do something good and help others can be a powerful force when unleashed in the right direction. Let's do a little exercise. I want you to close your eyes and reflect on your life in its current form." Jamie flipped open her sketchbook and began to doodle while she spoke.

Dani closed her eyes and took a deep breath, preparing herself to tackle the tough questions.

"What in your life now makes you smile?"

"My aunt's friends and neighbors, the guy across the hall, Mrs. Grady's dinner parties, prepping Mrs. Grady's dinner parties."

"I'm hearing that you enjoy being with people. What is it about these friends and neighbors that draws your sunny smiles?"

"They remind me of my aunt, and the fun times we shared, her funny and interesting stories. They've all lived such rich lives and are so generous in sharing their experiences and time. It's a very tight community, and they were so kind to Aunt Helen while our family was far away."

"And the guy across the hall?"

"Nick?"

"Is that his name? What about him makes you smile? You listed him separately."

"Um..." How open she should be with Jamie? Odds were slim to none that she'd ever meet Nick, and she was no good at dissembling. Deciding on full disclosure, Dani replied, "He's hot! Melt your bones, fan your face, hot. He's recently returned from a deployment and is struggling to readjust to civilian life. We've agreed that neither of us is in a position to pursue the sparks that seem to fly between us. But that doesn't mean I can't appreciate a beautiful man." The goofy grin had returned.

"An excellent reason to smile in my book! Not sure how to turn lusting after a hot guy into a career, but I'll put my mind to it and figure something out! Next question. Imagine that you are coming home after a long day at work, at your ideal job. How do you feel?"

Dani closed her eyes and imagined kicking off shoes and tucking up her feet on the couch. "I feel tired, but in a good way. Like I put in a lot of hard work, but I'm happy with the results. I made people smile today. I made their life better somehow. And I know that I'll happily get back up to do the same thing tomorrow."

"Have you ever felt that feeling before in your life?"

"Yes, when I was taking care of my Aunt Helen at the end. We had hospice helpers, who handled a lot of her medical needs, but I was responsible for a lot of her personal care. It was grueling. She needed constant help, but I was so glad to be doing it. I know I was able to bring comfort and laughter to her when she needed it. That meant a lot to both of us."

"Do you think you want to pursue something medical or hospice related?"

"No. I think I could only do that for family, or someone I really cared about. It got very personal."

"Is there anything currently in your life that gives you that feeling of satisfaction? That feeling that you've done something to help someone else feel good?" Jamie sketched frantically.

"Well, I cook for Mrs. Grady's dinner parties. I know she feels good when she can visit with her friends and make sure they're eating well. I like being a part of that. I've always enjoyed cooking for people. It's a way I can show that I care, and these people were so good to Aunt Helen. I like knowing that I can give them a meal to look forward to every week."

"Are they good to you?" Jamie's hand paused in her sketching. She looked up at Dani with a deeper concentration, as if this question was more important somehow.

"Yes, of course."

"Well, you keep saying they are your aunt's neighbors, and

they were good to her, but you are the one living with them now. It almost seems like you're trying to earn their approval or pay them back."

"I've only been there for six months. I guess I don't feel like I really belong yet. But I am happy to help them out."

"There it is."

"There what is?"

"You are using your skills to break into a well-established community. They welcome you, but you still feel like an outsider. You need to build your own community, on your own terms. There is the root of your motivation and your skill. Take a look." Jamie had been sketching as Dani spoke, catching her ideas as pictures. She revealed the idea board she'd sketched. It showed Dani surrounded by people, laughing and smiling, while cooking at a stove. "You enjoy caring for people, because it makes you feel useful and gives you joy. It makes sense that the desire to be helpful surfaced yesterday in your homework session. You enjoy cooking, recognizing that it's nourishment for the body and soul of the people you love. There's the skill, the vehicle you use to bring that care and help to your target audience. Take this for inspiration and feel free to add to it, if anything else occurs to you."

Dani took the drawing and stared. It was like a thousand puzzle pieces were starting to line up and fill that hole in her heart. She took a deep breath and felt for the first time in years, maybe the first time in her life, that she knew which direction to go. She couldn't see the destination yet, but there was a path in front of her.

"Now comes the next step." Jamie's business voice broke through her thoughts. "How can we take that skill and motivation and shift its target to one that could potentially earn you a living? Is there another target audience near you who would benefit from home cooked goodness served with a healthy dose of kindness and community? Think about that now, and we'll touch base this afternoon to see where we are."

Dani stared at the sketch as she whispered to Jamie. "Wow. You're good!" It was so clear. Something in her heart shifted and things felt "right" again.

"Ha ha ha! That's what they all say."

"No, I didn't mean it like that! Just that, wow, you saw me so clearly, so quickly. That's a gift. Thank you for inviting me."

"I am so happy to help, Dani, but I have to admit it was a little selfish on my part, too. I've been feeling caught in the whirlwind lately, a bit drained from all the press and attention. This weekend has been great to refocus on what drew me to my ideal career, namely helping friends see in themselves all of the wonderful qualities that I do! It's been really great to see you. I spend so much time surrounded by clients, I have not been taking time to connect with people I love."

"I hear you! OK, as part of Aunt Helen's decree, I'm supposed to get a life, not just a career. Let's have a girls' night out! I'll pull together a couple more people, and we'll hit the town."

"God! A real honest-to-goodness GNO? It's been ages since I had one of those! I'm in!"

"Great! Check your schedule and let me know when you're free."

"I will! Oh, you just gave me the boost I needed to get through the rest of the morning! I don't think the rest of my clients will be as easy to pinpoint. After all, I had a head start with you. I've had your chocolate chip cookies...Now go do your homework, young lady!" Jamie admonished with mock severity, while shooing her from the room.

"Girls' Night Out! Woohoo!"

Nick sat on his couch Sunday morning with his laptop open. He skimmed the sites that Dani had pulled for him. The VA website showed him resources at various sites and clinics around the Bay Area. As he read the information on warning signs he could see that he could fit the description of several, but not all. There were links for vets in crisis, concerned family members, confidential chats, and more.

The more he read, the more he convinced himself that his problems weren't that bad. He went to the Connect With A Vet site and began clicking on video clips to watch. He glanced up at the clock to find he'd been listening to stories from other vets for over an hour. This he understood. He heard himself in their stories, and he had his own network of veterans to connect with right down the hall. He'd be fine. He shook his head at the idea of a residential program. He basically had that here. He muttered as he puttered around the kitchen getting chips and beer, as if trying to convince himself aloud of his decision.

"It's not like I'm suicidal. I just want some space. And yes, I get the panic attacks, and I'd like those to stop, but it's not so bad most of the time. I just feel a little nervous. Look, I've gone out to dinner with strangers twice in one week. I'm not hiding. And I have Dani willing to help keep me moving forward."

Thinking of Dani brought a smile to his face. She'd be back tomorrow, and he was looking forward to it more than he should. Maybe once he was better, he could be good enough, whole enough, to be in her life as more than a friend. Given how much he wanted her, he needed to get on this counseling thing quickly. Who knew how long he'd be able to keep his feelings hidden... "I'll just go and see about getting someone to talk to. I can do that from here. I don't need to be taking up a bed at a facility. There are other guys worse off who need that."

He decided to call a counselor at the VA Monday morning, and start the process. The outpatient counseling would be enough. He cringed at the thought of going inpatient into a rehabilitation program. He'd just gotten his independence back. He wasn't about to hand it over. He didn't need all that. Especially if he had Dani keeping him on track. Satisfied with his decision, he shut down the computer and settled back with Sunday morning baseball on TV and a freshly bathed Taco on his lap sound asleep.

NINE

Dani sat back out on the porch doing her homework. She was making a list of groups that would benefit from her particular skills. So far it was a long one. Homeless, shelters for women and children, preschool programs in rougher parts of the Bay Area, nursing home residents, and the list went on. There was no shortage of people who needed consistent access to affordable quality food. But none of those groups really fired her up. Her list was almost obscured by the random doodles in the margins. She was stalled. She knew she hadn't hit upon just the right audience yet. If only she could keep cooking for Mrs. Grady and the others.

The image sprang fully formed into her head. All of her aunt's friends sitting around a table in a diner type restaurant, and Dani serving her signature meals from the kitchen in the back. Her imagination continued to fill in the picture. Who else would eat here? Other vets in the area might like getting out a night or two a week. They'd fit right in with her friends. If she put the restaurant close to the VA, they could stop in after their appointments.

Excitement bubbled in her veins. She had so many veterans

in her life whom she cared for and whose sacrifices she respected. It was her most satisfying moment of the week watching them enjoy her cooking. Why not just expand the table? Surely there were other people who would want home cooked meals. But what would set her apart from any other restaurant on her street? Why didn't these people use other restaurants? Price. Most vets lived on a limited income if they were retired. And if they were homeless vets, price was even more of an issue. That's why she helped provide the groceries for her meals with Mrs. Grady. If she kept doing dinners just like she was at home, could she keep costs low enough? Sandwiches at lunch with fresh fruit and a salad, a family style dinner with a main protein, starch, and veggies, some kind of dessert, and coffee, tea, or water. Keep the options limited to keep costs low, and she could pass all those savings along to her customers. Maybe even add a "Pay It Forward' scheme to prefund dinner for the homeless. It just might work!

Her mind swirling with ideas, her hand struggled to keep up, jotting down notes and questions as they flittered through. At the end of an hour, she had a plan. There were still tons of details to research, food costs/suppliers to price, menus to plan, permits to apply for, and probably small business and food prep classes in her future, but it was a plan! She struggled briefly to contain her excitement, and gave up, doing a happy dance around the porch and grinning from ear to ear. She looked at the clock and realized that it was time for the final session of the retreat. Gathering her notes, she ran inside.

She slipped into the last open seat around the circle of cozy chairs that had been set up in the parlor. The other five participants and Jamie were already seated and discussing the realizations the others had reached. The range of responses was quite varied but all overwhelmingly positive. Clearly, Jamie was very good at her job.

"I'm going to turn my crafting hobby into a cottage business. Now that I'm not sitting in the bleachers for games, I can use that time to make the wreaths and buntings my friends request. I'm going to turn one of the bedrooms into a craft room and open a storefront on Etsy." This was from Angela, who was grinning from ear to ear.

"I'm going to finally retire from my company, and let the young bucks take the reins. Because I'll be busy setting up a non-profit project to run in my retirement that will provide job skill training and mentoring for young people looking to enter the tech field." The CEO seemed content with her decisions, where at the beginning of the retreat she had been unable to disengage from work until Jamie had taken away her phone.

Everyone around the circle had found a new path to follow on their way home. When it came to her, Dani smiled and described her vision.

"I know and love a lot of veterans. These are people who made sacrifices for our country and came home to try and pick up the reins of a normal life. Some have adjusted better than others. Many of them are aging and beginning to live on fixed incomes. They face monetary and health challenges. There is the added struggle of dealing with the memories of their time in the service. They tend to be isolated unless they are lucky enough to live in my building where isolation is a foreign concept. There are vets in every generation, many forgotten by all but history.

"There is a group of people that I cook for every week, and I know that for many it's the only home cooked meal they have all week long. I know they are not the only ones with this struggle. I live around the corner from the VA clinic, and I see people with similar challenges every day, waiting for the bus or walking back home. So, here's my idea: a restaurant and gathering place, open to everyone, but initially advertised to the vets coming and going in the neighborhood. A healthy, home-cooked meal at a low, fixed price, and the company of other vets. A place to come and grab a cup of coffee and a slice of pie and shoot the shit with other vets. A place to build community, and provide steady nutrition to a needy population. What do you think?"

The chorus of positive thoughts from around the circle warmed Dani's heart and buoyed her enthusiasm. This could work. This could really work.

Jamie ended the session with a follow-up plan.

"You have all made a lot of progress this weekend. I know it has been intense, and you've done a lot of soul searching and creative processing. I don't want you to lose the euphoria and excitement of this weekend as you go back into your daily lives, your demanding routines, and your commitments. I'd like to schedule follow-up phone sessions every other week so we can keep this positive momentum.

"I am also going to charge you each with setting up a support system at home. We get so focused on making it, that we think we have to make it on our own. This is not true, and very rarely possible.

"Picture the most put-together, successful person you can think of, and I guarantee there are between 5 and 10 people who have actively supported them and helped them get to where they are today, if not more. Take Oprah, for example. By the time her show went off the air, she had an entire company whose focus was helping her get it together to share her gift with the world.

"Your last homework assignment of the weekend is to imagine your failure. Get specific. What will get in the way of making this happen? Are there toxic elements in your life that will attempt to derail your plans? Will you sabotage yourself and how? This may seem like a big downer at the end of this great weekend, but if you can see the pitfalls ahead of time, you can plan to avoid them.

"Once you have your list, think of specific people in your life who you can ask for help. Do you need time away from your current job to do the planning necessary for your new idea? Talk to a co-worker about switching shifts or approach your boss for a more flexible schedule. Are childcare duties going to draw your time away from getting your goals accomplished? Get a regular sitter or your spouse to come and free up some of your time. Do you get distracted easily or lose steam? Designate one or two friends to check in with you and keep you motivated. Tap your biggest cheerleaders for support. I'm so proud of all the progress you've made this weekend! I'll talk to you soon!"

TEN

MONDAY MORNING, Dani knocked on the door across the hall with a rapid series of taps. High pitched barking behind the door surprised her, and she stepped back to double check the number. Nick opened the door wide, and his new roommate ran out to say hello. The small, sprightly pup ran out between his legs and barked as he ran circles around Dani in the hallway.

"You're back!"

"I am. Who is this?"

"I'm calling him Taco. Found him in an alley this weekend. After a much-needed bath and a few solid meals, this handsome pup emerged. I need to get some signs up around town. I'm sure someone is missing him. So, I've got a temporary roommate until we find his family. How was the retreat?"

"You've had a busy weekend. He is a cutie." She reached down to pet the pup behind the ears and made an instant friend. "The retreat was wonderful! I think I have a plan."

"Me, too. Come on in."

"Really?" Pleasantly surprised, she followed him into the kitchen. "That's great. What's the plan?"

"Well, I called over to the VA this morning, and I have an

appointment to see a counselor tomorrow afternoon." She made herself comfortable at the table, while he poured her a fresh cup of coffee. He even pulled out a packet of fake sugar for her from the stash she'd tucked into his groceries. He'd remembered. She was impressed. He dropped an old sock he'd tied into knots onto the floor for Taco, and joined her at the table.

"You were right. I was avoiding dealing with it. After a few visits from the Wednesday Crew, I felt a bit better about taking that first step. I looked at the websites you pulled for me, and figured out my plan of action. So, thanks for the push."

"That's great, Nick. I'm glad it helped."

"So, what's your plan?"

"I'm going to turn Wednesday dinners into a business model. I want to open a restaurant that serves veterans a healthy, fixed-menu meal at a low price. I want to meet their nutritional needs and their social ones by providing a place to gather, eat good food, and chat with friends, new and old. What do you think?"

"You figured all that out in one weekend? I think it's great. I can think of no group more deserving of your magic chocolate chip cookies than my fellow vets. Have you thought through a business plan yet?"

"Ha! I just had this epiphany yesterday. Jamie was a great sounding board. I don't even know where to start. But I'm revved about something for the first time in forever, and that has to be worth something. I just need to buckle down now and do some leg work. I'm so excited!"

"That's really great, Dani. I can see why they call you Sunny. You're literally beaming." Grinning, Nick reached across the small table to tuck a stray strand of hair behind her ear. She blushed and turned her head. If he kept that up, there was no way she was going to be able to keep her "just friends" promise.

"So, what do you want to do today?" Change the subject. Deflect his interest.

"I don't know. I don't have any plans. How about a movie?"

"Sure, as long as it's not too violent or scary. My overactive imagination likes to keep me up at night reminding me of all the things that go bump in the night." She imagined violent movies weren't real high on his list right now, either. It was easy enough to give him an out.

Dani scanned the available movies on demand and settled on one they'd both seen about the boy wizard who lived. She dashed across the hall and returned with a big cozy afghan and a bowl of popcorn.

"I refuse to sit on that ugly couch." She draped the blanket over the offending sofa with a grin. If only covering the couch could bury the memories of what had happened between them on it. If she had any chance of keeping their truce, those memories had to stay covered. *Although if he wanted to uncover his abs again*...No. She cut off her thoughts. She couldn't go down that road in her mind, and then sit with him on the couch for two hours. Control. She would just have to find some. She claimed one end of the couch, resting her head on the armrest, and curled her legs towards the back of the couch. Nick took his spot on the other and propped his feet on the table. The couch wasn't' very big so her feet ended up touching his leg. It was very cozy and, Dani quickly realized, a big mistake. Huge.

It shouldn't have been romantic, but it was. They were watching a kid's movie, for goodness sake! Dani was struggling to make sense of her feelings as she thought about the last time she'd been this turned on just by touching feet with someone. During those heady hormone laden days of high school, Dani had found herself sharing a love seat with a boy she'd been crushing on for a solid month. Casually lounging, her legs tangled with his as they idly watched some horror flick at a house party. She didn't remember a bit of the movie they'd been watching, since every shift of his toes against her leg had refocused her senses and built the tension inside her, until she was convinced he was doing it on purpose. That day had been a let down, because the boy she'd been interested in had left the party alone without ever making a move, clearly not as active a participant in her seduction as she'd hoped. The roiling emotions she'd felt that day so long ago paled in comparison to what she was fighting now.

Her toes were tucked up against his thighs, and she could feel the sinewy strength beneath them. He kept shifting trying to get comfortable, and every time he did, she had to wiggle her toes to find a new comfy spot. He pulled his feet up onto the couch, and Dani blushed again. She had to get that pesky blushing under control. The man was going to think she was a prude. *It might be easier if he thought I was a prude. If he knew how badly I want to jump him right now, this cease-fire would be over before it began.*

The slide of his legs along her calves sent goose bumps up her legs and was as thoroughly arousing as if he'd been stroking her bare legs with his hands, those wonderful strong hands with long, firm, agile fingers...*Stop it!* She reached for some popcorn and accidentally touched those tempting fingers. She yanked her hand away as if she'd been burned, the warmth traveling all the way up to her arm. *We are friends. Just friends.* She fought desperately to ignore the pinging sensation deep in her belly and the pressure growing between her thighs. She clenched her legs together in an effort to relieve some of the pressure, sliding her toes from beneath him and turning sideways. *Focus on the movie. Ignore the sexy man under the blanket.* Sure. She had no idea what was happening in the movie, as it took all of her mental powers to keep herself on her end of the couch. If he would just stay still, she could ignore these disturbing impulses.

When the movie ended, Dani leapt up from the couch.

"Let's get some fresh air. I could use a trip to the library. You know, dive into my research. Want to come?" She mentally slapped her forehead. Had she really just asked him if he wanted to come? Her mind clearly hadn't found its way out of the gutter, despite her two hours of effort.

"No, you go ahead. I'm going to do a few chores around here."

She followed him to the door, and after a fraught moment where she passed too close to him and almost exploded, she made it out of his apartment, integrity intact. This "just friends" thing was going to be much harder than she'd anticipated.

ELEVEN

For the next few weeks, Dani tested his will and, so far, he'd managed to keep his impulses under control. She wasn't doing it on purpose, but whenever she was near, he was tempted. His tension switched from resisting memories of war to resisting the urge to hold her in his arms, but he would take frustration over the fear any day.

That first week they'd spent most of their time in each other's apartments. Nick's fear and anxiety had kept him pretty house bound. He had to leave to see his VA therapist and to walk Taco, but those small excursions exhausted him.

When the groceries had run out, he'd attempted another trip to the store. Hands shaking, senses on high alert, he forced himself walk the aisles and to select his own food. He needed to know he could handle something as simple as feeding himself, but it took a toll. He was emotionally done by the time he made it home. But he had done it. He'd counted that as a win.

Safe within the walls of his small apartment, he had unpacked his bags and discovered that several six packs of beer had made their way into his cart. He didn't remember adding them. Later that night, he'd been too low to fight the demons when they came. When he woke, on the couch, he discovered far too many empty cans and a new hole in the drywall. He'd pushed too far, too fast. Despite wanting his privacy, the empty rooms gave him too much time to think.

As a result, Nick found that he sought Dani's company more often than not. Days were better when she was around. By the end of the second week, Dani had decided he needed to get out and explore. She designated herself his personal tour guide. Although his anxiety outside was still high, being near her helped. And he couldn't deny he enjoyed the hum of sexual tension skating through his system whenever she was near. Her determination to introduce him to the beauty of his new state had brought them to the coast this morning. He'd mentioned that he'd never gone surfing, and here they were, preparing to enter the Pacific for a surfing lesson in Santa Cruz. Thankfully, there was no ocean in Iraq, so the water didn't trigger him as badly as the city did.

Still, Nick fought to keep his attraction and his anxiety under wraps. As she'd stripped down to her bikini, Nick's mind glazed over. He quickly turned to don his wetsuit, praying she hadn't seen the tent in his trunks. When he turned back, she was fully covered in her wetsuit, and the fraught moment passed. The lingering glow of his arousal kept him warm as he stepped into the chilly water. The professional she'd hired was very laid back but thorough, and soon they were paddling out into the waves.

"I can't believe you convinced me to do this."

"Doesn't everyone who comes to California dream of surfing?"

"Sure, but I grew up in Chicago. The waves of Lake Michigan don't get high enough for this."

"What's life without a little adventure? Besides you can't really say you live in Cali until you've been out on a board."

With that she paddled ahead of him to catch the first wave. Nick admired her form as she gracefully got vertical and eased her way along the curl. Her athletic curves, encased in black neoprene, twisted and turned ,effortlessly suspending her on the leading edge of the water. Now he understood why everyone found surfers so sexy.

Sadly, his first attempt was not as smooth. He drank a lot of salt water just trying to pop up on the board, but between the sun and the waves and the company, he found he didn't mind.

"So, you learned to do this as a kid?"

"I grew up over the mountain in San Jose, so the beach was just 30 minutes away. My sister and I both begged our parents for lessons in middle school. I spent a lot of my summer weekends here at the beach."

"Muscle memory is a beautiful thing."

"Don't worry. You'll get it. It just takes some practice." He doubted he'd make it back out on the waves without her, but he couldn't say that. He picked up the thread of conversation that seemed safest.

"So, you've got a sister?"

"Yeah, Jen. She's two years older than me. She lives up in Seattle with her husband, Brian, and my beautiful nieces. My parents moved up there two years ago, once they retired to be closer to their grands."

"And you went to Houston." He let the implied question hang.

"I may not have known what I wanted to do, but I knew I didn't want to follow in my sister's footsteps. She stayed close to home for college, and I didn't want that, so I left."

"And once you graduated?"

"I'd made connections in Houston through school, so I stayed. It didn't seem like there was much left for me here."

"What does your sister think of the café idea?"

"She thinks I'm crazy for trying to open a low-cost restaurant in the most expensive real estate market in the country. She doesn't get that that's exactly why I need to do it." She turned that grin on him, the one that melted his brain. "Race you for that wave!" And she took off paddling, leaving him trailing in her wake. Of course, she beat him. And, of course, he got flipped again.

Once he'd regained his board for a breather, he turned and grinned at her. He was more energized than he'd been in months.

"Next time you want to change to the subject, just do it. I don't need the dunking."

She grinned back at him, and he contemplated paddling closer for a kiss. The comfortable silence stretched into tension, and thankfully Dani popped back onto her stomach and paddled off to chase another wave. At least one of them had their head in the game.

Don't ruin a good thing. She is just a good friend. Quit thinking about kissing her again. The trouble was his mind kept running their first kiss on loop, and damn if he didn't crave another. He let the wave roll him, counting on the cold to wash all those tricky thoughts from his mind.

THE DAYS they spent apart stretched time. Nick knew that she was busy researching and planning for her new business, and he didn't want to distract her. He resisted the urge to knock on her door every morning and ask her to spend the day with him. She had a goal. It wasn't her fault that he wasn't making as much progress with his own goal as he'd wanted. He found himself staring at the door, waiting for her special knock. As his recycling filled with more cans, and he learned how to patch drywall from YouTube, the only time he felt really grounded came when he could forget his troubles in her sunny smile.

On the days when she was available, he always made an effort to be up for whatever she suggested. When she suggested a hike and a picnic, he was wary, but the thought of saying no and losing her company was untenable. He second-guessed himself the entire car ride. Dani pulled a backpack lunch from the trunk, and they hiked the trails in the open space up the side of one of the mountains surrounding Silicon Valley. Once again, she knew exactly what he needed. The quiet of the woods, the cooling shade interspersed with hidden meadows full of sunshine, the companionable silence they maintained, lulled him.

Spreading a blanket beneath a tree, Nick watched as Dani unpacked some layered sandwiches, homemade pesto pasta salad, and chocolate chip banana bread, all recipes she was testing for the restaurant. She handed Nick his portion, and he tried not to notice how gorgeous she looked kneeling on the plaid, with the dappled afternoon sun turning her curls to gold. He took a quick bite of pasta, because he really wanted to nibble on her collarbone.

"God, this is good Dani. If this is what you've got in mind for the café, I'll be a regular in no time."

"I should hope that's already a given. You don't think there's too much garlic in the pesto?"

"Uh, I'm probably not the guy to ask, but it tastes damn good to me."

Dani offered a small smile and ducked her head.

"I'm glad to know that food is the one part of this restaurant I don't have to worry about."

"Does that mean you're worried about the rest of it?"

"Pretty much. Slogging through all this legislation is killing me. I mean, I've got a tentative timeline worked out, and a list of action items to tackle, but more and more things keep cropping up, throwing me off. Permits, and certifications, and then there's the grant and non-profit funding paperwork... I don't want to make a mistake and get shut down, but I feel like I'm bound to mess up something because there's just so much to keep track of. And I keep losing focus mid-thought because I look up and there's Aunt Helen's postcards or her favorite book or the throw blanket she always asked for. I spiral into memory, and I lose hours... I can't seem to stay focused, and I'm really getting overwhelmed." The words flowed out of her like a dam had broken somewhere inside. Her shoulders drooped, and her face lost its glow. Why had she kept all of this from him? Didn't she realize that he would help her with this stuff?

"Come here." Nick patted the space on the blanket in front of him. "Turn around." She sat down with her back to him. He placed his hands on her drooping shoulders and began to gently knead away the tension knots he found there. Even touching her like this was risky, but she had done so much for him. He could certainly control himself long enough to return the favor.

"Don't get so stressed about it, Dani. It's not good for you. You've got plenty of time. Let's look at it together tomorrow." She nodded and stretched her neck to the side, silently requesting his attention. She couldn't know what that trust did to him, or she wouldn't still be sitting there.

With each glide of his fingers over the bare nape of her neck, Dani went a little more limp. She let out a low moan as he worked on a particularly sore spot, and all but collapsed back into his lap. Nick's hands froze, cupping her shoulders, desperately fighting for control. If he leaned forward just a bit he could bury his nose in her neck, kiss that spot by her ear that had made her moan like that on his couch. His breath blew hot and unsteady past her ear. She shivered. He couldn't tell if arousal or fear had prompted the chill. If she was smart, and she was, it would have been fear. He didn't think he could stand it if she was afraid of him. His grip tightened, his decision made, and he gently pushed her forward into her own space. Dani didn't immediately turn to face him, but spoke over her shoulder as she packed up their leftovers.

"Thanks, Nick. I guess I needed that."

"Dani, I..."

She turned with a blank smile determinedly plastered across her face. He was certain it would pass for anyone else, but he could tell it wasn't a real smile. "So, we'll meet tomorrow to go over the paperwork?"

"Yeah. Yeah, we can do that."

Despite the near miss, Nick realized this was the most at peace he'd felt in weeks, as they hiked back down. The complete lack of interference from other humans helped Nick let his guard down almost completely and just be in the moment with Dani. Even the ever-present chemistry between them couldn't break the simple peace of a walk in the woods. Nick reached for her hand as they ambled back towards her car, relishing the connection. The day took on a surreal feeling in his mind. Even though they'd only known each other a short time, Nick felt like he was walking with his oldest friend.

"Why are you picking those up?"

He looked down at his hands and smiled. He'd unconsciously collected interesting bits of wood as they walked.

"I didn't realize I was. It's something I used to do when I was a kid. I'd get them home and build little forts or fences for my toys. I had one that I had rubbed with my thumb until it was completely smooth. I just loved the way it felt in my hands."

Glad to have found a happy memory to share, his heart felt lighter in his chest. Dani handed him a smooth and round bark chip. "Why don't you take this with you, just to have something to hold while you think your deep thoughts?"

"You know, Sunny, I could handle the cooking for the suppers if you need the time to work on your plans." Mrs. Grady sat at her kitchen table, while Dani juggled the prep for the week's resident dinners.

"I'm happy to help."

"I know, and I appreciate it, but now that you've got something better to spend your time on..."

"I've got plenty of time. Besides, it's good practice for the café."

"I just don't want you spreading yourself too thin, honey." Mrs. Grady took the spoon from her hand, and bumped her aside with her hip. "Just because I like the help doesn't mean I'm helpless. So, have you heard the buzz about the new Hardcart mystery coming out next week? I'm almost afraid to try it after the last two."

"Actually, Nick said he heard that this one was going to be much better than the last two. Apparently, he ditched the co-author after the flak he took from his fans." She accepted her ousting from the stove and turned to prep the Caesar salad. Mrs. Grady glanced up from the béchamel sauce she was stirring to give Dani an arched look.

"Oh, Nick said, huh?" Innuendo colored her words with good-humored ribbing.

"Yes, *he* did." Dani could feel the blush warming her cheeks.

"He's saying an awful lot these days. How often are you over there?"

"We hang out a lot. So? We're helping each other out."

"Is that what they're calling it these days?" Mrs. Grady teased.

"It's completely platonic." Dani assured her. Well, mostly platonic. There were still pesky sparks that threatened to flame up, but she was doing a good job of ignoring them. "The day I finished sorting the storage units and loaded the charity trucks, he came to support me. I don't think I could have done that without him. I still find myself losing entire afternoons, just missing her." Dani remembered how he'd tagged along on the first day she had done the read aloud at the library. As she ended the session with her beloved copy of Goodnight Moon, she could barely finish through the tears. She still couldn't bring herself to make the beef stroganoff that had been her aunt's favorite meal. Little things were keeping her tied to the past. His support had gotten her over some difficult moments.

"I need a friend right now, and so does he. It's working. He makes me think about myself and my life in a different way."

She'd gotten used to seeing herself as the designated caretaker for the building. She had been spending her days immersed in the lives of her elderly neighbors. Being with Nick was opening new doors. She began to think about herself as a young attractive woman with a plan for her future, instead of an unemployed caretaker with no one to care for. Dani realized just how long it had been since she'd had regular interactions with people her own age. Now that her career project was stumbling along, maybe it was time to bring more people into her life. She recalled her promise to Jamie for a Girls' Night Out and added it to her mental to-do list.

"Well, then I'm happy for you both. Although how you're keeping it platonic after seeing the man's chest on moving day is beyond me!"

"Mrs. Grady!"

"Sunny, if I were thirty years younger, you'd have some stiff competition."

Laughing and turning back to the stove once more, Dani assured her, "If you were thirty years younger, I wouldn't stand a chance!"

TWELVE

MONDAYS WERE HARD. Nick got home from his therapy session by noon, and Dani usually popped over with lunch. So when she showed up with a tray of homemade mac and cheese, he wasn't surprised. When he opened the door, Dani held up the casserole like a peace offering. Silently, he stepped back from the door, wishing that a tray of tasty noodles could solve his problems.

"Do you want to talk about it?"

"No. I just spent all morning talking about it."

"You know you can tell me anything. If you ever need to vent, I'm here."

"No. I mean, yes, I know, but no. I'm OK."

He was far from OK, but the last thing he wanted to do was drag her into his personal hell. He didn't want her to see the dark side of him, didn't want her touched by the ugliness he couldn't get out of his head. Dani was his sunshine, and he didn't want to bring up the clouds. When she suggested an afternoon of paperwork, he nodded, grateful that she didn't expect him to head out when he was so drained.

She pulled her work out of her bag and got busy.

Completely at home in his apartment, she spread her work out at the table. They tackled it together, Dani wielding a pen, while Nick picked up a piece of wood and his carving knife. Idly he played with the piece in his hand while they worked. He'd bought some woodworking tools, his high school interest sparked by their walk in the woods. It was soothing to work near Dani, as she finished up a form. He patiently sanded hardwood at the table next to her, as she crossed things off her to-do list and asked his opinion. He admired her drive and dedication in the face of her sadness. He wished he could find that same grit and determination he'd relied on for so many years. Damn it! Where had it gone? He hadn't created anything, but he kept sanding away, hoping the repetitive action would somehow bring him someplace new.

By the end of the month, Dani took stock of her progress based on her business plan and was encouraged. She had enrolled in a Food Safety course online, signed up for an entrepreneurial class at the local College, and scoured every link on the Small Business Association's website. Every day her resolve to devote her time and energy to this project strengthened. Nick was in large part responsible for this progress, as he had kept her from wallowing and getting distracted. Her dream was beginning to take shape.

She picked up the phone and dialed Jamie for her conference follow-up, confident and pleased with her progress.

"Hi, Dani. How is everything going?"

"Things are going great. This café project is just what I've needed to help me work through my grief. I still miss Aunt Helen, but I know that I'm doing something positive with her legacy and that helps. Every time I cross something off my to do list, I know she's smiling." Dani filled her in on the classes she was taking and her search for a location.

"I'm so glad to hear that you're doing well with it. Do you need any help? I'm proud of what you've managed to tackle, but don't be afraid to ask for help."

"Nick, the sexy neighbor, has been helping me out quite a bit."

"That sounds promising."

"We are still just friends, but the time we spend together feels so right. We'll see. But I do have something to ask you."

"Anything. Shoot."

"Can you be free on Saturday night for that Girl's Night Out I mentioned?"

"Are you kidding? Of course! It's a date. I can't wait to hang out without a single work agenda attached."

"I'm inviting some other girlfriends, too. My friend from the law office, Olivia and my yoga instructor, Stella. You're going to love them."

"Send me an email so I can pop it into my calendar, OK? I've got to run. My next appointment is here."

"No problem. Take care!"

Dani sent out a quick email to Jaime, Stella, and Olivia to see if they'd be up for a new bar that had popped up on her radar while trolling Yelp for things to do with Nick. "Flipped" was described as a fun mix between relaxed dance club and small plates restaurant with an emphasis on international cuisine. Something for everyone. She made a reservation for Saturday night and sent out the invite with a triumphant click.

"There you go, Aunt Helen. Reconnect with friends: Check." She turned to look at her aunt's picture, still hanging on the wall. "I am going to build the life I need. I just wish you could have been here to see it."

She swung from giddy anticipation to grief so quickly her

head literally spun. She had thought it would get better with time, but each reminder of Helen still had the power to overwhelm her. She needed to get out and away from her memories. Closing her laptop, she headed across the hall to Nick's to see if he was up for a walk in the sunshine.

FRIDAY AT NOON, Nick sat on his couch breathing deeply, trying to get calm again. He had gotten home from his counseling session nearly an hour before and still couldn't quite settle his rough edges. His counselor had poked at some pretty difficult memories and had made him re-process what had happened in Iraq. Those were memories and emotions that Nick had buried deep for a reason. He knew that pulling them back into the light was part of the strategy. It was supposed to help him process those emotions in a safe place, so they would eventually lose their ability to cripple him.

Unfortunately, he hadn't gotten any more comfortable revisiting that time of his life in the last few weeks. It still put him right on the edge of an attack. He found himself staring at the door, as if he could will Dani to come and knock. He didn't want her to see him like this, didn't want to need her, but the fact remained. Dani was a ray of sunshine pushing away the lingering clouds. Usually she was right there when he got back from his sessions. His appointment had gotten bumped to Friday, because his therapist, Alex, had to go present at a conference. He hadn't gotten a chance to mention it to Dani. So now he was stuck, going over and over all the things he'd talked about with Alex. Mentally exhausted, Nick leaned his head back on his couch and closed his eyes trying to will away the images lurking there. Instead of finding peace, he found himself asleep and right back in the nightmare of war.

His company was out escorting an inspector from USAID, checking on the progress of updates being made at the electrical plant at the dam in Samarra. Chatter had been quiet, and the inspector had been visiting similar sites all week. They loaded up the convoy. His Lieutenant, who was supposed to lead the group out, had come down with a nasty stomach bug and Nick confined him to quarters. Nick led the convoy himself through the local neighborhoods and up the river, which had not been part of the original plan. After six years of working his way up the chain of command he rarely had to participate in the field any longer. But he pitched in for the sake of the mission, and this was his reward.

When they pulled up at the dam, the scene looked normal. Nick and half the company went inside with the inspector and toured the facility. It was clear where the new machinery was being installed and the workers, communicating through an interpreter, were able to explain in detail what they were working on and how it fit into the overall function of the plant. Nick felt encouraged by the fact that progress was being made on the infrastructure and that the workers were invested in the process. The inspector smiled and took notes in his journal as the tour ended, when one of the exterior guards crackled a warning over the COM.

A group of insurgents had heard about the inspections, and they were angry. They were angry about the war. They were angry about the threat to their local power, both literal and figurative. They were angry about perceived threats to their religion. They were angry young men that had never known a different life.

The ambush was set just outside the fence surrounding the electrical power station, along the road leading away from the plant. The remote location of the plant upstream at the dam, outside of the town limits and surrounded on three sides by water, restricted Nick's options for avoiding the insurgents and returning safely to base. He could feel his mind cycling through every possibility. The rebels had gotten close enough to the plant entrance to be a threat, but too far to pick off with the weaponry they'd brought along. Conflict was inevitable. Nick barked out orders, scrambling his troops, assessing the situation and making the call to engage. His gut told him he had to engage them. There was no other option.

Nick knew he was dreaming, but as hard as he fought, he couldn't pull himself out of it. He couldn't change the course of the events about to unfold.

With his adrenaline pumping, and his senses keenly focused on the task at hand, Nick led his men into a protective shield around the civilians traveling with them and emerged from the building trying to gain their vehicles. If they could reach the armored Humvees, they would have a chance to get past the roadblock by plowing through the main gate and taking the back road down the river, following the train tracks south and crossing the river further down, to circle back to Baghdad.

Every detail was burned in his brain, the sun, the heat, the sand, the murky water just a few yards distant, the helmets of his men as they ran in front of him. His eyes scanned the yard, taking in the various positions of insurgents, and he called out orders accordingly. For all his training and preparedness, there were just too many of them. When his troops began to sprint for the vehicles, weapons drawn, the firefight began.

The inspector and his interpreter were both wearing full protective gear thankfully, but the heavy armor and helmets made their movements slow and clumsy. The interpreter fell, and when Nick bent to help him up, a bullet whistled over his helmet. Shoving the civilian to his feet and forward, Nick glanced over his shoulder and saw that the bullet intended for him had struck down a young soldier, Private First Class

Carling, who had just transferred to the unit. He'd been hit at a downward angle, shattering his kneecap, shot by a sniper positioned atop the wall. Nick turned back and hauled the man up onto his shoulder and continued running for the trucks.

Handing the injured soldier to Henderson, his medic inside, he turned to assess the progress of the rest of the group and saw that another soldier had been hit about 20 yards from the trucks, lying motionless on the ground. Nick recognized the man. Specialist Finn was a seasoned soldier, with a wife and two kids waiting for him at home. Not about to leave a man behind, Nick tapped Sergeant Banks next to him, gestured silently his intent, and they moved in tandem to pick up the fallen soldier.

They drew heavy fire, and Nick felt the searing burn of a bullet graze his lower abdomen just above his hip on his right side. His scar burned just as vividly as the day it had happened. Ignoring the pain, he pushed onward, and reached Finn. A quick assessment indicated that his soldier was still breathing, but that he was seriously injured. While Banks provided cover, Nick hauled Finn on his back all the way back to the Humvees.

With everyone loaded, he gave the command to pull out and begin firing on the makeshift blockade as they barreled towards it, hoping to clear out as many insurgents and also detonate any IEDs that might have been planted there. Confident that his men were carrying out his orders, he called out over the net to ensure that Henderson was attending to Specialist Finn. He prayed to a God he wasn't sure was listening that they would make it back to base in time to save him.

The chatter over the net was almost incoherent, and what Nick could make out was unsettling. Henderson was applying pressure to the pulsing wound on the soldier's upper arm but there was a lot of blood. When she pulled the emergency release on Finn's vest to get a better look at the injury, she could see that the bullet had gone straight through and lodged into his side.

"There's no way to apply a tourniquet. He's losing a lot of blood." Finn was looking real pale, and the medic's worry bled into her trembling voice.

"It's not good, Sir," she yelled over the static on the net.

"Just do what you can, Whiskey." Nick yelled into the hand mic. He wanted it to sound encouraging, but it came out as an order. His adrenaline high, Nick could feel his heart racing and the cold sweat on his forehead. In his dream he could feel the searing desert sun roasting the Humvee.

The Humvees made it through the blockade, but had to take the long way around to get back to base. They had immediately taken Finn and Carling to the hospital, and Nick went with them. Finn had lapsed into unconsciousness from blood loss, and the surgeons looked at the arterial damage caused by the insurgent's bullet and shook their heads. It was too severe, and Finn was too weak. They tried to stabilize him with blood transfusions and IV's, so they could prep him for an amputation, but he was too far gone. He died there, on the table, with a team of doctors and nurses working desperately to save him. Nick could tell the instant they walked through the double doors that Finn was gone. His heart sank. No matter how many times he had this dream, the end was the same. He was never fast enough to save Finn.

Sitting there in triage, with the dead man's blood on his vest and his own slowly seeping through a bandage, Nick raged internally. How could they not have saved him? How would he tell Maggie, whom he'd last seen sitting at a picnic table at a summer barbecue on base, that her beloved husband had been shot down by the very people he was trying to help? That the people who would benefit from their mission had turned around and attacked them? Had specifically targeted the people who were trying to rebuild their country?

For the first time in his military career, he felt useless and disheartened. He could understand getting shot at for coming in and trying to rout the insurgents. He couldn't understand getting shot at for trying to provide functional reliable electricity and water sources, schools and hospitals, for a population in need. It didn't make sense to him. How could he try and make sense of it for her?

Nick felt the familiar swirls of futility, remorse, guilt, anger, and pain spiraling through the dream. He was drowning, the pressure of all those emotions making it hard for him to breathe. He struggled to surface from sleep. A cool touch on his forehead, made him shiver. He was burning up. That touch shifted to his cheeks and then his shoulders, shaking him, trying to pull him up from the depths.

THIRTEEN

Dani leaned over him, taking his shoulders and shaking him, trying to wake him. She had knocked on the door, and heard him inside. She let herself in with her old key when she identified the sound sneaking beneath the door as quiet weeping. She doubted he even knew that tears were streaming down his face. Sleep was the only state that he couldn't control. He couldn't keep up his walls and barriers. She doubted he'd thank her for coming in and finding him like this, but she couldn't leave now. She leaned closer and gripped his flushed cheeks in her cool hands again.

"Nick! Wake up! Come back to me." She gave his head a gentle shake.

His large hands came up to grip her wrists, holding her bent over, facing him, her face inches from his. When he finally opened his eyes, the sorrow and anger she saw lingering in the unfocused brown depths made her heart clench in response.

"Nick. It's me, Dani. I'm here. It's OK. I'm here." She wiped the tears from his cheeks with her thumbs and wished she could carry a part of his burden for him, just to lighten the load for a while. He didn't deserve to be hurting like this after all he'd done for his country.

"Dani..." He exhaled a deep sigh and pulled her down into a desperate hug. She was straddling his lap, while he sat on the couch. Wordlessly, he laid his head on her chest, and she slid her fingers back around his head to his nape, holding him in her embrace. She ran her fingers through his hair, marveling at how it had grown out in the short time she'd known him. He leaned into her caress, closing his eyes. This she could give. Simple physical comfort to a friend in pain.

"It's OK, Nick. I've got you. It was just a bad dream. It's over now. Shhh." She kept up the flow of soothing reassurance as his breath began to even out. She tried to keep her body in check, but his head resting on the crest of her breasts, his breath sending warm drafts down her cleavage, put her senses on high alert. She should pull away, but after months of feeling alone, it felt good just to be held close. His hands released her wrists and moved around to her lower back to pull her closer, until her entire front was molded to his. She stroked her hands up and down his back, reveling in the opportunity to trace all of the muscles she'd been dying to touch since she'd seen them on display on moving day. When he began to shake again, she held him tighter.

"Stay with me. Listen to my voice. I've got you, Nick, and I'm not going anywhere. I'm here. You're not alone. You don't have to be alone."

He opened his eyes and pulled back to look at her. He seemed to be coming out of it. His eyes were clear, and he recognized who he held in his arms.

"Dani. You came. How did you know?"

"I didn't. I heard you through the door. I'm sorry. I used my key..." He shook his head to deny the apology.

"I needed you, and you came." He dropped his forehead to

her sternum and shook his head. She brought her hands back to soothing his hair and down his shoulders. She hated to see him so beaten.

"I will always come when you need me, Nick." When he met her eyes one more time, they were deadly serious.

"What if I said I needed you right now?" His hands cruised under the hem of her shirt to grasp her lower back, skin to skin. "What if I asked you to stay?" He pressed his lips to the opening left by her V-neck t-shirt, kissing her collarbone. "Would you come, Dani? Would you stay and come for me?" He shifted beneath her, and she could feel his impatient erection nudging her where she sat straddled across his lap. She rocked her hips in response, savoring the sensation.

After fighting her attraction for weeks, it felt too good to stop. Her body had been starved for this kind of attention, and after looking at the sweets from afar, she was finally being offered a taste. Although the taste quickly turned into a feast when Nick raised his head from her chest, and took her lips with his. *Finally.* They had been dancing around their attraction for so long, she was relieved to be able to give in and let her guard down.

She crushed her lips to his with an urgency that overtook any finesse she might've exercised. Once she'd sampled the goodies, she had a craving for more. Nick pulled back and tried to speak, but all he could manage was, "Dani...I need...more..."

She cut him off, placing her fingers on his already swollen lips.

"Me, too." She leaned back, gripping the hem of her shirt and pulling it over her head. She reveled in the look on his face. Her nipples pebbled even harder, now clearly visible through her demure undergarments. She certainly hadn't planned on anyone seeing her bra when she'd gotten dressed. He didn't seem to mind. She trembled as he reached up to trace her flesh along the edge of her bra, before tugging it down to reveal her. Repeating the maneuver on the other side, baring her fully to his gaze, he cupped her firm breasts before rubbing his thumbs over each crest. Each teasing sweep and pinch drove her farther out of her mind, until she rocked her hips forward, sliding herself against his shaft, eager to find some relief. Nick's hips jerked in response, pushing him against her again. Dani reached down between them and swiftly pulled his shirt over his head. His trance broken, Nick leaned in and began to taste. She gripped his head in both hands, holding him tightly to her, willing him silently to continue pushing her higher. She could feel the delicious tension building just from rocking against him, still separated by two layers of denim.

Convinced that he wouldn't cease his attentions, Dani allowed her hands to roam, tracing every indent and curve. She felt the ridges of a nasty scar at his waist, but she was immediately distracted from her discovery. His movements jerky and frantic, Nick pushed up off the couch enough to flip her over onto her back, and reached for the button on her jeans. Dani pushed his hand away, and set about doing it herself.

"Go get yourself ready, because I'm about to explode, and I want you inside me when I do," she commanded, tugging the tight denim down her legs.

Nick reached for his wallet, pulled out his emergency spare, and shucked his pants. He rolled on protection, and levered himself down over her waiting body. She lifted her arms in welcome. He leaned down to kiss her, as he slowly slid inside.

Dani gasped as he stretched her wide. It had been a long time since she'd made love, and everything felt deliciously tight. He slowly inched his way deeper and deeper until she relaxed and he slid home. She adored his weight on top of her, holding him so deeply inside her. He held still, breathing rapidly, and Dani could tell he was fighting for control. But she was too close to allow him stillness for very long. She was moments from a climax herself, and she wanted it, wanted him, badly. Drawing his head back down to her breasts, she made her needs clear, rocking her hips beneath him. He quickly took the hint and began kissing her nipples, letting her set the pace. It felt so damn good to lose herself in him.

She began the climb to oblivion and urged him to go faster, harder, more. She pushed him to give her everything she wanted. Her back arched as she skimmed the peak, before she clamped down hard around him. She shook endlessly, completely shattered by the power of her release. Nick quickly let his own orgasm overtake him, his rapid deep thrusts catching her on the way down.

He collapsed on top of her. When she gasped for breath, he rolled to the side, pulling her close to keep her from being crushed and from tumbling off the couch. Still inside her, he pulled her leg over his hip, tucked her head under his chin, and held her close. Lulled by her own release and his deep breathing, Dani quickly joined him in sleep, content to let thinking about what had just happened wait until later, much, much later.

Nick felt the soft arms holding him and the sweet smelling hair tickling his nose. He snuggled closer, enjoying the feeling of warmth and comfort, until he realized it wasn't a dream. Reluctantly opening his eyes, he looked down and saw that it was, indeed, Dani tucked into his arms, nuzzled against his bare chest. Damn it. Anger welled up in his chest. Panic was right behind. He'd hoped it was just another dream. Had he just ruined the best thing in his life, their friendship? Why the hell was he so weak when it came to resisting her?

He couldn't deny that the passion between them had been explosive, and that he no longer had his post-therapy hangover. But what now? He still wasn't OK. He wasn't whole. How could he ask her to be with him when he had nothing to offer her in return? It would be a one-sided relationship, and she deserved so much better than that. She was so kindhearted that she'd probably just sleep with him to help him feel better if he asked her. Oh, God. Is that what had just happened? Was this a pity fuck? That thought made him sick to his stomach. He slid back from her, unwrapping her arms from around him. He couldn't stay in her arms, not knowing why she was holding him. He left the room to take a shower and try to get his head on straight before he had to talk to her. He was afraid of the rage that was swimming in his blood, and he didn't know what would come out of his mouth if he tried to explain right now. Stalking into his bedroom, he put his fist through the nearest wall and added another drywall patch to his to-do list.

FOURTEEN

Dani woke on the couch naked, cold, and alone. Uneasy, she pushed her hair out of her eyes and searched the floor for her hastily dropped t-shirt. Then she heard the shower running. He hadn't left. Relief flowed through her. She hugged the warm and fuzzy emotions that flooded back close to her chest. She'd promised him no complications, no relationship, but surely that had changed given how close they'd already become over the last few weeks. He must be ready to let her in, share some of his burden. He wouldn't have taken things to the next level if he hadn't changed his mind. She didn't know anyone with as firm convictions as Nick. They could talk about the change in their relationship later. He'd need to process, and she could give him the space to do that. With a contented smile on her face, she gathered her scattered clothes, dressed quickly, and retreated back across the hall.

Glancing at her clock, she realized it was only 2:30 on Friday afternoon. She took a gamble and called Stella, hoping she'd catch her before her evening classes started. Her friend picked up on the third ring.

"Hey honey! I got your email. Flipped looks great! I'm dying to try it now that I've seen the menu online, and I can't wait to see you. It's been too long since you made it to class."

"Good! I was trying to find a place that would appeal to everyone. I can't wait to see you, too. But I have a little problem."

"What is it? Are you OK?" The instant concern in her friend's voice made her smile.

"I have a fashion emergency. I have accountant clothes, and workout clothes, and grubbies for cooking and cleaning. But I have zero going-out clothes! Help!" When Stella laughed at her tone of mock horror, she switched to begging. "What are you doing this afternoon? Can you meet me for a wardrobe intervention? Please, please, pretty please."

"That sounds dire! I can meet you in half an hour." Dani hung up the phone with a huge grin splitting her face. It was turning into an excellent afternoon.

When Nick got out of the shower, he discovered that he was alone in the apartment. His first reaction was relief. Tension drained from his shoulders. Maybe it made him a coward, but he was grateful he'd gotten a reprieve. He didn't feel steady enough yet to not lash out at Dani. Why the hell had she gotten right up in his face when he was in the middle of an attack? Didn't the woman have an ounce of self-preservation? Or was that why she'd run? He started to second-guess himself. Turning to Taco, he searched for answers.

"Why didn't she stay? Don't most women want to talk about what sex means? Is she angry at me for losing control? Or is she regretting her impulse to have pity sex? What do you think, Taco?" The dog had no reply, except for his soulful brown eyes that reflected Nick's own confusion back at him. Had he completely ruined the best friendship he had? And damn it, why hadn't she stayed so he could ask her these questions and get some answers, instead of pacing his apartment in a towel talking to a dog?

He'd lost control, but he could get it back. He could fix this. He'd explain what had happened and everything would go back to the way it had been. He just needed to cool off before he talked to Dani. Then everything would be fine. After he apologized, they could go back to being friends. He had to believe that, or the weight of his guilt would crush him.

Maybe it was naïve of him to think he could be a friend only, especially after she'd proven to be even sexier in reality than she'd been in his very creative and detailed dreams. Resisting her was going to be nearly impossible. He'd want her again, and again. His mind was already rising to the challenge, filling his head with images of all the ways he'd want to have her.

With a firm mental shake, he shut down that line of thought. He couldn't afford to go there, even in his mind, if he was to have any chance of resisting her in real life. He'd have to rely on his Army discipline, but he was sure he could do it, especially if she was in the same frame of mind. The one thing of which he was absolutely certain, was that he needed to keep Dani in his life. She was his anchor, his touchstone. She had become an integral part of his life in such a short time. Maybe too integral. He was afraid of what might happen if she suddenly wasn't there. That was the problem. He'd gotten so used to having her around, that he'd forgotten how to be by himself.

They'd been spending too much time together, just the two of them. It had caused all of that charged energy to build up. That wasn't healthy or smart. He would call Seth, and get out to spend some time with his buddy. He'd been cooped up long enough. He needed some guy time.

"Hey buddy! How've you been? I wondered when you'd crawl out from under your rock," Seth teased.

"Ha ha. I'm good. I wanted to see what you're up to tomorrow night. You want to go out?"

"You are in luck, my man! Killeran and Santos are in town for a bit of training out at the base. We were going to go check out this new place, Flipped. I heard it's great for checking out the ladies. You game?"

"Sure, that sounds great." Maybe that was what he needed. Meet some new girls, get Dani out of his head for a while. "I'll meet you guys there."

"Perfect. Listen, man, it's really good to hear from you. Don't let it go so long again, all right? You had me worried."

"No need to worry about me. I'd be worried for you. Now that I'm coming, there's no way the ladies will even spare you a glance."

"Ha ha, smart ass. In your dreams. See you tomorrow."

Nick hung up with a smile. This was what he'd been missing. He could admit that he'd made a mistake spending so much time with Dani, to the exclusion of his other friends. He needed his guys, too. Feeling a little more settled, he crossed the hall and knocked on her door, ready to get things straight and re-establish their ground rules. He waited and waited, knocked again even, before he realized that she must be gone. Surprise hit him hard that she wasn't there when he wanted to talk to her. Had he run her out of her own place? Was she that upset? That she would leave without telling him unsettled him again, but he didn't want to think too deeply about why that was.

Dani trailed Stella as she scoured the racks at one of the boutiques lining the corridors of the outdoor mall. Dani had joined Stella's studio as a way to de-stress while caring for Aunt Helen, and became fast friends with the owner/instructor. Although her attendance had fallen off since she'd begun spending her time on the café and Nick, she could still rely on her friend for support. Though the tall redhead looked nothing like her, Dani trusted her style sense. She always looked put together. She also knew how to push Dani out of her comfort zone, so she was the perfect person to call for this mission.

Stella was picking out way more outfits than Dani, so Dani just rolled with her friend's enthusiasm. She had no idea what would look good on her figure. She looked down at her jeans and t-shirt combo, so perfect for cooking or caregiving, so blah for everything else. Playing on the social scene had never been big on her to-do list, so her clothes were helplessly outdated. Not to mention she had added a few pounds to her curves with all the trial cooking and grief eating she'd been doing, so nothing fit. She had no idea what current fashions would suit her new curvier frame. Apparently, Stella did and was amassing a stockpile of outfits for her to try on.

"You do realize I only need one, right?"

Stella shot her a patronizing look and patted her cheek.

"You do realize that's crap, right? If you're serious about rejoining the world of the living, you need to look the part. You'll need outfits for girls' night, true, but what about first date night? Second date night? Sex-date night? Not to mention the general updating that your wardrobe needs. You asked for an intervention, and by God, you're going to get one!"

"Hallelujah! I have seen the light! Let me get started on what you've got there, or we'll never make a dent."

Dani tried on the dresses, all cute, but all ridiculously short. "Um, Stella, I think you forgot to hand me the pants that go with these tops!" She tugged the skirt to try and make it reach her knees.

"Ha ha. You have fantastic legs, of which I am ridiculously envious, and over which men should drool. They can't drool if they can't see them."

"I'm not so sure I need to have men drooling over my legs."

"Of course you do, honey! With those legs and your assets on top, we'll make them beg..."

"No, that's not what I meant. I want to look cute for our night out, but I may not need to attract a guy. I might already have one."

"What?" Stella barged into the dressing room with her. "Spill it, now! Who is he? Why haven't I heard about this? What do you mean might?"

Dani deliberately kept her gaze on her reflection in the mirror.

"You're so cute when you go all big sister on me. It's Nick. He's the vet I told you I was helping out."

"The vet whom you were careful to not describe in any flattering terms? The vet I *assumed* was just like all the other vets in your building? I thought you were bringing an old guy his groceries!"

"We have young vets, too, you know. People seem to forget about them, but they are just as needy as our aging veterans."

"OK, off the soap box! I will not be distracted. You deliberately didn't tell me he was young."

"I didn't want you jumping all over me about him! We've been just friends. That's what he needed from me, and I didn't want any pressure to change that before he was ready."

"Well, what's with the 'maybe' now?"

"I'll admit I've gotten closer to him than any other man in my life. This is nothing like asshole Matthew. I won't say it's the big L yet, but I feel like that's maybe where we're headed. I've tried to keep my distance and give him the space he's needed, but this afternoon we had a breakthrough, of sorts."

"A breakthrough?"

"Yeah, as in we broke through our clothes and made love on his couch!" Grinning and holding her arms around herself, she tried to contain the giddy laughter that threatened to break free.

"So, what did he say, you know, after?" Stella pressed for details.

"Nothing."

"What do you mean nothing? Did he brush it off? Or did he beg for more?"

"No, no, just nothing. I didn't really give him a chance. He was in the shower when I woke up, and I just left. I thought he might be embarrassed over how the situation came about, so I gave him some space. It'll be fine. He's the best man I know. Stella, I've never been so comfortable so quickly. We hang out together almost every day. We talk about everything, but we are completely comfortable in each other's silence too. It's amazing. I'll admit I was a little spooked to be falling so quickly for someone who was off limits, but now that we've crossed that line, it feels like the most natural thing in the world."

"Why was he 'off-limits'?" Stella asked.

"For starters, he lives across the hall. Rule of Dating #7."

"Don't date people in your building or at work. Obviously, but I don't get the feeling that's it. He doesn't seem the type to be put off by a simple dating rule, no matter how logical."

"No, that's not all. He just got out of the army, after a very difficult tour in Iraq. He's been struggling with his memories and some PTSD reactions. He's open to my help, up to a point, but he doesn't want me to know what he's done and how he's suffering. He said that he just wants to protect me from the crap in his life right now, but I think he's avoiding dealing with it still. That's the big reason we've been fighting our attraction. He hasn't been in a good spot to be in a relationship. And to be honest, neither have I. Grieving Aunt Helen, getting her estate in order, starting a new life... I put myself off-limits too. It just seems like none of that matters right now. This thing between us makes all of that seem like excuses. It just feels...right."

"Dani, I don't want to rain on your parade, but it sounds like he's dealing with some pretty serious stuff. You've known him less than a month. I just want you to be careful. Are you sure you want to get involved? I mean what if he gets violent? Or goes into a spiral? You're just starting to come out of a spiral of your own. Are you sure about this?"

"I am. It's never felt so right before. I know he's got issues, but he's working on them. We're working on them. The friendship we have is incredibly special. He's special." Dani watched her best friend bite her tongue, literally, and change the subject.

"Well, that's all the more reason to knock him on his ass with a spectacular outfit for your official first date!" Grabbing a coral mini dress, Stella pushed it and Dani back into the changing room. "Try this one next!"

Dani looked at the dress on the hanger skeptically. It looked like one of her V-neck tank tops. It was pretty, with some beading and sequin detailing on the top half, but it definitely seemed to be missing a few inches off the bottom. Then she checked the price tag. Jaw dropping, she popped her head back out of the dressing room. "Stella! What rack are you shopping from? How can a tank top cost $300?"

"Just humor me and put it on!"

Shaking her head over the ludicrous thought of spending $300 dollars on a dress to just wear on a date, she slid the silk/lycra frock over her head. She tugged it down to mid-thigh, and turned to evaluate the dress in the mirror. For the second time in less than a minute, her jaw scraped the floor. What had looked simple on the hanger was anything but when it was stretched over her figure. The dress showed off her toned arms and dipped in the front to show just a hint of the cleavage that would drive him wild. Every sparkle drew her eyes to her chest, while every seam pulled the fabric in just the right way to highlight her curves in a subtly sexy way. The abbreviated hemline made her legs seem a mile long, and the coral shade brought out the warm highlights in her skin. It could have been a sausage casing dress, but it wasn't. The designer of this dress knew a woman's body and had created the perfect showcase for it. When she moved, it moved with her. Suddenly $300 didn't seem so outrageous...

"You're awful quiet in there. Did you get stuck?"

"No, I'm good. I'm great! Stella, you're a genius." She opened the door and had the pleasure of seeing Stella's jaw drop too.

"That's it. That dress is coming home. Don't you even dare argue with genius."

"I wouldn't dream of it. Holy cow! Who knew this was hiding under my jeans?"

"Nick certainly doesn't, or he'd never have lasted three weeks."

Laughing, Dani gave Stella a big hug and turned to look at the rack that had appeared conveniently across from her changing room.

"Who knew dress up as an adult could be so much fun? What's next?"

Dani happily spent the next three hours chatting, trying on clothes, and refreshing her friendship with Stella. She left with several cute tops and jeans along with the amazing dress, a pair of nude heels, and two more fun date night outfits. Dani was on top of the world. Nothing like great sex, bonding time with a girlfriend, and kick-ass, new clothes to round out a perfect day.

FIFTEEN

DANI ENTERED the bustling bar and bistro with her girlfriends and watched heads turn to track their progress to their table. Dressed to the nines for their night out, four beautiful women were bound to attract attention. The coral sheath and nude stilettos made Dani aware of her body and her walk, in a way she hadn't been in a long time. She had donned her dress and applied her makeup, arming herself with her femininity in a ritual as old as time, ready to take on the world of men. She bolstered her power, finding the confidence to walk into the place as if she owned it. Every male gaze that she attracted gave her a secret thrill. It had been too long since she'd let this side of herself out to play. Attracting men's attention, in the company of good friends, shot her confidence even higher. The fact that she already had a particular man in mind freed her from worrying about following through on any of flirtatious glances coming her way.

"Julia Quinn must be right," Stella teased as a flight of champagne arrived at their table almost before they did, sent by two suits at the end of the bar. "Men are like sheep—happy followers. Now that one of us is taken, we're irresistible."

"What? Who's taken?" Olivia chimed in.

"Dani, of course. Can't you see the glowy, I-just-got-laid vibe she's still sporting?"

Dani felt her face flush, as her friends immediately pounced on this news.

"Details! We need details! I bet it was the sexy new neighbor. Am I right? Tell me I'm right." Jamie bounced in her seat.

"She got it in one! How did you know?" Stella replied.

"Something about the 'he's so sexy, he turns my knees to Jell-O' story a few weeks ago stuck with me. So, what's the story, Dani?" Jamie took the lead and engaged the men in suits with smiling nods and flirting eyes, while Dani filled the girls in.

"I'm not sure yet. We haven't really spoken since the explosion."

"Explosion?"

"Well, when you keep sexual tension under that much pressure, it's bound to explode sooner or later. And oh my, does that man know how to let go..."

They placed their orders for small plates to share, and between Stella and Jaime flirtatiously sampling bacon wrapped dates and lemon roasted asparagus spears, they reduced the men at the bar to drooling fools. Laughter and that secret female power glowed in every eye around the table. Dani knew she'd been right to call for a Girls' Night Out. Every woman deserved to recharge with the girls, and it had been too long for all of them. Grinning at the response of the men at the bar to her friends' antics, Dani let her gaze scan the rest of the room. She did a double take when she spotted a pair of very familiar broad shoulders across the room.

Nick leaned back in his chair, trying to angle it away from

the table so he could see the door. He'd showed up last and had gotten the seat facing the wall. He could feel the prickles of anxiety climbing up his spine. He couldn't sit still and leaned forward to cup his hands around the single pint of beer he was nursing. He tried to refocus on the conversation his buddies were having about the upcoming playoffs. He hadn't been following the season closely, and couldn't let his guard down enough to follow the debate. Every time a waiter passed behind him, his attention shifted, following their movements until they were safely past.

"So, Nick, how're you settling into your new place?" Killeran asked. "Seth told us you got a place across town?"

"Uh, yeah, Killer. It's good, you know, a little quiet, but good."

"Anyone special in your life?" Killeran prodded.

"Nope."

"What about the babe across the hall?" Santos put in. Nick glared across the table at Seth.

"What? She's hot! She's the only positive thing your building has going for it. Of course, I mentioned her. Guys, you should've seen her! Blond hair, blue eyes, and a plate of home-made chocolate chip cookies? Doesn't get more perfect than that!"

"She's not some fantasy girl." Nick replied with a hint of anger. Dani was the last person he wanted to be talking about right now. He hadn't spoken to her since "The Incident." He'd been trying to talk to her for over twenty-four hours now, and had failed miserably. She had to be avoiding him. He'd crossed a line, and now she was pissed. He'd gone over and over it in his mind and hadn't made peace with it yet. If he could just talk to her, and explain...but no. She didn't even have the decency to let him down face to face. "She's got flaws, too." Like loving him so well he'd lost his damn mind.

"Everyone's got flaws. She sounds great. I'd be willing to overlook quite a bit for regular homemade cookies," Killeran said.

"I'd be willing to overlook anything for regular sex!" Santos chuckled and sipped his beer.

"And that explains your last girlfriend." Seth tossed out the easy joke. "But seriously, Nick, are you telling me you're not interested? Because I'd be more than happy to tap that! Give her my number!"

His anger surged over his friends' crude remarks. "Touch her, and I'll break your fingers!" He bit back any further comments and clenched his hands trying to control his temper. His friends traded looks of concern over the outburst. Seth ventured a quiet comment, "But there's no one special, huh?"

"Dammit! I just said there's no one special in my life! No one! Ok? Now back off!" Nick shot back at a near yell. Seth's concerned look shifted from his face to over his shoulder, and a flash of horrified dismay was quickly replaced by his usual happy-go-lucky social mask. Nick's stomach clenched with dread.

"Hi, Dani! What are you doing here?"

His words were a punch in the gut. Her breath literally whooshed out of her lungs, and she curled protectively, an arm wrapping around her stomach. "No one special," he'd said. She had heard it as clear as day. She was no one special to him. The pain of betrayal was instant and stunning. Her heart broke in half, the pain in her chest mirroring the pain in her belly. Hours passed in those few seconds, as she reeled from his words and the fierce anger behind them. How could she have been so wrong? How could he not have felt how right it was between them? But she pulled it all inside, to be dealt with later. She still had enough pride and awareness to paste a carefree smile on her face and respond when Seth greeted her.

"Hi, Dani! What are you doing here?"

"Hey, Seth. Hi, Nick. My friends and I are here for our Girls' Night Out." She gestured over her shoulder. "I saw you guys and thought I'd come say hey."

"Killeran, Santos, this is Dani. Dani, these are some of our buddies, in town for some training." Seth made the introductions. Dani carefully kept her attention on the three men facing her. "It's nice to meet you."

Nick raised a hand, reaching for hers. *Like hell.* Dani stepped back out of his reach. "Well, I'll let you guys get back to your dinner." She watched his expression as he raised his gaze from the floor to her face, taking in every inch in between. She saw heat flare in his eyes, and it took every ounce of her control not to slap it out. She kept her eyes cold, her smile empty. As regret replaced the flames in his gaze, she delivered her parting shot.

"Goodbye, Nick." She used her remaining scrap of feminine power to sway her hips and make him stare as she walked away with her head held high.

Dani barely made it back to her table before her façade started to tremble.

"Oh, shit. Something happened! Code red ladies!"

"What's going on?"

"Who was she talking to? Is she OK?"

"I think that's the guy."

"What guy?"

"THE guy?"

"Oh, shit!"

"Bathroom intervention?"

"Immediately."

Her friends collected their purses and circled around her. She numbly allowed them to guide her through the crowded bar. They swept her into the ladies' room, just in the nick of time. Her mask cracked as soon as she looked in the mirror, and the tears began to flow. Jamie pulled her into a hug and Olivia ran into a stall and returned armed with tissues. Once Dani's sobs quieted to mere tears, Stella broached the sensitive subject.

"What happened, honey?"

"I was wrong."

"Was that Nick?" Dani nodded. "What did he say to you?"

"To me? Not much. About me to his buddies? Quote: There is no one special in my life. At full volume, about five seconds before I walked up. You never do hear good things when you eavesdrop, do you?" The tears still streaming down her cheeks spoiled her poor attempt at humor and a smile. She relayed the gist of the conversation and how she'd said goodbye. "I thought this was it. I really thought we were great together. Wow, was my radar way off."

"Are you sure he wasn't just being razzed by his friends?" Jamie wiped away the neglected tears.

"Does it matter? The man I slept with yesterday just disavowed the existence of anyone special in his life to his friends. And he knows I heard him. How can I just ignore that?"

"You can't. He's a complete ass who doesn't deserve you. Either he should've been man enough to keep his hands off you if he didn't have the feelings to back it up, or man enough to admit those feelings to his friends if he does have them. No matter how you look at it, he's handled this poorly, and hurt you in the process." Olivia rubbed her hand up and down Dani's arm. Her logical analysis, while solid, didn't help Dani feel any better.

"Want me to go out there and kick him in the balls? I will,

you know. That's how deep our friendship goes!" Stella said vehemently, coaxing Dani's first true smile.

"Ooooh, instant revenge! I like where your head is at, Stella!" Ever the cheerleader, Jamie rubbed her hands together.

"Nope," interjected Olivia. "That's too obvious and could get you hauled in on assault charges. I don't have money for bail. Besides it doesn't hurt long enough. But if you really want revenge," Olivia caught and held Dani's gaze in the mirror. "Don't let him see you hurt. You are hot enough to make any red-blooded male in the room swallow his tongue. Show him that if he's not interested, many others are. Jealousy is a bitter pill, and the image of another man's hands on your hips as you dance close, swaying to a slow song? That'll be burned on his retina for life."

"Why would he be jealous? He obviously doesn't want me. Why should he?"

"Hey, none of that negative crap in here." Jamie cut her off. "Of course, he wants you. That's why he fought for three weeks to keep his hands off you. I'd bet money that he's upset he lost control. Olivia's idea is brilliant. It'll make him suffer now and later, when he can't get you out of his head. Can you pull it off?"

"Of course, she can pull it off! Didn't you see her balls of steel as she kept it together for the whole conversation? Let's do it!" Stella cheered.

Dani gathered her courage and channeled her anger and hurt into resolve. She nodded decisively. "Let's do it. Olivia, can you help me get my face back together? Stella, I'm going to need another drink. And Jamie, go work your wiles on those two guys who sent the champagne. Let's give him something to think about."

"Yes! That's my girl. Screw the bastard, on three." The ladies huddled up and put their hands in on top of hers. "1-2-3 break!"

Her friends scattered to tend to their assigned tasks. Dani pushed her pain deeper inside, determined not to ruin their GNO. She would make her pain and her pride push her through the next hour's charade. Then she'd allow herself to poke all the sore spots and have a good cry when she was home and alone. Her falsely bright smile was back on display when Stella returned with a fresh flute of champagne.

"Atta girl," Olivia whispered as she pulled out her emergency stash of cosmetics. "Let's go kick his ass." And she got to work.

SIXTEEN

"THAT'S THE GIRL NEXT DOOR?" Killer asked, his eyes still glued to her ass, as he watched her walk away. "She looks like that and cooks, too? I'll take her number, and you can fight me for her, Seth." His attempt to add a little levity to the situation fell flat. Nick shot him a baleful look.

"You are such a fucking idiot." Seth said quietly, shaking his head.

"Finally, something we agree on," Nick muttered, and he dropped his head back down on his arms.

"Come on. Let's go get another round." Seth dragged Nick up to the bar and away from their loud-mouthed friends.

Like the complete ass that he was, Nick kept trying to surreptitiously look over his shoulder, hoping for a glimpse of Dani. He wanted to make sure that she was all right. Hell, he just wanted to see her in that dress again. Her crew had swooped down and hustled her into the bathroom, but he hadn't seen her come out yet.

"Stop craning your neck. I'll tell you when she comes out." Seth said.

"What?" Nick asked, trying to sound innocent.

"Do you really think I don't know what you're doing? I said, I'll tell you when she comes out of the bathroom. I haven't seen her yet. How badly did you just fuck up?"

"About as bad as you can. I'm out of control, man. The last thing I wanted to do was hurt her. I was trying to protect her, dammit. And then, I just lost it. And now she's hurting, and I did it."

"Protect her from what?"

"From me."

"Listen, man. You need to level with me right now. You haven't been the same since Samarra. What's going on that you're afraid you hurt her?"

The only one he'd been fooling was himself. He grimaced and spilled his secrets to Seth.

"I keep going back to Samarra and losing Finn. I can't stop looking over my shoulder for an attack. Shit, sitting with my back to the door tonight almost killed me. And the rage... it comes on so quick. Dani got me to see a counselor, but I'm still struggling. I'm no good for her right now. I have no right to touch her the way I did."

"Wait, did you physically hurt her?"

"No, no! Jesus! She came in after a therapy session, and I was in the middle of a flashback. I lost control, and we ended up having sex on my couch, yesterday. I'm all messed up about it, and you guys go pushing my buttons, and shit, I fucked up big time."

"I wish you'd told me all this before. You don't need to do this alone. I've had my own struggles since we got back too. We are not done talking about this. But Killeran and Santos are heading back, and I get the feeling that you'd rather not share this with everyone. You know Killer can't keep his mouth shut."

Nick nodded. "Thanks, man."

A hot redhead settled at the bar next to Seth.

"Are you here with the idiot?"

"Yeah. I'm Seth. You're here with Dani."

"Stella. What the hell happened?"

"Does the phrase FUBAR mean anything to you?"

"Fucked up beyond all recognition? You've got that right, soldier."

"Listen, he screwed up, and he knows it." Nick listened to his friend try and salvage the situation. Seth scribbled his cell phone number on a napkin and slid it to her without making eye contact, but Nick caught the exchange. Stella reached for the two flutes the bartender had set down in front of her.

"All I can say is he's sorry."

"One of the sorriest," Stella shot back, not one ounce of sympathy in her hard eyes.

Nick nodded, taking the direct hit, as Stella headed back to the restroom.

"Damn, sir, she shut you down." The bartender came back over wiping her hands on a bar cloth.

"Excuse me?" Nick looked at the young woman behind the bar currently grinning at his misfortune. He took in her dark spiral curls and her flashing eyes, but it was her smile that stuck in his mind, naggingly familiar.

"What did you say to piss her off? I gotta tell you, sir, I wouldn't want to get on her bad side. She looks pretty fierce." It suddenly hit him.

"Whiskey? Is that you?" Seth's eyes widened as she confirmed Nick's guess.

"I wondered how long it would take you."

"You look great!" She raised an eyebrow at Seth's remark. He quickly clarified. "Oh come on, the last time I saw you was in Mosul. Hair back, in uniform, covered in dust. I'm surprised I even recognized you. What are you doing here?" Nick was glad that Seth had picked up the conversation. He sincerely doubted he'd be able to handle words around any woman the way his night was going.

"Working. Can I get you something?"

"But weren't you a medic? Why are you slinging drinks?"

"Gotta keep Mama's bills paid. Do you know how much an EMT makes? I wanted to get out and be a nurse but there's almost a two-year waitlist just to get into school. I have to make ends meet in the meantime. I'm still in the reserves, and I picked up some side jobs like this one."

"Well, good luck. I hope that all works out for you."

"So how badly did you just screw up?" She turned her attention back to Nick, and he met her question with a baleful stare.

"You caught that, huh? Pretty bad."

Whiskey poured a round of Jameson shots, and filled up a pitcher with a light beer. "This round is on me. Your girl just came out of the bathroom, and she looks like she's gonna make you pay."

Nick pushed his shot toward Seth, and turned in his seat. He was going to need a clear head to get through this night. Seth grabbed his shoulder to hold him steady.

"Come on, man. Let's take this back to our table. We'll have a better view of the show from there. Thanks, Whiskey. I'll see you around." Nick's jaw clenched at Seth's playful tone. How could he treat this like a joke? Oh right, it wasn't his life coming apart at the seams.

Santos sat back down at the table. "You really stepped in it, man. I heard her friend, the tall sexy brunette hitting up those guys at the end of the bar."

Killeran chimed in. "You sure did. And oh man, is she going to make you pay for it. Here she comes." All four heads turned to focus on the table where the gorgeous women had been sitting. Nick sat still as a stone, waiting for the crowds to part, dreading his retribution.

His mouth dried to sawdust as he watched her walk into the room, more beautiful than he'd ever seen her. That dress in motion did things to her figure that were nearly criminal. His hands curled into fists on the table, and his body vibrated with restrained energy as he watched her walk away from him, and directly toward the two men entertaining the brunette. Seth reached across the table and laid a restraining hand on his wrist.

"Easy, buddy. Unfortunately, you earned this. And if you break their pretty faces, I'm going to end up in county, because I won't let you take them on alone. Those suits look like the type who'd sue. Do you want to leave?"

Nick forced his shoulders down from his ears, and smoothed his hands on the table. "No, I'm okay. I'm fine. I just won't look." That's what he said, but he couldn't help torturing himself. His heart cringed at every smile, every touch, every laugh she gave to another. It was his penance for screwing up the best thing in his life.

Dani emerged head held high, make-up flawless thanks to Olivia's expertise, hips swaying. She flipped her loose blond curls back over her shoulder, and smoothed her hands down her hips. She steeled herself to not look at him, instead focusing on Jamie and flashing a smile at the gentlemen who met them at their table.

"Dani, this is Jake and his friend, Bill."

"We had to come meet the most beautiful women in the room. I hope you don't mind if we join you."

"Of course not. I'm flattered. Have you met everyone?" Dani

inwardly rolled her eyes and slipped into hostess mode. She would make it through this torture if it killed her. She flirted and laughed as if her life depended on it. Jake asked her to dance, and she agreed. While he was a pleasant enough partner, she had said yes mainly to antagonize the man watching from across the room. When his hand slipped from the small of her back to the curve of her ass, she didn't like it but resisted the urge to move away. She hoped Nick's eyes were burning in his head, but she had little confidence that he cared enough for that to be happening. She couldn't even confirm that he was watching. Every time she turned her head he was studying his beer, but when she turned away she swore she felt a tingle down her spine.

If only she'd felt something for one of the two guys paying her attention tonight, but neither one aroused anything more than casual interest. Not a blip, not a ping, not a tingle. Stella kept giving her encouraging smiles, but her nerves were shot. The stress of fending off leading suggestions from Jake and obsessing over eye contact with a certain miserable but silent jerk coalesced into a headache that was threatening to explode through her skull. When Jake and Bill went to the bar for another round, Dani made her exit.

"Ladies, I am beat, and I have a horrible headache coming on. It was great to see you tonight. Thanks for everything. Stella, it's your turn next month. Set us up with something fun for our next GNO. I promise less drama!"

As her friends shared good byes and promises to stay in touch, Dani shrugged her purse on to her shoulder and headed for the door. Outside, she fumbled in her purse for her car keys. She was so focused on getting home before the tension headache turned into a migraine, that she was completely surprised when Jake grabbed her arm on the sidewalk.

"Hey Dani! Wait up," Jake spun her to face him. "That was great."

Too close. Too fast. Her head spun, and she couldn't think as she tried to regain her balance.

"What was great?" Dani asked in a near whisper, barely keeping her frustration and her headache from boiling over.

"The excuse about a headache to get us out of there. No offense, Jamie's great, but I am definitely looking forward to a little one-on-one time with you." Dani rolled her eyes at his innuendo and immediately regretted the impulse as pain stabbed through her eye socket.

"Should we head to your place or mine?"

"Listen, Jake. It was nice to meet you and all, but the headache is no excuse. I really have to get home, alone."

"You're kidding me, right?"

"No, I'm afraid not. Goodnight, Jake."

"That's it? You little tease! What was all that in there? The flirting, the dancing? I bought all four of you drinks! And all I get is, 'It was nice to meet you?'" He grabbed her arm to stop her forward progress and spun her around to face him. Dizzy and nauseous, Dani clutched his shoulder for balance. "That's bullshit and you know it." He pulled her in closer.

"No!" Dani brought her hands up between them to try and fend off the unwanted contact. Suddenly her hands were pushing empty air. She opened her eyes a crack to try and figure out what had happened without blasting her retinas with too much light. Apparently, Jake wasn't the only one who'd followed her out of the bar.

Nick stood with his hand around Jake's throat, pushing him up against the side of building. Jake struggled against the iron grip that was cutting off his air supply, and as he kicked his legs, Dani realized that Nick was actually holding him up off the ground.

"Nick, put him down before you hurt him."

Nick ignored her and continued to pin the struggling man

against the wall. "I believe the lady said, 'No.' Didn't you, Dani?"

Afraid of the unleashed anger she saw in his eyes, Dani put a hand on his arm and tried to deescalate. "It was just a misunderstanding."

"No, it wasn't Dani. I heard you tell him very clearly that you needed to go home alone and weren't interested in his company. What I want to know is if this asshole heard you say no. His answer will determine how many bones I break." His voice had gotten very hard and clipped, unlike anything she'd heard from him before. His tone brooked no argument. Dani was afraid that he would do serious harm to Jake. The man's veins were beginning to bulge, and his face was turning an unpleasant shade of purple. She wasn't sure Nick could back down from this level of engagement.

"Nick, stop this now. Jake is going to go home now. Alone. Aren't you Jake?"

The pinned man attempted to nod his head, but only succeeded in quivering. Grabbing Nick's arms more forcefully now, Dani yanked.

"God damn it, Nick! Stop it! Let him go! You've made your point. He'll leave. Nick look at me. I'm fine."

"I'm not," he muttered as he finally turned and made eye contact with her. The self-loathing and regret she saw swimming there beneath all that anger staggered her, but she held firm. Gripping his face in her hands, she tried to break through the red haze again. His arm was beginning to tremble.

"Put him down, Nick. I'm not hurt. Don't do this."

Nodding, Nick slowly lowered the trembling man to the ground and loosened the death grip around his throat. But before he let him go completely, he leaned in close and uttered a quiet, flat statement that was bone chilling and effective.

"You won't ever go near her again."

Jake backed away from Nick, rubbing his neck and desperately gasping for air. He glanced at Dani, and then back at Nick. Dani felt the growl as it rumbled up her arm. Good Lord, he'd actually growled! Dani tightened her grip. Jake nodded almost imperceptibly, and then took off in a hurry for his car.

"You'll be lucky if he doesn't charge you with assault." She finally released her grip on his arm now that the imminent crisis had passed.

"He's lucky I didn't break his arms. Are you really OK?"

"I'm fine. I just need to get home." Dani turned and continued up the street to where she'd parked her car. Glancing over her shoulder, she saw that Nick was still trailing her, shoulders hunched, hands shoved into the pockets of his jeans.

"What are you doing? Leave me alone."

"I...can't. I'm just going to make sure you make it to your car safely, OK? I promise I won't bother you."

Unable to expend another ounce of energy on fighting him, she simply turned and resumed the slow walk to her car. Sliding into the driver's seat, she closed the door and laid her throbbing head on the steering wheel. How was she ever going to drive home like this? The migraine was winning, and she fumbled in her glove compartment for the small bottle of medication she kept in there for just such an occasion. Squinting at the bottle, she struggled with the childproof cap. She let out a yelp when the driver's side door swung open, and Nick leaned into her car.

"Scoot over."

"What?"

"I said, scoot over. You're in no condition to drive, are you?" Dani was beyond arguing. Hell, she was beyond moving. He took the bottle from her clumsy hands and opened it for her. "Come on. I'll drive you home. We're headed the same direction anyhow."

Dani assessed him warily. She did not want to accept his

offer, but she realized it was probably the fastest way to get home and in bed. The thought of being in bed, with him, made her heart clutch, and she started to knee-jerk refuse him.

"Dani, please. Let me do this for you."

Whether it was the soft plea in his voice or the lightning spike of pain that was radiating through her left eye, she awkwardly pushed herself over to the passenger side and chased her pill down with a forgotten bottle of stale warm water she found in the door. Nick folded himself into the front seat of her compact, slid the seat all the way back, and pulled out into traffic. He lapsed into blessed silence.

Dani was grateful that he didn't try to talk to her about what she'd overheard. She didn't think she could bear it, on top of everything else. She rested her cheek against the cold windowpane and quickly fell asleep to escape the pain pulsing in her head and in her heart.

She roused slightly as he lifted her sleeping form from her car and carried her upstairs. Dani rested her head against his shoulder and breathed deeply in her half sleep. Scents of soap, beer, and warm man filled her head, and she burrowed closer into his heat. The last thing she remembered was a brush of lips across her forehead before she blessedly fell asleep.

Nick placed Dani gingerly down on the bed. What he'd found with Dani was special, and she deserved to be protected and cherished. He buried his nose in the hair that tickled his cheek and inhaled, enjoying the privilege one last time. Removing her stiletto heels was a special kind of torture – those shoes had driven him crazy all night, making her legs endlessly long and her hips sway to the music. He battled the urge to run his hands up those legs now, but knew he hadn't earned the right. More than anything he wanted to crawl in bed behind her and pull her close. It was what he wanted, but not what she needed. Leaning down and pressing a kiss on her clammy forehead, he tucked her in under the comforter and forced himself to turn away.

Nick stumbled as if he was drunk across the hallway, even though he hadn't even managed to finish his one lukewarm beer. It was like walking through quicksand trying to reach the sanctuary of his own apartment, desperate to get himself away from her before he completely fell apart. The minute the door closed behind him, the fear and anger and self-loathing erupted and he lost it. He was worthless. He'd hurt the one person in the world who gave a damn about him. Lamps crashed as he translated his breaking heart into actions.

He threw pillows and cushions off the ugly couch, trying to erase the fatal actions that had killed his soul for good. He deserved every minute of torture she'd put him through tonight. But when his mind replayed that asshole's hands on her, grabbing her, forcing her, more holes appeared in the walls. He was sick with fear and remorse. Who would save him from himself now? He blacked out as the rage he could no longer control took over.

When he finally wound down, he had no idea where he was and how much time had passed. He surveyed the damage. Taco was cowering in the corner shaking and whimpering. Horrified, he looked down and saw the blood on his hands, and he knew what he needed to do. He cleaned himself up, packed his bags, and took one more trip across the hall.

Even in sleep, she glowed with an inner radiance that took his breath away. Sunny, indeed. He settled Taco on her bed, and retreated to the doorway. He kicked himself again for the pain he caused her. He would never forget the look in her eyes at the bar. She deserved so much more. She deserved someone whole, someone sane, someone else. He wouldn't be able to stay away from her, but he couldn't be with her, either. His struggle with his own will power that evening had proven it in spades. With one last anguished look at the amazing woman asleep on the bed, he said, "Good-bye, Dani." And walked out of her life.

SEVENTEEN

Dani slept through the rest of the migraine that kept her in bed until ten the next morning. The fact that she'd managed to take her medicine before the headache incapacitated her meant she was only suffering from the hangover she'd earned and not the hazy muddle that usually followed a migraine episode. As she contemplated leaving the cozy confines of her bed in search of water, the true horror of the evening before came back to her full force. *No one special*, he'd said. Feeling her heart breaking anew, she vetoed the water in favor of burrowing back under her covers. The familiar empty feeling spread through her chest leaving her numb and cold. She yelped when something furry brushed against her leg.

"Taco? How did you get in here? Did he toss you aside too?" Pulling the pup close for a cuddle, she let the tears flow. "It's all my fault. I shouldn't have let him get so close. He warned me, didn't he? I should have understood that he wasn't interested in me that way. We got caught in a moment of weakness, and we lost our heads. That's all. Except it didn't feel like that was all, you know what I mean?" She looked down at the pup trying to lick her chin, as if he was going to give her a response.

All of the negative thoughts circled through her head on a repeating loop. He'd said he only needed a friend. And really, who would want her as anything else? It seemed she was good enough to sleep with, but not good enough to keep. Just plain old Dani. Granted she'd looked pretty hot last night, hence attracting the asshole Jake, but that wasn't the real her. Nick had known the real Dani and hadn't found her attractive enough to be "someone special" in his life. Old wounds from her break up with Matthew blended with the fresh cuts left by Nick. She had trusted the wrong men with her heart twice now.

The loop repeated, each time adding more details and doubt. She was an idiot for thinking that they had developed anything but a friendship.

The knock at the door pulled a groan from her heart and the covers back up over her head. He wanted to hash things out now? Well, she'd be damned if she'd give him the satisfaction of seeing her face now, splotchy and puffy eyed. The knocking became more insistent. He wasn't going to take a hint. Well, it would serve him right to see what he'd caused. With a head of steam building, she stalked to the door and yanked it open.

Stella stood there with a cardboard coffee carrier in one hand, and a copy of the latest ParaNora in the other. Her big smile turned quickly into a moue of concern. Dani's anger shifted back to sadness as soon as she realized it was her best friend and not her not-boyfriend waiting to be welcomed in. Pushing the book and a large skim mocha, extra chocolate, no whip, into Dani's hands, Stella moved into the room and shut the door behind her.

"What happened? You look like you were hit by a truck! Last I knew, you were heading out, and Jake left too. Then 20 minutes later, Seth comes by asking if we'd seen Nick. I expected to hash out some revenge nookie stories this morning, or at least a steamy kiss. I did not expect to find you like this!

What happened to the kick-ass warrior woman who shoved his words down his throat last night?"

"She's not here." Taking the first sip of her favorite fancy coffee, she closed her eyes and hummed. "Don't take this the wrong way, but will you marry me?" She worked up a genuine smile as the sugar, fat, and caffeine hit her system. "Who needs men, with a best friend who will bring the perfect coffee and a new book for the morning-after debrief?"

"I'm flattered, but there are some things that are better with a man."

"I think we could manage. Really, what man would do this?"

"Don't think flattery will distract me. I need details!"

"I screwed it all up." Dani sighed and related the events of the evening from the moment she left the bar. She picked up Taco who was pacing in circles on her bed, before she plopped on her couch. "And now he's angry with me. Our plan backfired. He felt he needed to protect me, like some big brother. It's no wonder he didn't want anything more with me. Who would?"

"OK, I realize that we had to suppress the pity party last night and shift right into crush his balls mercilessly mode. Let's get it out of your system right now. I assume you've been at this awhile. You have 30 more seconds to feel sorry for yourself. Go." Stella intently followed the second hand on its trip around the face of her watch. "There. Done now. As an outside observer, here's what I saw last night. He watched your every move in the mirror behind his table, even though he tried not to. Every time Jake put his hands on your ass while you were dancing, he gripped his glass so hard I'm surprised it didn't shatter. His buddy Seth watched you, too, though his eyes were more speculative. You might have an ally there."

"An ally? You make it sound like we're at war."

"We are. What I saw last night was a man being eaten alive by emotions that he refused to set free. You are going to have to go to battle for him. Are you going to let the man you love go so easily?"

"I didn't say I loved him."

"You didn't have to, honey. My point is he was not acting like a big brother, or a good friend who didn't give a damn. He was acting like a jealous boyfriend watching someone else hitting on his girl. Given that he almost tore Jake apart outside the restaurant just confirms that. You are not alone in this situation, and you sure as hell aren't at fault. Are you sure you're ready to walk away?"

"I think I have to, Stella. You didn't see his eyes last night. He was so angry and hurt. If I make him feel that way, I'm not good for him. And I won't push myself on someone who clearly doesn't want me in his life in that way." Admitting that her friend had seen what she'd been willfully ignoring stung. "I can't pull back from loving him. You're right about that. I do love him, but what I need and what he can give are clearly not the same. And because I love him, I won't cause him any more pain. I'll just have to try and get over him."

A knock on the door had her taking a deep breath, steeling herself to face him. "I can do this," she muttered under her breath. "I can set him free."

She pulled the door open again, and for the second time it was not the person she was aching to see. Seth stood there, shifting awkwardly, working a small white envelope between his fingers.

"What do you want?" Dani asked. Her irritation that Nick hadn't bothered to confront her in person won out over her manners.

"Nick asked me to come over this morning. When I got here, I found a key on the mat and instructions on the table. He asked me to clear out his fridge, clean up the mess, and give you this." He held out the envelope.

"He's gone?"

Seth shrugged. "I don't know. He didn't tell me. But it looks that way."

She looked back to Stella sitting at her kitchen table. "He just left..."

"Well then, I guess that makes it easier to leave him alone."

A million thoughts raced through Dani's head as she stared at the unopened envelope.

"Well, I'll get out of your hair."

Dani, still absorbed with the envelope closed the door behind him.

"Should I open it?"

"Of course you should open it! Hello! Dying of curiosity over here!"

Dani returned to Taco on the couch and carefully tore the envelope open to reveal a sheet of folded notebook paper inside. His nearly illegible masculine scrawl covered the page. She caught a hint of his scent, and her gut clenched. With a deliberate breath for strength, she began to read.

Dear Dani,

I'm sorry. I'm sorry about what happened the other day. I'm sorry about what you heard last night. I'm sorry for what happened outside. I'm sorry that I am not a good enough man for you. I'm sorry for causing you pain. I'm sorry I couldn't tell you any of this in person. I just couldn't find the words. But you don't have to worry about running into me. I'm going to go away for a while. Please keep an eye on Taco for me. I know it's a lot to ask, but I don't want the little guy feeling abandoned twice. I can't live like this, always afraid I'll hurt you. I hope you can find it in your heart to forgive me while I'm gone. I don't think I could bear to lose your friendship.

-Nick

"He's gone."

"What do you mean gone?"

Dani handed over the letter to Stella.

"What are you thinking right now?"

"This is all my fault. I drove him away. He doesn't even feel comfortable in his own home. I can't believe he would just leave, though. Damn it, Stella. This hurts so much. Why does it hurt more that he's left, when I was going to set him free? I really thought we had something, that this was building towards something solid and good. And now I've blown it." Dani curled into a ball around Taco, trying to hold herself together. The little dog licked her cheeks furiously offering his unique brand of comfort. How could she not explode, when her heart was shattering in a million pieces? Stella pulled her into a hug, holding her and stroking her hair, as the dam of emotion she'd been suppressing since the night before finally broke. Dani sobbed and let the tears drain her mind and soul, until she was empty. As the weeping quieted, Stella broke the silence.

"Are you ready to listen for a minute?" she asked softly.

"I can't stop you, can I?" Dani pushed herself up to sitting, looking her friend in the eyes.

"I know this hurts. I know you feel like you caused this. But it's never your fault for being true to your own feelings. If he can't handle those feelings, that's on him. I'm sorry that it had to come out like this, but you will be OK. And I'm going to be here to help you."

"Thanks, honey. I appreciate the support. I will be OK. I

will." Someday soon, God willing. Even if this love gripping her didn't go away, it would fade in time. It had to.

A WEEK LATER, on Saturday morning, Olivia came over to try and cheer Dani up. The scones and homemade strawberry preserves had certainly perked up her appetite, but Liv had little success on the emotional front.

"How are you doing, sweetheart?"

"I'm fine."

"Let's try that again. How are you really doing?" Liv poured Dani some strong black English Breakfast tea and leaned back with her own mug.

"I'm trying to be OK. I still cry sometimes, and I don't know who I'm crying for, him or Aunt Helen."

"You're crying for yourself, Dani. You've lost so much in such a short time. Cut yourself some slack. Tears are allowed."

"For how long? How long should I feel this miserable? This broken?" Dani picked up Taco and snuggled the small dog under her chin. He responded with licks to her chin, well attuned to his foster mama's moods. He was such a sweet little thing. After putting up all those Lost Dogs signs with Nick, she was surprised that no one had stepped forward to claim the little guy. She kept the smart pup for company, and for a reminder of Nick if she were being completely honest. The irony of finding comfort in his dog was not lost on her.

"You are not broken! A bit bruised perhaps, but never broken. I know what broken looks like. You'll get through this." Liv's mother had literally broken down after her father left, leaving Olivia with the heavy responsibility of keeping their little family afloat and thriving.

"I just feel lost. I'm trying to focus on work, but it feels so futile most days. I'm pouring myself into the business plans. On days when I can exhaust myself, I am actually able to get some sleep. I'm not getting very far with the funding proposals, and...I miss him. Oh God, I miss him." Dani burst into tears, and felt Liv scoop her into a side hug. As her friend smoothed a comforting hand down her back, Dani poured out a bit more of her grief. It helped to get the sadness out, but what would be left when it was all gone?

"I keep dreaming, of what we had, of how he made me feel, of what I had hoped we would build. And inevitably, I get the replay of that night in the bar. I can't change the script, and I can't make it stop. Any other time I would pour my heart out to Aunt Helen, and this mess is making me miss her even more. Somehow, the apartment seems even emptier now."

The double edged grief was just too much. She desperately needed something to spur her out of this slump.

"Hang in there, honey. We're all here to help. I can't do much about missing him, but I can sure as hell help with a funding proposal. Paperwork is my jam! Seriously, let's make a plan, and I'll stay and help you tackle some of it today. I've got your back."

Nodding, Dani walked to the bathroom and rinsed her blotchy face for the umpteenth time that week. She faced herself in the mirror, unflinching. A plan. If she could just focus on the plan, she'd get through this. *Please God, let me get through this...*

EIGHTEEN

At least baking gave her something to focus on for a few hours. She wrapped up the still warm coffee cakes and headed down to the VA to drop them off for the nurses who had helped Aunt Helen during her many appointments. Getting out in the fresh air before the heat of the day set in was just what she needed. No more wallowing. As she walked, Dani noticed that the donut shop on the corner was going out of business. She stopped in to chat with the owners who had supplied Aunt Helen's Sunday morning apple fritters.

"Hi Rose, what's with the sign?"

"Oh sweetie, Herb and I are getting too old for this 4 a.m. baking! We're going to retire."

"That's exciting. What's the plan?"

"We're going to get us an RV and go cross country, see the grandchildren. I'm just worried about the shop. We own the building, and need to find a new tenant, but we've had no offers. I told Herb we should've renovated a few years ago with the tax refund, but did he listen to me? No, of course not! 'What do we need new bathrooms for?' he asks me."

As Rose rambled on, Dani got a funny tingle in her belly, a

niggling sense that something important was about to happen. She looked around her and realized that this space would be perfect for her fledgling business.

"Can I take a look around?"

Dani found an industrial kitchen setup that was optimized for efficient donut production, but she could see the potential. The back-office area was small and cluttered with forty years of records and receipts, but it would be plenty of space for her desk and computer once it was cleaned out. The flutters in her belly got stronger, and she just knew. This was The Sunshine Café.

"Rose, Herb, this might sound crazy, but I want it. With the money from Aunt Helen, I want to open a café specifically serving local veterans. I want to give them a good meal and a solid community. I've been looking for a location, and I think this would be perfect. What do you think?"

"I think I'd like to hear more."

By the end of her pitch, Rose had tears in her eyes. Herb offered his hand to seal the deal.

"I'm a vet, and I know a few guys who come in here regularly. I've worried about where they'd go when I shut down. I think you're doing a wonderful thing. I'll rest easy knowing that our building is being put to good use by someone we trust."

They decided to meet again in a few weeks to formalize things and hash out the details. That gave Dani yet another deadline to push towards, but the push was more difficult this time around. She sent in the paperwork to incorporate The Sunshine Café as a non-profit and applied for the necessary permits to upgrade the facilities. She opened a small business account and applied for a line of credit at the local bank. She used some of Aunt Helen's seed money to secure the building and start renovations, but she didn't want to blow through all of that up front. Dani had gotten the expected run-around from various offices online trying to find out what she needed to do next. She also applied for several state grants for women business owners. Researching used restaurant supply houses to get deals on the industrial range and ovens she knew she'd need to upgrade proved to be the easiest task on her list. She even contemplated setting up a kickstarter campaign to build community interest. Details. She was swimming in details.

Every step of the way, there was a snag or unexpected paperwork or unavoidable delay. Completely overwhelmed by the task she'd taken on, Dani slogged through with little enthusiasm. Her high from finding the building wore off quickly. She really missed having Nick to cheer her on.

One particularly low day, she flipped through her notes from the retreat trying to get reenergized. Jamie's parting advice resonated loud and clear. Angry with herself for having pinned so much of her support network on Nick, she took steps to change that. She began doing her paperwork over at Mrs. Grady's apartment for the company and encouragement. She invited Olivia over to look at paint swatches and plate designs.

Once they'd settled at the table with their design magazines, coffee, and blondie bars, Olivia dove right into her list-making mode.

"So, we'll need a color scheme for the whole restaurant, dishes, cutlery, glassware, mugs, stools. I'll start a list for that, and one for recipe ideas. Ooh, and another for your helpful business links. We'll get you sorted in no time." Nerves skittered through Olivia's voice, and sent Dani's skittering in response.

"Whoa, whoa, slow down! You just got here. What's with the manic list making? You only do that when you're stressed. What gives?"

"Ugh! You're right." Olivia took a deep breath. "I'm just frustrated with work. I mean, you know it's a good job, and I know Michael values my contributions to his legal team, but something just feels off. I'm bored. I'm very good at being a paralegal, but now that my brother has finished grad school, I feel like I just don't have the motivation to keep doing it, just because I'm good at it. Is this making any sense?"

"Of course it is. I'm in the same boat, honey. And I just got pushed off into the deep end by a well-meaning relative. It's OK to do what you need to do for a while, but sometimes it's important to go after what you want to do instead."

"Do you have any idea what that might be?" Mrs. Grady joined them at her table, tea in hand.

"No, and that's part of what's so frustrating. I know I want a change but I don't know to what, and it's got me spinning my wheels. So, give me a break and let me spin them for you! The Sunshine Café, right? I see lots of yellow in my future..."

Building on her positive energy, Dani called Jaime and asked her for some advice on how to keep herself moving forward in a positive way. She couldn't afford to let herself get sidetracked into negativity again. She had gotten too close to giving up.

"I just need to be able to keep my eye on the bigger picture. I know there will be snags and delays, but I can't let them hit me so hard. What should I do?"

"Have you made a vision board?"

"A what?"

"I'll take that as a no. A vision board is a way to build your ideas on paper so that you don't lose track of them when you're caught in the doldrums.

"You can do it on Pinterest or the old-fashioned way. Go out and get a big poster board. Then take your favorite magazines, photos, Etsy finds, etc. that inspire you or your project. In this case, you could create your vision for the café. Then the next time you get frustrated, go look at the board, and let yourself imagine it done. Imagine yourself successful and standing in your brand-new restaurant serving your first customers. It's a way to keep your positive feelings in your sights."

"Brilliant! You're brilliant! Why didn't I think of this?"

"Because you were stuck in those doldrums. Now go and keep your chin up. It's a great dream, a great plan, and you can totally achieve it!"

"Thanks! You're the best!"

"Anytime, honey!"

Dani spent a few hours hunkered down with her scissors and glue, feeling very much like she was back in elementary school making a collage. She found herself drawn to bold colors like bright yellow and navy blue, with white trim to pop out the details. She began to build the detailed image of The Sunshine Café in her mind. She added to Olivia's lists as she found things she loved and started a new one for renovation ideas. She'd knock out the dividing wall between the kitchen and the dining room. She wanted to recreate the function of Mrs. Grady's dinners on a larger scale. Dani knew that people needed to feel at home to heal, so a home she would create. She dreamed of her bright yellow and white kitchen with a few pieces of kitschy artwork where she could create her meals and still talk to friends sitting at an island countertop built-in where the current display cases sat, splitting the restaurant in half. She wanted to pull out the ugly old booths, too, maybe sell them online. There's a fine line between vintage and old, and the red vinyl booths that had been duct taped in several places to cover the holes were just old.

She had this vision of big family tables instead of small booths, serving family style to foster conversation and connection. How could they connect if everyone sat alone? She wanted to encourage people to talk to their fellow diners, and what better way than by sitting elbow to elbow with a stranger while sharing a meal. For men and women used to eating in a mess hall, she assumed this wouldn't be a problem. She'd remove the booths and try to sell them. Someone with vision could make them beautiful again, but they didn't fit in with Dani's vision, so they had to go.

Most of the front of the restaurant was framed by two plate glass window walls, which she planned to camouflage with lace curtains. She had one firm wall on the far right, and she knew exactly what she wanted to do there. One of her favorite walls at her house growing up was the memory wall. It had been covered with framed pictures documenting her family's history. She stared at that wall for hours as a child, building stories in her mind about the people in the pictures. When her parents moved north, they had boxed up all those memories, but Dani hadn't forgotten.

She would paint that wall a bold navy blue and hang bright white picture frames in varying sizes. She'd fill it with pictures of Aunt Helen, her family, her friends in uniform. She wanted it to be a memory wall of military service, a reminder of good times, and a living testament that no one had to be alone in their memories. As her clientele grew, she imagined asking regulars to bring in pictures to add. Smiling, she continued clipping yellow tablecloths, white milk glass vases, and several fun mismatched place settings. With her vision for The Sunshine Café taking shape, more of her frustrations slowly faded.

On the social front, she was taking baby steps. She went out with Stella a few times, and practiced her smiling and flirting, even though her heart wasn't in it. Stella even convinced her to go back to Flipped to try and bury the bad memories.

"Let's get you a drink."

"Thanks Stella. I have a feeling I'm going to need it tonight."

"Why do you say that?"

"Because none of this feels right. I'm sitting here all dressed up trying to attract a man, when the only one that I want has disappeared. What's the point?" She twisted her cocktail napkin. "Maybe if I drink enough, I'll stop worrying about him long enough to enjoy a conversation."

"Oh Sweetie, that's no solution. You've got it bad. Let's sit here at the bar tonight. We can just have some girl time."

"I hate to ruin your evening. I don't know why I'm such a downer."

"I know why. You're in love."

"No. I am absolutely not. I can't be 'in love' by myself."

"Uh-huh." Stella raised her hand to call over a bartender. A woman with bobbing black curls and a mile wide smile hustled down to their end of the bar, and Stella greeted her with her signature warmth.

"Hi, I'm Stella. What's your name?"

"I'm Brandy." Stella reached over the bar to shake Brandy's hand.

"Brandy, this is my friend Dani. She's a bit lovelorn tonight. The guy she's fallen for has gone AWOL. We need an appropriate cocktail."

Brandy leaned back considering Dani's slumped shoulders and miserable expression.

"Hmm, well judging by your face a Painkiller might be in order, or maybe an Orgasm. There's nothing quite like getting The Last Word when it comes to men, but if he's not around that will be tough. No, tonight I think you need a Flirtini, just a little something to help you get your groove back, so you can have a little fun." She began expertly mixing the vodka, pineapple, and champagne cocktail.

"A little fun would be a welcome change." Dani sighed, hoping her drink would indeed fix her mood.

"Oh, you are good!" Stella beamed. "What would you make for me?"

Brandy's almond face split again with a mischievous smile.

"Hmm, for you? A Harvey Wallbanger or a Redheaded Slut."

Stella's bark of laughter drew the eyes of men all over the bar. Even Dani felt a grin tugging at the corners of her mouth. That deep throaty laugh was infectious. "I think I'll stick with the Flirtini as well, thanks. Can you join us for one?" Brandy made a larger drink and poured a little into a third glass for herself.

When each woman had a martini in front of her, Stella raised hers in a toast.

"To Love, Lust, and all points between. May we find what makes us happy."

"Anything I can do to help with that?" Seth said from behind Stella's shoulder, making her startle and slosh a good portion of her drink over the treacherous rim of the martini glass.

"Jesus, Seth! You scared me!"

"And here I thought seeing me would make you happy."

"Why on Earth would you think that, sir?" Brandy chimed in.

"I've been known to make a woman happy a time or two. You only know one side of me, Whiskey."

"Not that I'm doubting your prowess, but it's highly unlikely you'll be making anyone over here happy tonight. And I thought her name was Brandy." Stella fired back.

"Long story. Army nickname." Brandy clarified.

"You could make me happy, Seth." Dani said quietly, her

eyes completely earnest. "Where is he? Is he OK? Have you seen him?"

"Uh, no, I haven't seen him, but I know that he's fine, Dani. We talk."

"Why do you get to talk to him, and I don't? Where did he go?"

"Somewhere safe. Trust me on this. He's doing fine. You don't have to worry."

"I don't think you're helping, Seth. Is this about Captain Gantry, and the trouble he caused in here last time? You guys almost got me fired." Brandy turned an accusing eye on Seth.

"You know Nick?" Dani asked.

"Yeah, I served with him in Iraq. He was my C.O. I was the field medic in his company. That's why my nickname is Whiskey. My specialty code is 68W, or 68 Whiskey. With my first name being Brandy, it was too easy. We went through some tough shit together."

"Yeah, I've heard about some of it. Thank you for your service." Dani was dying to ask the young woman more questions about Nick and those tough times, but she got the feeling they wouldn't be welcomed. She turned her attention back to Seth. "Listen, I get that he doesn't want to talk to me. I get that whatever was between us is probably over. What I don't understand is why we can't have a fucking conversation about it! He dropped off his dog and a note, for crying out loud! I deserve better, Seth."

"Yes, you do, Dani. I'm sorry I can't tell you more, but it's not my story to tell."

"Here's a story you can tell. I got a call about Taco. His owner got back from a trip and discovered him missing from the dog sitter who bailed. I'm meeting with her in the morning. I guess he won't need to say goodbye to him, either." Dani felt her anger spiking and she downed half of her Flirtini in one gulp.

"Yeah, I'll, uh, pass that along..."

"Great. Now if you'll excuse me, I feel like dancing."

In addition to pissing her off again, this encounter gave Dani's active imagination fodder for another week of disquieting dreams. The negative thoughts swirled her emotions into a frenzy again. He was doing just fine without her. He wasn't suffering through any of this. He hadn't even checked in on Taco, who had cried at the door for days after he'd left. Dani knew just how the poor dog felt, and now that Taco had been reunited with his real mama, Dani had completely lost her last thread of connection with Nick. He clearly hadn't been nearly as attached to her, as she had been to him. Taco leaving had widened the hole in her heart. She blamed Nick for that, too, since she wouldn't have gotten so close to the sweet pup if Nick hadn't run away. Finally, her anger kicked in, and she vowed that she would move on.

Riding high on the wave of anger, Dani flipped open her laptop and logged on to a popular local dating website.

"It is past time to get over this ridiculous crush," she muttered.

The little voice in her heart warned that this wasn't a crush. Dani muted that little voice and resolutely set up a profile. She needed to widen the pool of applicants, cast her net out for someone who was actively available and searching for some kind of connection as well. It wasn't like she was meeting anyone at her job (*what job?*) or in her building (*yeah, that worked out real well*). She'd met a few guys out with Stella, but none of them were really her type. She might as well start screening guys online. At the very least, she might enjoy going out for dinner with someone she knew had some shared interests, rather than randomly meeting up with whoever happened to be at the bar that night.

In just a few clicks, she had her basic profile set up. She was able to input her interests, hobbies, and physical traits. Before she had even uploaded a picture of herself, the website had supplied a full page of available gentlemen in her area. Yes, she thought. This is a move in the right direction. She sat up a little straighter in her chair. She was strong, powerful even, for taking control of her own love life. No more relying on the whims of fate. She would tackle this goal just like she tackled the other goals in her life, with forethought, logic, and strong positive actions. And she would get Nick out of her head, and her heart. She had to move on. She couldn't keep going like this.

NINETEEN

Nick was doing the hardest work of his life. After his meltdown with Dani, he'd checked himself in to the VA inpatient PTSD program. Trying to heal on his own was going to get someone killed or worse. He worked with his therapist almost every day using a Cognitive Processing Therapy approach. They worked on identifying all of his symptoms. His therapists coached him to be actively aware of his thoughts and feelings surrounding the trauma. Next, they'd work on developing skills to help him decide how he wanted to feel and how to readjust to a "normal" life. To that end, he practiced Guided Meditation twice a week to help retrain his brain and body to be in a consciously relaxed state.

Nick also had group sessions with other vets to share their experiences. He'd made a few friends with the guys in the group, but no one was really in a good place to put in the effort. Would they even want to be friends when the whole treatment deal was over? He worked his body to exhaustion on the physical therapy equipment, hoping to give his mind a break. He slept more in those four weeks than he had since he'd come home.

Sitting across from his therapist in the one-on-one sessions was the hardest. Dr. Adrian Broman certainly didn't go easy on him.

"We've spent a lot of time processing your flashbacks, your triggers. Today I want to talk about what brought you into our program here. What took you so long to enroll?"

"At first I thought I'd get better on my own, if I could just have a little peace and quiet. I could ignore it or rationalize that I was OK as long as I wasn't hurting anyone else." Nick pulled the small round wood chip from his pocket and rubbed his thumb over its now smooth surface. The repetitive motion focused his thoughts.

"What changed?"

"I wasn't alone any more. I met a girl, a really great girl, maybe even THE girl. And I fucked it up. I lost control. Thank God I didn't hurt her, but I almost choked a man who didn't take her no for an answer. I can't say with certainty that I would have let him live if she hadn't managed to get through to me. I scared her, and I scared myself. When I got back home I went into a rage blackout. I don't remember a few hours of the night, but I came to in a completely trashed apartment and my knuckles were bloody from punching the walls. I've never been that out of control. I don't ever want to feel that way again."

"Why does it scare you?"

"I could have hurt her. Hell, I already did hurt her emotionally. I can't get the look on her face out of my head when I said that she was no one special. I think I lo...I might be in...I really like this girl. I cannot hurt her any more. I need to be back in control."

Their relationship had been brief but intense. His reactions had shocked and scared him.

"And you think by being in control of your emotions again, you can get her back?"

In trying to deny his own feelings, he'd bruised hers. Maybe it was for the best. What did he have to offer her? A battered mind and shattered soul? That's not what Dani deserved.

"I don't know about winning her back, but she sure deserved better from me than she got. Whatever lies I was telling myself have stopped working. I want to be me again. I want to know that I am not the person she thinks I am."

No matter how many times he told himself she was better off without him, though, she remained his motivator throughout his treatments. He wanted to be good enough for her. He wanted to be the kind of man she deserved, whether or not he got to prove it to her. He knew who he was, who he had been. He had to believe he could be that man again. He kept that desire foremost in his mind as he worked on healing himself.

He checked in with Seth every few days, just to talk. His best friend had pinned him down after Nick had asked him to move his car from the bar and check his mail every few days. Once Nick explained that he'd checked himself in for treatment, Seth was immediately helpful and promised to take care of all the details, on the condition that Nick keep him in the loop. Sometimes it hurt more than it helped, but he couldn't resist asking about Dani.

Seth dropped into an armchair across from him in the lounge at the VA.

"Hey man, how's it going today?"

"Not bad. I've got group in a little while, but this morning was pretty mellow."

"That's good to hear. Guess who I ran into last night."

"Who?"

"Dani, Stella, and Whiskey."

"You saw Dani? How did she look? Is she ok?"

"She looked OK, a little down maybe, but she is not OK.

She is still really broken up over this whole thing. Asked me where you were, why you wouldn't call. It broke my heart. She asked me to deliver a message."

Nick rubbed his chest where his heart felt like it was breaking all over again.

"Yeah, what'd she say?"

"She said that Taco's owner showed up to claim him, and she's giving him back." His heart hitched a little at the thought of losing his little buddy. That apartment was going to seem really empty without him. He added to the running tally of painful moments to discuss.

"Fair enough. How was Whiskey doing?"

"She's making ends meet. I asked her for her number in case you wanted to talk to her about any of this. She was there and might give you another perspective. Your therapist was asking if anyone could come join you for sessions. She might be a good choice."

"I don't know..."

"Do me a favor and call her, alright? She thinks I was scamming her number for myself. I want to prove her wrong."

"OK, I'll call her..." Nick got real quiet, thinking about Dani, trying to picture her talking to Whiskey at the bar.

"Are you sure you don't want me to tell Dani what you're up to?"

"No. Don't tell her. I don't want her trying to help me while I'm in here. You know she would. She's just that kind of person. I'm afraid I might hurt her again. I'll tell her when I'm better. I can't risk being near her until then."

"OK. Listen, don't worry about Dani. She's got her friends supporting her and her new business to keep her busy. I'm sure she'll be just fine. You just focus on you."

"Yeah, like I need an excuse to be a selfish bastard."

Seth punched him in the shoulder.

"That's not what I meant. You're doing hard work. It takes guts to admit you need help and to go get it. I'm proud of you, man."

"Thanks Seth. You'll keep in touch right?"

"You got it, Nick. Whatever you need."

As HE SAT in group session, he listened to his fellow soldiers recount their episodes and try to pin down their triggers. One man had taken his kids out for breakfast on a Sunday morning, and the local pancake house had a clown in making balloon animals for the kids. One balloon doggy had gotten a little too friendly with a kid's fork and popped. In the next breath, he'd been halfway over the table trying to cover his kids, pancakes and scrambled eggs flying. The terrified look on his kids' faces had been the last straw that pushed him into the inpatient program. Another guy had confronted his neighbors about their barking dogs, with his service pistol in his hand. He hadn't even realized he'd been holding his weapon until he got back home. After apologizing for scaring the shit out of them, he asked his neighbors to collect his mail and water his plants while he came to get help.

Hearing their struggles had helped him feel a bit better about his own. He was coming to the realization that, although he'd been on his own dealing with his troubles for most of his adult life, he no longer had to. In fact, it was much healthier for him to share some of his emotional load right now onto shoulders qualified to help carry it. He still fought every day over those impulses to hold his weaknesses close to the vest. Then, he'd picture Dani's face, eyes blank, smile forced, and would make himself share whatever piece of the puzzle he'd been holding back. Her pain and his role in causing it pushed him to dig deep and sit with his own pain. A bit of penance for the hurt he'd caused. He realized it was actually helping him face his demons. He just hoped he'd be able to make it up to her somehow, and soon.

TWENTY

Dani was sitting in Mrs. Grady's apartment, cursing over a letter from the city about her permits, and nursing a cup of coffee. Needing a mental break, she flipped over to her dating website and checked her inbox for messages.

"Who are they?" Mrs. Grady leaned over her shoulder to inspect the pictures of men scrolling down her screen.

"Just some guys."

"How does it work?"

"I made a profile and put it out on the site. Men interested in finding someone have done the same thing. Then we search and see who we find that might be a match. They are complete strangers right now, but based on my description they've found me and are interested in saying hi. I'll see if I think any of them fit."

"Well, of course they want to meet you. Why wouldn't they? One look at your picture, and I'm sure your inbox flooded."

"Actually, I didn't get around to putting a picture up, and now I think I'll leave it blank. It's serving as a good filter. The guys responding are interested in my personality details and have no idea how I look. I can weed out some of the random creepy dudes. It's kind of nice after being ogled out at the bars with Stella. All they know is SunnyD likes to cook and read and is starting her own business."

"And what about Nick?"

"What about him? Do I still miss him? Yes. Has he spoken to me in over a month? No. I think it's pretty clear that ship has sailed, no matter how much I might've wished to be onboard." Dani paused and took a deep breath. She was not going to let that hurt and anger bubble back up now. "This is a good distraction. I'm not ready to meet any of them yet. I'm going to chat with them a while longer. I just need something to be moving in a positive direction. Between Nick and all these delays, I'm going crazy."

"Well, don't you lose momentum. Delays are part of the game. It's OK to let them bug you, but don't let them stop you. Let me call my friend Suzanne. Her niece works for the city. I'll see if I can get her to look in to the problem with the permits."

"Is there anyone you don't know?" Dani teased, smiling.

"If I don't know them, they're not worth knowing!"

While Mrs. Grady worked her contacts at City Hall, Dani got busy at the donut shop. She had signed her lease and helped throw a going away party for Herb and Rose. She reassured many of their loyal regulars that she'd be reopening soon, and invited them to leave their phone numbers on a list so that she could contact them when the new restaurant was ready. She could not contain her enthusiasm, and laughed and joked with her prospective clientele as she circulated through the party.

The morning after, Herb handed over the keys with a big bear hug for luck and hopped in his RV with Rose, ready to zigzag their way across the States with an eventual destination of Florida. The older couple gave her free rein to renovate the place, excited by what they'd seen of her vision.

Finally, she could dive into some good physical labor. Maybe it would help clear away some of her mental cobwebs. Dressed in her grubby jeans and a ratty old t-shirt from high school, hair pulled back under a kerchief, Dani filled a bucket with hot soapy water and began scrubbing the place top to bottom. Years of accumulated dust and grease yielded to the vigor of her scrub brush. She set up fans to help keep the air moving. Even with the fans, she felt the temperature rising as early morning transitioned to noon, and she was grateful for the kerchief keeping the sweat from dripping in her eyes.

The beige walls slowly became lighter and lighter as she wiped them down. She would prime and paint them, of course, but she relished the symbolic clean slate. She attacked the glass donut cases running across the width of the restaurant with vinegar and newspaper until they shined like new. Although she had plans to remove most of them, she wanted them all to shine when she got them up on craigslist. She was also going to have to troll the for sale portion of the website for some barstools and hopefully some kitchen gear while she was at it. She also needed to find some replacement tables. Her arms and back screamed with tension as the ever-growing to-do list swirled through her head, her anxiety grew to overwhelming proportions. She sat down in one of the booths, and cradled her head in her hands. Was she crazy? What made her think that she could do this?

"Aunt Helen, what was I thinking? I can't do this...at least I can't do it without you. It's too much." She spoke aloud, hoping that her aunt could hear her, wherever she might be. In her mind, she heard her aunt's voice, laughingly repeating an oft-heard phrase. "Even if you fall on your face, you're still moving forward." Dani had to laugh at herself a bit. Helen had always been good at defusing a situation with a bit of humor. And as usual, she was right, Dani thought. What do I have to lose but time? Yes, it's hard. If it weren't hard, it wouldn't be worth doing.

Knock off the negative thoughts. Keep moving. She tried to silence the clamoring to-do's fighting for her attention. Movement was progress. One step at a time. She could make this work. She wasn't buying that particular line yet, but she figured if she repeated it often enough she might start to believe it.

Dani cursed her height as she struggled to reach the top of the wall, batting at cobwebs that were just out of reach even when she balanced on a chair on tiptoe. Adding a ladder to her mental shopping list, she sighed and climbed down. Resigned to another delay in her progress towards her goal, she moved on to cleaning the booths, attacking every nook and cranny with renewed frustration. Why couldn't something just go right for a change? It had all looked so rosy at the beginning, but now? Were all these setbacks a sign that she'd made a mistake? And why the hell were there so many sprinkles shoved down in between the cushions on this damn booth?

"I am not going to give up, but man, could I use a lucky break," she muttered.

Then she screamed and dropped her scrub brush when someone knocked on the large plate glass window behind her. Silhouetted in the noon sun, she didn't immediately register who was at the door. All she saw was a tall dark shadow with broad shoulders as she slowly walked to the door. Surely, it couldn't be, she thought. How would he even know where to find her?

Shading her eyes against the sun, she gestured him to the door. As he stepped around the corner of the building, the bright sunshine illuminated a face she hadn't expected to see again. She reached for the lock, and hesitated. Did she really want to let him in again? The literal and figurative meanings of the question ricocheted through her mind, as she stared at him through the safety of the glass door.

Nick put his hand out and touched the glass, mouthing the word "please." She read the remorse in his earnest brown eyes and decided to hear what he had to say. Maybe it would help her secure the closure that she was still struggling to find. She flipped the lock and turned her back, tucking her stray bangs back under her kerchief and attempting to wipe some of the sweat and grime from her forehead with the back of her hand. Of course, he would find her to chat when she looked like a mess. What was karma punishing her for?

She steeled herself to hear his excuses and not give him the satisfaction of knowing how much his abandonment had hurt her.

"Hi, Dani."

"Hi." She turned to face him and leaned back against one of the tables, arms crossed over her middle, as if she could protect herself from whatever was coming. A strained silence filled the air between them.

"What do you want?" she finally blurted, her anger and hurt making her voice sharp.

"To apologize, again, and maybe explain a little bit."

"I'm not sure you have an explanation I care to hear. There's no excuse for the way you behaved."

"I won't insult your intelligence with excuses. You are absolutely right. Just let me explain what happened."

"You've got five minutes, and then I'd like you to leave."

"Thanks, Dani. It means a lot to me that you'll listen."

"Your clock is ticking, four and a half..."

"Right, so let me start of by saying I was a jerk, a certifiable asshole, a real idiot, and I'm sorry. My loss of control put you in an awkward and painful position. I'm sorry. But I'm glad it happened."

Dani's jaw dropped open and her eyes widened.

"Excuse me? You were doing so well with the 'I'm sorry's.' What the hell do you mean, you're glad it happened?"

Nick held his hands up in defense and hurried to explain.

"Don't take this the wrong way, but hurting you, someone who had gone out of her way to help me, someone I care about, was rock bottom. I let my friends and the situation goad me into a panic, and I lashed out, unfortunately at the one person who had given me the gift of her strength and stability. I'm deeply sorry for it, but it forced me to see just how out of control I was and how badly I needed to get better."

"Well, bully for you. Are you 'all better' now?" she asked flippantly, unwilling to let her guard down just yet.

"No, not all better. That night I lost control. It wasn't the first time or the last. I knew I had to quit pretending everything was fine. I checked myself into the VA's inpatient PTSD treatment program. I learned a lot over the last six weeks, about what I was doing and what I can do to handle it. It was rough. I'm better than I was, but I'll still deal with this for a long time. It's a long road to recovery. I'll be in therapy for years." He moved over to grasp her hands in his. "You are incredible for trying to help me, but I realized I wasn't being fair to you. I'm sorry." When she looked up and met his eyes, he repeated. "I'm sorry."

Suddenly it all made sense. She thought back to that night. The nightmare. The crowded bar. Her broken heart. Jake's purple face. *Oh God, he went to get help, and I have been mad at him for it.* Her arms wanted to reach for him and pull him into a big hug. She wanted to tell him how proud she was that he'd gone, and how glad she was he'd come back. He was doing what he needed to do to be healthy. How could she be mad at that?

She wanted to kick herself for thinking poorly of him. She knew he was a good guy.

And then she froze. He was apologizing because he was a good guy. He hadn't said anything about wanting her back. He wasn't here with declarations of love. The pain in her heart flooded back, but she held firm against the desire to crumble. Dani felt like she'd lost something precious, her hope. He'd come back, and stripped her of her anger and her hope in one gut-crushing speech. And he was going to be back. Right across the hall. Living, and loving, and moving on with his life. And she would watch it all from the safety of her own life, because much as he deserved to move on, so did she. She shrugged her shoulders, pulling her hands free, and turned to pick up her scrub brush.

"Apology accepted. Now if you'll excuse me..."

"Actually, I believe I have one more minute left on the clock."

"Make it quick," Dani fired back not looking up from her scrubbing.

"I'd like for us to be friends again."

Dani looked at him over her shoulder, mouth agape, a dead ringer for a trout on ice.

"Look, I know I screwed up, but I want a chance to fix it. The idea of you hating me forever is killing me. Right now, it's pretty justified, but I want a chance to change that."

"You're asking for an awful lot," Dani murmured. Damn him for being reasonable. Why couldn't he just keep being the asshole she'd painted him as so she could walk away clean? Why did he have to be the good guy who messed with her heart-strings? This would not end well. She felt that in her bones.

"I know it. I need to do this. Let me start by helping out around this place. If you can scrounge up another sponge, I'll get the high corners for you."

She caught and held his gaze. She saw only earnest hope in his gaze, not even the slightest hint of desire. Small wonder, given how I'm dressed. In the next breath, she scolded herself for even wishing to see desire. Desire is what had gotten them into this mess. One day after having sex with her, he was checking into therapy. Getting involved with her had broken him, and she couldn't do that to him again. She should be happy that he was stable enough to even have this conversation. Even knowing it would likely cause her pain later, Dani couldn't suppress her innate impulse to reach out to other human beings. Despite it not being the best idea for her, she'd give him a shot at friendship. She couldn't say no. She just wouldn't get over-involved like she had last time. Steeling herself with a deep breath, she finally broke the tense silence as he waited for the sponge and her decision.

"You're right and wrong. I don't hate you. I hate what you did and how it made me feel. But I'm willing to give you a chance. I miss our friendship, too, but that is all I'm open to rebuilding. *Friendship*," she emphasized.

"Understood. Thank you." Nick grinned, his whole frame visibly relaxing. Inexplicably annoyed, Dani chucked the sponge at him, catching him square in the chest.

"Get to work, big guy. That ceiling isn't going to clean itself. You've got some serious manual labor in your near future. Start scrubbing."

Nick laughed, climbed up on the chair, and began scrubbing the ceiling corners. He worked quietly and efficiently, and silence filled the room. Dani moved on to scrubbing the tables and booths with intense focus, willing herself not to be distracted by the very large, very handsome man in the corner. Gradually the tension left her shoulders as she relaxed into the soothing monotony of cleaning. She was a bit startled when she looked up and realized that Nick had gone outside. He'd begun working on the exterior and windows with the vinegar. She'd gotten lost in the quiet and hadn't noticed him leave.

She took a moment to observe him, muscles flexing and bunching, as he scrubbed at the spider webs in the rafters over the door. Tantalizing hints of chiseled abs peeked out beneath his shirt as he stretched high with the broom. Sweat and soapy water had combined to mold his t-shirt to his very defined physique. His golden brown hair no longer resembled the buzz cut it had. Now, it was a shaggy sun-kissed mop that curled at his nape and ears. From the side, he looked like a mischievous little boy who'd managed to evade the comb yet again. That was until he turned those intense eyes and sculpted face towards her, and she realized that he was in fact a very dangerous man. Not physically. She refused to believe he would have hurt her that night. But he was dangerous to her peace of mind and her self-control. In light of the pain he was dealing with, the fact that he still had the power to turn her into a slack-jawed, weak-kneed, pulsing bundle of lust did not bode well for her friendship only decree. She sternly shook herself and vowed to make more of an effort with her online dating profile. Maybe if someone else distracted her, she'd have better luck keeping Nick on a platonic plane.

Though her emotions were having trouble getting on board with the new plan, she was determined to be the friend he needed. No matter how much her heart wanted to be his someone special. Bottom line, she couldn't say no to having him in her life. Not when he needed her.

TWENTY-ONE

Nick made a point of helping her regularly at the café, cleaning, making repairs, installing the new floors, and helping with the heavy lifting. He helped her keep an eye on the sub-contractors, making sure they showed up and did the work they promised. He even did some sketches for the island she wanted, and was toying with building it for her. With both of them working hard, they passed the preliminary inspection two weeks into renovations.

When he wasn't helping at the café, Nick desperately tried to fill the hours. He tagged along with Seth to his family's woodshed. Valenti Contractors were known for their custom woodwork, and Nick was a welcome addition to the crew. He entered the workshop and inhaled deeply, letting the smell of the shavings, and the whirr of the tools fill his mind. Nick immediately calmed. The sights and sounds reminded him of his brief patch of stability in high school. Memories of woodworking with his friend's dad during the two years he'd lived with their family still brought warmth to his chest and a smile to his face. He'd forgotten how much he loved it until Seth had suggested he tag along.

"Hey, Nick! Good to see you!" Antonio Valenti, Seth's dad, clapped his big hand on Nick's shoulder in a bone-shaking welcome. "What are you working on today?" Tony had generously offered Nick the use of the workshop for his recovery, and he spent part of each day working with the wood.

"Nothing in particular. You got anything you need done?"

"Always, son. Always. If you want to do some of the fancy work for that custom kitchen built-in, I'd appreciate it. I'll leave the cut-list on the counter." Nick pitched in when they got busy, happy to return a favor, but mostly he was left to follow his own inspiration. A sense of calm and peace suffused him when he was creating something. He had built a custom fit bookcase for his place and a rocking chair with carved arms for Mrs. Grady. He also began work on the table and an island for Dani.

"I'll check it out, see if I can help."

"Are you sure I can't convince you to hire on? I'd love to pay you for the work you've done."

"Nah. Letting me use the shop is payment enough. But you'll be the first to know if something changes."

"You and my son. Both of you lazy as ever. I thought for sure the Army would have fixed that. You come for dinner on Sunday." He shook his head and left Nick in the workshop. The Army had changed many things. He wasn't lazy, just not whole. Every time Mr. Valenti started hinting about joining the crew full time, a flare of anxiety singed him. It was clear he could handle the work, but the idea of someone depending on him freaked Nick out. He was terrified to disappoint someone else. He picked out several pieces of scrap walnut and maple. While he thought of the other person he'd disappointed, he measured and trimmed, glued and clamped. An idea sprang into his mind, and he knew exactly what he was building and why. He set it aside to dry and turned to the more straightforward trim work. All of the loud, solitary work gave him a good chance to think.

He wasn't ready to give up his time with Dani for a full time job, and he wasn't sure he was steady enough for one yet either. He was still doing outpatient counseling two days a week and often, after a session, he was useless for a few hours while he recovered. No, he was content to help her get her dream off the ground and take care of himself. That was enough for now.

DANI REMAINED a driving force behind his recovery, even if she didn't know it. He was committed to her success. He spread the word during his weekly counseling visits at the VA about her grand opening and helped her keep up her spirits when repeated email exchanges with city hall slowed her progress. He was determined to make up for his behavior and to show her his better side. Although he hadn't quite given up hope of redemption, he was reading her "friends only" signals loud and clear.

He continued to follow up with his therapists, and tried to be as open as possible.

"I'm lonely," he blurted, into the silence of the counselor's office.

"That's a normal reaction, adjusting to life on your own after the camaraderie of the Army. Is this about Dani? I'm worried that you are pinning too much of your recovery time on her."

"No. I'm just helping her out, trying not to be an asshole. I know I need to recover for me. I see a lot of friends and neighbors during the day, but the apartment is really quiet at night. It's starting to get to me."

"What do you want to do about it?"

Images of moving Dani into his place raced past his mind's eye, but he quickly rejected the fantasy. "I don't know."

"What about a dog?"

"What about it?"

"Many vets have found it rewarding to have someone to take care of. Rescuing a dog from a shelter, caring for a companion, being responsible for another living being, all of these are great steps back into normal life, normal interactions. Think about it. There are lots of dogs who need a loving home. There's a great organization down in San Martin called Operation Freedom Paws that trains vets and their dogs at the same time to help with the PTSD. I'll get you the info."

Nick thought about Taco and how quickly he'd bonded with Dani. At the time, he hadn't been able to pin down his feelings, but he realized now that he had been jealous. Deep down he'd hoped that Taco would be his. Abandoning him shortly after finding him was probably not the best way to build loyalty though. Now that Taco had gone back home, Nick was really missing him. Getting another dog wasn't a bad idea. He could start fresh.

Once the idea was in his head, he couldn't shake it. Nick ventured out to the Humane Society of Silicon Valley, just to take a look and give the idea a trial run. He walked past the puppies as they gamboled over each other in their pens. He paused by the smaller dogs, each yapping at the gate. When he reached the special room for older dogs, he knew he'd found his mark. All those sad eyes, just waiting to be chosen. Looking at the shiny plaque over the door, he smiled. Of course it was Helen's House. Nick remembered Dani talking about her aunt's bequest to fund care for older dogs that were less likely to be adopted.

Once he was taken into the viewing room, a pair of big brown eyes set into a resigned face won his heart. Bella, her tag said, an eight year old coonhound/lab mix, with eyes that saw right through him and offered comfort. When they brought her out of the kennel, she sat at his feet, put one paw in his lap and laid her head down on top of it. He'd been claimed with such quiet dignity, such sweet relief, and his heart melted into a puddle on the floor.

"When can I bring her home?"

Once again, his therapist had been spot on with his recommendation. He started to work with the trainers at Operation Freedom Paws, learning how to connect with Bella and to teach her how to help him. He spent several hours every evening training with her. His new routine taking care of Bella, going for walks and runs and cuddling on the couch, helped fill the empty hours and gave him a sense of purpose and pride. She was extremely intelligent and active. She thrived in the trainings and quickly picked up the lessons. Bella learned to recognize when Nick was getting anxious as well. She would go and lean her head calmly against his thigh in silent support. It was often enough to prevent a full-blown attack. The training classes were another safe space for him. Everyone was a vet training their dogs. Everyone was hurt and trying to become whole. It felt good to be around people and pets who understood without all the questions.

As he built on his positive progress, Nick thought about Dani more and more. He needed to get back to his plan. Despite wanting to fix things with Dani, he had some work to do to get ready before actively pursuing her.

"Man, you have to get back out there." Seth prodded him over a shared beer at Flipped.

"I'm not ready." Nick leaned back on his stool. The idea of dating anyone but Dani made him feel sick to his stomach. Whiskey joined them at the end of the bar.

"What if you tried online dating? No pressure, you can think about what you're saying, practice some lines."

"Is that what you're looking for Whiskey? Someone with good lines?" Seth teased.

"Anything would be better than what I've had lately, which is a big fat nothing. But if Nick is going to need to do some fancy talking to convince a certain someone special to forgive his sorry ass, he should practice first."

Nick thought about what they said. If he was going to have to grovel, he might as well practice online first. He joined an online dating site with the intention of relearning how to talk to women, set up his profile carefully and when he clicked to submit, a list of possible matches in his area popped up on his screen.

Chuckling, he leaned back in his chair and stretched. Of course. Top of the list. SunnyD, joined recently, loves baking chocolate chip cookies and surfing. It had to be her. Fate was not quite done playing her hand, so he added Sunny D to his favorites list and logged off. He could tell Seth he had joined in all honesty, but he also recognized a sign when he saw one. He'd spent years relying on his gut instincts. They had kept him alive and almost well through multiple deployments. He wasn't about to start ignoring them now. Dani was special, and he didn't need to talk to anyone but her. Bella nudged her head under his elbow.

"That's right girl. Let's go get her."

TWENTY-TWO

"So, Dani, how are things going with the café?" Stella sat across the table from her at a trendy Italian trattoria, trying to keep the awkward flow of conversation going. This was Dani's first attempt at meeting a person from an online dating site, and it was already a disaster. Thank God she had Stella to help her get through this.

She and Felix had been chatting for a while, and Dani had offered a double date. Felix had jumped at the opportunity, so Felix and Dani, and Stella and her Mr. Right Now, Blaine, were sitting around a table wasting an evening. The food was excellent. The company was not. Felix had posted a profile picture that was very flattering and taken probably 10 years earlier. Not wanting to judge a book by its cover, Dani had been willing to overlook the blurring of the truth and consider him based on his character and conversation. Unfortunately, both were severely lacking.

"OK, I guess. It's been a challenging week."

"This is why pretty women shouldn't work so hard. Trying to make it in the business world is just too much stress. Women can't handle the pressure like a man." Felix tossed off that comment as calmly as if he were remarking on the weather.

"Excuse me?" Dani was stunned. Felix seemed to think she simply hadn't heard him clearly, because he elaborated.

"Women just aren't built for the workplace. We all know what women are best at. That's why any woman of mine is gonna stay close to home. Wouldn't want to get caught too far from the bedroom. Right, man?" Felix had turned to Blaine for backup, but Stella's friend just stared, dumbfounded.

Stella opened her mouth, likely to burn the little hair left on Felix's head right off with her flaming retort. Dani deliberately cut her off.

"I can handle the stress just fine, thank you. It's just been a bad week."

"Well, maybe I could help you relax later, if you know what I mean." He leered at Dani dropping his gaze to her chest. As if his verbal innuendo hadn't already been too much. Ugh.

Phrases and compliments that had sounded charming in text were smarmy coming from his lips accompanied by a knowing leer. His continued references to sex and intimacy couched in euphemisms grated on her nerves. How many ways could a guy find to bring up sex in subtext? Apparently thousands. His commentary on the roles of women in his life and wider society were repulsive. He did not register the effect his conversation had on the ladies at the table. Blaine had picked up on it and had the grace to look ashamed on Felix's behalf. Dani locked eyes with Stella in disbelief. Was he serious? Were they being punked?

When Blaine had blessedly turned the conversation to baseball and the Giants' chances at another ring, Dani excused herself from the table. Stella followed her.

"Gotta go together, huh? Need any more company?"

The man did not know when to stop.

"No, we're fine, thanks. Be right back."

Safe inside the privacy of the bathroom, Dani ran her wrists under cold water, desperate to cool her rising temper. Stella's tirade wasn't helping.

"Is this guy for real? Does he truly think that women want to hear this shit?" Stella was pacing, and Dani followed her friend in the mirror.

"I'm so sorry I dragged you along for this."

"No. It's a good reminder that sexism is alive and well in the world. Thank God Blaine was able to deflect."

"How are things going there?"

Stella leaned against the sink, and fluffed her red waves in the mirror. "He's fine, I guess. Perfectly polite, and he has great taste in music, but we just aren't clicking, if you know what I mean. Life's too short to settle for average sex."

"Well, after tonight, you might not have to worry about that anymore. Felix might run him off."

"Felix is about to run me off. I don't know how much more of his crap I can listen to."

"Let's just stay for dessert. There's a grilled peach napoleon on the menu that I wanted to try."

"Well, I do deserve a reward for making it through this date without punching him in the throat. Give me your credit card, though. I'll slip it to the waiter now, so we can make a quick retreat. I'm not staying here one minute longer than it takes you to satisfy your sweet tooth."

"I promise I'll be quick."

"That's what he said..." Stella wiggled her eyebrows, and Dani snorted.

"Too soon."

The joke broke the tension, and they returned to the table to tough it out. She couldn't do it. When their waiter came with dessert menus, Dani quickly declined and asked for the check.

"That's right, baby. We'll have some dessert later," quipped Felix, that leer returning to mar his slightly fleshy features.

"No, we won't!" Dani snapped back, her disgust and anger infusing her tone. "Not only will we never 'have dessert,' we won't even have dinner again! Good-bye. Don't call."

Frustrated and upset, she stormed out of the restaurant. How had she gotten this so wrong?

The door opened, and Stella marched out behind her.

"Thank God. I couldn't take another minute of that. I know in dating you have to kiss a lot of frogs..."

"Hell, no. Never kissing that frog. Not now, not ever. Let's go home."

Dani felt her disappointment weighing on her heart the whole drive home. Stella blessedly left her to her own thoughts, but that meant she had no escape from them. She tried not to compare Felix to Nick, but she couldn't help it. He'd set her bar awfully high, and Felix didn't measure up in so many ways. This was a disaster.

Now she was sneaking in, so she wouldn't have to dissect the whole mess for the edification and amusement of her neighbor. Tomorrow, it would be funny. Tonight, it just made her sad. Dani opened the door to her apartment quietly. She didn't think she could face the temptation of the sexy man across the hall after the hellacious double date she'd just endured.

She opened up her laptop and waited for it to wake up, so she could permanently block Felix from her inbox. She made herself a cup of tea, changed out of her date wear into a cozy t-shirt and yoga pants, and pulled up SanJoseSolos.com. In her inbox she had 2 unread messages. The first was from Felix saying he'd had great time and couldn't wait to see her again. Amazed at the man's audacity, idiocy, optimism, or some combination thereof, she checked the time stamp. Either he'd texted her immediately after her brush-off outside the restaurant, or he had someone else writing for him. She really hoped it was the latter, so she wouldn't have to feel quite so foolish for being taken in. She clicked the block sender button and switched over to the next message in her inbox.

This one was from someone new, a CaptAm. It took her a second to come up with Captain America, but when she did, she smiled and clicked to open the message.

Hey SunnyD,

Are you as sweet as your namesake? That taste on my tongue still takes me right back to hot summer days. I used to beg for it every chance I got. Anyhow, it looks like we've got a lot in common according to your profile. Want to chat and get to know each other better?

-CaptAm

She almost deleted the message without replying. Seriously? How slimy could you get? Before she could click to delete, another message from him showed up in her inbox. She clicked on it instead out of curiosity.

Hi SunnyD,

So...I re-read my message to you and realized how bad the first few lines sound if you read them the wrong way. I DID NOT mean it that way. I just really liked the juice when I was a kid. Your name made me smile and remember. Just didn't want you to think I was a creep. Good night.

-CaptAm

His earnestness reached out to her and made her chuckle. She *had* read that email in Felix's voice. What did it say about him that he re-read his message and worried about perception? She was inclined to cut him some slack, but then she remembered her Cyrano suspicions about Felix and wondered if someone else had tipped him off to the potential tenor of his note. She would vet her suitors more carefully this time around.

She pulled up his profile, noting vital stats as well as his lack of picture. Hmm, she thought. No wonder the computer matched them up. They really did have a lot in common. She opened up a message back to him.

Hi CaptAm,

I'm glad you sent that second message. Definitely creepy LOL. So is Captain America another childhood joy? How do you like the site so far?

-SunnyD

She hit send, determined to keep things easy breezy. Let's see what he says. She got up to make herself some dessert to get rid of the bad taste left in her mouth from her spoiled dinner. The herbal tea wasn't cutting it. Time to call in the reinforcements. She spooned chocolate coconut ice cream into a bowl. By the time she sat back down at her computer, he'd sent her a chat request.

Willing to be diverted, Dani joined the chat, said hello, and settled into the corner of her couch, laptop settled across her thighs, ice cream in hand.

CaptAm: Hi there. The site has been...interesting. So far I've been propositioned twice, gotten into one political showdown, and picked up one crazy online stalker. You?
SunnyD: LOL Chatted with a couple of guys. No one got crazy, thank goodness. Although I did just get back from a date with a guy who thinks he is Don Juan, but has to be using a Cyrano online.
CaptAm: How'd they get in the same book? Seriously, not cool.

He caught classic literature references. *Promising...*

SunnyD: I don't know, but he was so skeevy that he's permanently out of my book. In fact, I read your message right after one of his. I'm glad you clarified, b/c I definitely read it a little creepy.
CaptAm: Yeah, sorry about that. I tend to write what I think and forget to filter for the Internet. Comes from being a pretty straightforward guy, I guess. I just don't do innuendo.
SunnyD: Good to know. What do you do?
CaptAm: I just started to work from home, freelancing. I'm still building my business.
SunnyD: That's funny. I'm starting a business myself, a restaurant. It's so frustrating. I'm going nuts with the delays from the city. I email and call at least once a week, but I'm getting nowhere.
CaptAm: Maybe you should try going down there in person. A smile and a plate of cookies open a lot of doors. I bet you've got a hell of a smile.

Dani did smile before she replied.

SunnyD: I also make a mean chocolate chip cookie. ;)
CaptAm: I'll have to take your word on that, unless you'd like to demonstrate for me sometime? I do love cookies.
SunnyD: We'll see. :)
CaptAm: Listen I've got to run, but I really enjoyed chatting with you. Is it too forward of me to ask if I can massage you later?

Dani blinked at the screen. She read it twice just to make sure she wasn't misunderstanding.

SunnyD: Yes, it is too forward! You may not massage me! Ick!
CaptAm: *message! MESSAGE! Damn Auto Correct!

Dani nearly spit out her ice cream, she was laughing so hard.

SunnyD: ROTFL! Yes, you can *message* me. Thanks for the laugh. I needed one tonight.
CaptAm: Happy to oblige. Goodnight, SunnyD.
SunnyD: Goodnight, Captain.

Dani leaned back, genuinely relaxed again after that good, long belly laugh. Maybe she'd give this online dating a second chance.

TWENTY-THREE

THE NEXT DAY, Dani walked confidently into City Hall, armed with her famous cookies, prepared to go head to head with Margie Templeton, the gatekeeper for all information on permits and new business clearances. The bank's loan statement had just come through, so she had made copies to bring in to the woman who ran the office with an iron fist. Emailing with her was driving Dani batty, and she really hoped that meeting face to face would smooth the flow of communication.

Dani knew from Mrs. Grady's intel that Margie was the key. Forewarned was forearmed. Margie had thirty-four years of experience and was indispensable to the Community Development Department. Given the recent cutbacks in city government, Margie had taken steps to improve her job security. She kept information flowing from her office under firm control. She had developed an annoying habit of emailing slowly and only including the next immediate step of the process.

No outlines, no information on the next few steps so she could multi-task while waiting a week and a half for the loans to go through... Dani fumed impatiently as she waited on a vinyl chair outside her office for the woman to return from her lunch break. The sign said, "Back at 1 pm," and it was now 1:37. Trying to keep her cool, but inwardly bristling over the further waste of her time, Dani rose quickly at the sound of someone coming through the door. It was not Margie who walked in, however; it was Mayor Jenkins. The older man with distinguished silver hair, and a not-so-distinguished potbelly, brushed past her into Margie's office. Not finding her there, he started muttering about long lunches, inefficiency, and payroll cutbacks.

"Where is that blasted woman?" he blurted out.

Seeing her chances at an expedited grand opening dwindling if Margie got fired by her blustering boss, Dani cleared her throat.

"Excuse me? Mayor Jenkins?"

He turned, startled, taking in her presence for the first time.

"If you're looking for Margie," Dani continued in her sunniest voice, "I believe she just ran down the hall to make some copies of my business plan. It seems her copier isn't working. I'm sure she'll be right back."

"Hmph!" With a disgruntled glare at the copier in the corner, he sighed and sat down to wait next to her. "So young lady, what kind of business are you planning to open?" he asked with his campaign grin hastily plastered on his face.

"I'm hoping to get the go ahead on a not-for-profit restaurant supporting veterans. It was my aunt's dying wish." She offered the mayor a cookie from the carefully arranged plate of bribes she held on her lap.

"I'm sorry for your loss. I hope you're finding everything that you need here."

"Margie has been very helpful."

At just that moment, the elusive Margie rushed out of the elevator. Her sharp linen suit managed to look fresh as she moved in impatient strides towards her office. She pulled up short and ran a hand over her carefully coifed French twist when she saw her visitors. Dani jumped into the silence, as Margie's eyes rounded at the sight of the Mayor waiting outside her office.

"So, were you able to copy those papers downstairs? I'm so sorry for the trouble," she said with the an overly bright tone and a wink concealed from the man on her left. Hoping Margie would play along, she smiled encouragingly and gestured to her office. "Maybe we could go over the next step in the process now. I was just telling Mayor Jenkins here about how excited I am for the restaurant to open."

Margie slowly agreed. "Yes, dear. They are right here in my purse. Let's go have a look."

"Just a minute, Margie," interrupted the mayor.

Both women froze.

"I need the minutes from the last development council meeting. No one else can track them down, and Bob is in my office waiting for me."

With a nearly audible sigh of relief, Margie opened the nearest file cabinet and extracted the required document.

"Here you go, sir. Sorry to keep you waiting."

"Thank you, Margie." With his good humor restored, he added, "And good luck with your restaurant. Just what this town needs, young people invested in its future." He leaned in to take another treat before adding, "These cookies are delicious! Let me know when you get the opening scheduled."

Recognizing the words from the most recent election's stump speech, Dani merely smiled and nodded, aware that he'd already dismissed her. He turned and left the office.

Margie collapsed into her chair, as Dani followed her the rest of the way into the immaculate office.

"I can't believe I was late! But Jean just became a grandmother and insisted on showing me all 75 shots of the little guy that she had taken on her iPad over the weekend, not to mention 4 videos of him sleeping. Sleeping! But, how could I say no?" Then recalling her audience, she pulled herself together and replaced the relaxed smile with a professional but blank mask. "What can I do for you, Miss?"

"That's it? No 'thanks for saving my hide'? No 'gosh, that was close,' or 'I'm so grateful'?" Incredulous that her risk would go unrecognized, Dani pushed. "He was ranting about inefficiency and payroll reductions! I covered for you!" Margie visibly blanched. Dani, more confident now that Margie knew the score, continued, "He seemed pretty happy about my plan to open the restaurant – The Sunshine Café. Hopefully that rings some bells since I have been emailing this office for weeks. How do you think he'd react to hearing that my plans had been delayed by this office?"

A flicker of recognition crossed her face, followed quickly by suspicion. "What are you getting at, Ms. Carmichael?"

Dani was impressed the bureaucrat knew her name without checking the file. "I want you to do something for me."

"I can't break any laws for you," Margie warned.

With a dry laugh, Dani replied, "I'm not asking you to. All I want is information. This is the thirteenth time I've been delayed, for the sole reason that I didn't know what to prepare for next. I need to be able to multitask and use my time better. Please, just tell me everything else that I need to do, so I can get on with it!"

After a brief pause, Margie turned to the third filing cabinet, bottom drawer, and pulled out an outline with the title, "How to Start Your Own Business." She made a copy on the miraculously healed copy machine and passed it across the desk, before carefully returning the original to its file.

With a smile, Dani asked, "Is there anything else you think I might be able to use?"

Sighing as if she was in pain, Margie handed over lists of preferred vendors and specs for zoning requirements. With a giddy smile, Dani passed her the bank statements, which she noted immediately disappeared into a folder neatly labeled with The Sunshine Café and a complete address. Thankfully Margie was competent, if a bit paranoid. Carefully storing the precious documents in her large purse, Dani prepared to leave the office. Impressed with the woman's organization, if not her efficiency, Dani offered the plate of cookies as a thank you gesture for the wealth of information Margie had parted with.

"Don't you dare leave those here. Do I look like I need any extra desserts?" The sour look was still firmly etched on her face, as she gestured to her plump waistline.

"Well, thank you again for all of your help today. I really do appreciate it."

Margie just shot her a baleful glare as Dani made her way out of the office, arms laden with her bulging purse and plate of cookies.

Turning back at the door, Dani whispered, "Don't worry, Margie. Your secret is safe with me. I won't tell a soul." Smiling, she strode into the hallway feeling like she'd finally gained a foothold in the quicksand.

DANI LEFT City Hall with a bounce in her step, a nearly full plate of cookies and optimism burning a hole in her purse. She couldn't wait to get home and dive into reading through everything. She had planned on popping in to one of the nearby restaurants, bustling with the downtown lunch rush, to grab a bite. Now she just wanted to get straight to work. As she hustled around the corner to get to her car, she almost tripped over a pair of legs sprawled out on the sidewalk.

"Oh!" she exclaimed, bobbling her plate of cookies.

"Pardon, ma'am," the young man apologized, as he tucked his legs back crisscross. "Can you spare some change or food?"

With a glance, Dani took in his half grown out buzz cut and fatigue pants, as well as the "Homeless, Will Work For Food" sign propped against his torn and threadbare rucksack.

"I'm sorry. I don't have any cash with me, but you're welcome to these," she said, gesturing to the plate of cookies she'd managed not to spill.

"Thank you much, ma'am. I appreciate that." He carefully took just one cookie from the tray and bit in. He surprised her by savoring the bite, instead of wolfing the cookie down whole when, judging by the sharpness of his cheekbones, he had to be hungry.

"Mmm, one of the best I've ever had."

"One of?" Dani probed, intrigued by this man's reactions and his slow drawl.

"Well, it's real buttery with plenty of dark chocolate to balance the sweet. It's real good, but my mama's were crunchy, with walnuts and a touch more vanilla. Those cookies were heaven on earth fresh from the oven, and even better a day later if you could manage to leave a few."

Impressed by his astute analysis of the flavors and his obvious appreciation for food, Dani again offered the plate.

"If you enjoyed it, you're welcome to more. Take the whole plate."

He looked at Dani skeptically.

"Are you sure they weren't meant for someone else, ma'am?"

"Someone else turned them down," she replied with a grin. "They're all yours, soldier."

His answering grin faded at the mention of his obvious former profession, but he accepted the plate all the same and tucked in.

"What's your name?" Dani asked, curious to know more about the young man she'd literally tripped over. Something in her gut told her that fate wasn't quite done with her today.

"James, ma'am, but everyone calls me Jimmy. What gave me away, as a soldier I mean?"

"A few months-old buzz cut, and an insistence on calling me 'ma'am' despite the fact that I can't be more than 5 years older than you. Where did you serve?"

"Iraq. Two tours." Jimmy's face closed up tight.

Dani was anxious to turn the conversation, aware of the younger man's discomfort.

"You seem to know food," she commented, pulling his attention back to her.

"Yes, ma'am. I guess you could say that. I was raised behind the counter at the diner in my hometown, while Mama cooked. She made certain I could hold my own in the kitchen. By the time I was 15, I was working the line and helping with the weekend baking."

"Sounds like a pretty good setup."

"It was, until my stupid ass, pardon my language ma'am, decided I should go see the world and serve my country. Joined up with the marines and.....well, here I am."

"I'm going to get nosy. Well, nosier I suppose. Why aren't you back in the kitchen with her, now that you're home?"

"Mama passed away while I was deployed. Never sick a day in her life, then goes and has a heart attack six months after I leave. I wasn't there for her. That kills me. I just...I just can't go back there." He swiped at his eyes as if he could erase the welling tears.

Dani nodded taking it all in. Every impulse was telling her to trust this young man and take a chance. Every impulse, except for the very large lump in her throat reminding her that the last time she had trusted a man, it had gone very, very badly.

Her heart still hadn't recovered from that breach of trust, but she couldn't change who she was just to avoid the difficult things in life. She was a helper, and when she felt called to help, she was going to do it. If she ended up disappointed, well that was life. She had many other instances where helping someone had filled her soul and repaired her heart. She saw an opportunity to help this young man and she meant to act on it.

"Do you mean it?"

"Mean what, ma'am?"

"Your sign. Will you work for food? I can't guarantee much of a salary up front, but I can guarantee some damn good food."

"You don't know a thing about me, ma'am. Begging your pardon, but I'm not a good bet for long term employment. I've got problems..."

"Jimmy, believe me. I think you'll fit right in. If you're willing to try, the job is yours. I need help in the kitchen getting my restaurant off the ground. You need a flexible understanding boss, and that's me." She wrote down her name and the address of the café on a scrap of paper with her phone number. "Think it over. If you're interested, come on by for a tryout. We'll see if we can work together."

Jimmy stared at the scrap of paper in his hand with disbelief. "Thank you, ma'am. Even if this doesn't work out, this is the first bit of hope I've had in a long time...And damn if it doesn't feel good."

Nodding at the fresh smile beaming out of his young face, Dani replied, "Trust me. Show up. I've got a good feeling about this." With a parting wave, Dani made her way to her car grinning until her cheeks hurt. It was a very good day.

TWENTY-FOUR

NICK WAS NAILING thin lauan plywood to the front of the new island he'd built to separate the dining room from the kitchen, when he was interrupted by a knock on the front glass. A young, somewhat scruffy man stood there, shuffling his feet and keeping his gaze averted.

Flipping the lock, he swung the door wide.

"Can I help you?"

Looking up, the young man instantly reacted to Nick's stance and tone. He straightened his spine, pulled his shoulders back, and met his gaze head on.

"Yes, sir. Miss Dani told me to come by about a job?"

Just then, Dani came from the back.

"Jimmy! You came! Oh, this is perfect timing. Nick this is Jimmy. He's going to be helping me out. I just bought my first batch of groceries to begin experimenting with larger scale production. I set it up with the VA to bring the meal over for their evening group therapy session. I figure it's good advertisement."

Nick caught the surprise on Jimmy's face at mention of the VA. Dani noticed, too.

"I guess I should fill you in on our mission. The Sunshine Café is going to be a place where people can come to get a good meal cheap. We are going to serve meals family style, with two options at lunch and one at dinner with multiple sides. Everything needs to be healthy and balanced. Good simple food for good people on a budget. I want people to feel like they are eating in a friend's home. I want to target the vet community: the older vets living on a fixed income, and more recent vets struggling to readjust. Everyone needs some comfort and sunshine, and that's what I can offer."

The young man just gaped at her.

"Is that something you think you'd like to work on?" Dani prodded, and Jimmy struggled to answer.

"Yes, ma'am. I'd really like to try. I don't want to let you down though." Nick recognized the shame and doubt that clouded the younger man's face.

Dani touched the young man's shoulder and waited for him to look into her eyes. "Didn't I mention an understanding boss? Just be open with me, and I'll do what I can." The young man stared at her for a moment, then blinked and nodded. Nick recognized that look. It was disbelief that someone was willing to take a chance on someone so unworthy. He'd worn it a few times himself in the face of Dani's generosity. Her open heart was just one of the many things he loved about her. Was he any closer to deserving another chance? It was a question he asked daily, and could not fully answer.

When Dani realized that Nick was standing there watching them intently, she shooed him out front.

"Go on. You've got a counter to finish. OK, Jimmy. Let's get cooking!"

Marveling over just how much goodness Dani managed to share with complete strangers, Nick got back to work. Eventually, he would install the new countertop, but he wanted to get the base finished before the custom curved counter arrived from their supplier. His time in the workshop had brought a shine back to his rusty skills. He spent happy hours designing and refining the counter. He'd also constructed her coffee bar area to mirror the design of the island, and one of the dining tables that needed to be an awkward size to fit right. He proudly put his personal stamp on the café. The simplicity and peace he felt working with his hands, knowing it was all for her, lulled him into a happy rhythm.

Before long, delicious smells drifted out of the kitchen and broke his concentration. With his stomach growling impatiently, he wandered back to investigate.

Dani and Jimmy stood side by side, facing the stove, though the young man was the one tending the pot. Nick sniffed his way across the room.

"What smells so good?" He came up behind Dani, deliberately placing his hands on her hips as he peeked over her shoulder. He kept it short, aiming for friendly, but even that brief contact flared his needs. He wanted her to be OK with his touch, and frankly, he had little will power to resist. He couldn't seem to stay away.

"Jimmy made a batch of his Mama's Chicken and Dumplings as a trial. I'll need some extra hands in the kitchen if I'm going to be running this place, too." She ladled heaping bowls for Nick, Jimmy, and herself. Nick inhaled the steam rising from the bowl cupped in his large hands, and quipped, "If it tastes half as good as it smells, you're hired!"

"Excuse me! I believe that's my call," Dani laughed. "But he's right, Jimmy. This smells divine."

"Like I was saying, Mama always hits it with some fresh parsley and thyme right at the end for a burst of fresh flavor without having to add too much salt. I could do that next time." Jimmy rambled, jittery nerves shaking in his voice. He watched

Dani anxiously as she took her first bite. Nick watched Jimmy, ready to jump into the situation if necessary.

Dani closed her eyes and hummed as the flavors burst on her tongue. Nick almost groaned. He remembered that look on her face. He'd seen it once before but he'd been in no state to appreciate it. God he hoped she'd give him another chance. He shifted his attention to Jimmy out of self-preservation, wondering if the boy had noticed the same thing he had. All he saw was rapt attention and nerves. When Nick deemed the boy calm enough, he turned his focus to the bowl in his hands. Normally, the hearty dish was a bit heavy or too thick, but this broth was lightly creamy and herby. The dumplings were perfectly steamed, light and fluffy, little pillows of buttery goodness floating on top.

Nick continued shoveling the delicious food into his mouth, heedless of the scalding his tongue was receiving. Dani put the bowl down, extended her hand, and simply said, "You're hired. Now sit down and eat."

With a whoop of excitement, Jimmy bounced on his toes, grinning from ear to ear. He shook her hand like a man pumping for water in a drought. His joy was infectious, and Nick couldn't help but return the grin, when the phone rang.

"Excuse me," Dani said, as she hustled to answer the line in the office.

"So," Nick switched to friendly but firm interrogation mode as soon as she was gone. "What's your story, Soldier?"

Jimmy's grin faded, and he just shrugged his shoulders in response.

"OK, you don't have to tell me. But there are two things you should know before you start here. One, I was Army. Handled a lot of shit over multiple deployments. I get it. You can talk to me if you need to. Sometimes it helps. Two, Dani is the real deal. No bullshit. She'd give you her last dime if she thought you needed it. If you take advantage of her, I will break you. You won't be able to run far enough fast enough." His tone dropped from commiserating to menacing, but he got the response he was looking for.

Jimmy's face turned to stone as he replied, "There are two things you should know. One, I would never take advantage of someone. I work for what I need, and I don't appreciate you saying otherwise. Two, my shit is my shit. I am handling it, and it's none of your damn business!"

"Well, we'll see how that goes, but know that you don't have to do it alone if you don't want to." Nick turned to leave the kitchen, placing his empty bowl in the sink as he passed. Turning back he asked, "Out of curiosity, how'd she hook you?"

Jimmy looked up from packaging the meal for transport.

"Chocolate chip cookies."

Nick burst out laughing. "They work every time! Welcome to the team."

Dani came back in and brushed her hands on her apron.

"OK, that was the VA. They're ready to take delivery. When we get back, we can start planning menus. What else can you make?"

Nick sat sprawled on his ugly couch with a cold beer and ignored the baseball game on TV. Seth assumed a similar position. Whiskey came in from the kitchen with a beer and a piece of toast.

"Man, you need to restock your fridge. This is pathetic. If we hadn't brought the beer, it would be empty now." She chewed her piece of toast with obvious gusto.

"I've been trying to keep beer out of the house. It's better that way. I get into less trouble."

"That's fair. But you still need food Nick. When's the last time you went to the store?"

Bella jumped into Nick's lap and snuggled under his chin. Just the thought of the store still set off his nerves. "It's been awhile. I've been waiting until Bella is trained enough to come with me. Besides most days Dani feeds me her practice meals. I'm not starving."

"OK, but you'll ask for help if you need it, right? I'm not going to have to kick your ass again, am I?" Whiskey and Seth had both shown up for him during his therapy sessions. Since they had both been with him at various points of the experience, they had perspectives to share that he had not considered. He knew they had both revisited some painful memories to help him out, and he was grateful.

"No, Whiskey. I'll call if I need you. I invited you here today, didn't I?"

"Yeah, you did and you've spent all of your time texting on your phone. Some friend." She teased, but she had a point. Nick's phone buzzed in his hand and he immediately checked the message. Seth got him with an elbow to the gut as he tried to pull Nick's attention back to the game.

"So, how's the online dating going?"

"Great." Nick quickly tucked his phone into his back pocket.

"Uh-oh! Evasive maneuver!" Seth rolled and tackled Nick trying to get the cell phone back out of his pocket. "What are you hiding? Is she ugly? Is she old? What is it?"

"Jesus! What are you, twelve?" They grappled for a few more minutes before Nick managed to pin Seth and rap his head against the floor. Whiskey watched from her perch on the arm of the couch. "That's for bashing my elbow into the coffee table and being an all around pain in the ass."

"So, who is she?"

"Who's who?"

"Come on! The girl whose messages you're hiding. Is she hot? Are you afraid I'll steal her away from you?" Seth could pester mercilessly when he tried.

"I could tell you, but then I'd have to kill you."

"Ha ha. But really, who is she?"

Nick heaved a sigh. He knew that once Seth had the bit between his teeth, he wouldn't let go until he had the information he was after. It made him a damn good leader of men, but a very obnoxious best friend.

"I'm swearing you to secrecy. Top Secret. For Your Ears Only."

"Now who's twelve?"

"I'm serious. I've worked too hard on this to have your big mouth fuck it all up."

"Understood."

He looked at Whiskey, needing her agreement too.

"OK, fine. My lips are sealed. Now who is she?"

"It's Dani."

"Seriously? I thought she was still pissed at you. Friends only, and all that." Whiskey took a slow sip of her beer, letting the quiet shock in her statement hang in the air between them.

"She is. She doesn't know it's me."

"Whoa."

Why did Seth look like he'd just been brained by a 2 x 4?

"Yeah, but the thing is I still feel the connection we had. I can't let that go. I just have to get her to feel it, too. Then we can 'meet,' and I'll explain everything."

"Dude, you'll be damn lucky if she doesn't slam the door in your face." Seth shook his head in disbelief.

"What? Why?"

"Because it is dishonest. Look, dude. I don't know Dani as well as you do, but I can't imagine she will be excited about this. You broke her heart when you disappeared without a word. I know you are working hard to rebuild her trust in you as friends. What makes you think she will want someone who lied to her?"

"But..."

Whiskey cut him off before he could defend his plan.

"No woman likes to be lied to. If she can't trust you and your reactions, there's no way she will trust her own feelings for you. Be careful, Nick. Be real careful. I don't want to see you get hurt."

Nick mulled over that possibility silently, taking a deep pull of his beer. He couldn't believe she wouldn't at least let him explain. No, they were wrong. They didn't know Dani's heart like he did. He'd explain, and she'd fall in love with him, and then maybe the ache around his heart would ease up. He couldn't keep his mask up much longer. He loved her and wanted to hold her close and never let go. He needed to have that right again like he needed to breathe. It was getting harder to hide every day.

He found reasons to touch her, like opening the door or bringing her coffee. Every time he did, he felt her flickering response. It was slowly killing him, ignoring his own reactions, but he couldn't resist reminding her that she felt something for him. It was torture to be around her and not with her, but he couldn't seem to stay away. Instead he poured his longing into long messaging sessions as Captain America. There he could share his thoughts and feelings with her in a way he couldn't face to face. No, Seth was being too cautious. He couldn't afford to change course now when his plan was so close to succeeding.

"You'll see," he muttered. "What's the score?" he asked, shifting his attention back to the game, and effectively shutting down the whole disturbing conversation.

TWENTY-FIVE

Mrs. Grady sat sipping her coffee at the front counter, while Dani bopped at the stainless steel workspace in the kitchen assembling a spinach and mushroom white lasagna. Dani was hosting the Wednesday night crew at the new restaurant as a dry run. The counter with a view into the open kitchen had newly reupholstered second hand stools, thanks to Nick's handiness with a staple gun and Olivia's keen eye at a fabric clearance sale. The bright sunshine yellow and white chevron pattern really popped against the navy blue that Dani had painted the bottom of the island. Mrs. Grady swiveled in the comfortable new bar stools.

"Nick built this counter, huh?"

The butcher block topped counter replaced most of the donut display cases that had dominated the front room. Removing the large wall of bins opened the kitchen to the dining room. Dani could keep an eye on the flow out front, while she was busy cooking in the back.

"He did. Isn't it gorgeous? He laid my new wood flooring, too." Dani cast a critical eye over her café and approved. She'd succeeded in turning a strip mall donut shop into a welcoming home.

Dani wiped her hands on the towel tucked into her apron before reaching into her pocket to check the chiming message on her phone. She laughed out loud before dropping the phone back in her apron pocket and turning back to her lasagna. She started humming and dancing to the music in her head, as she layered noodles, veggies, and béchamel sauce.

"So, who's put that wiggle in your hips?" Mrs. Grady teased.

"Hmm?" Dani's head jolted up, and then she realized she was grinning like an idiot. She had been mentally composing a funny rejoinder to the text that Captain America had just sent her. Blushing, she turned her head back to the task at hand before answering.

"Oh, no one you know."

"Really?" Mrs. Grady sounded disappointed. "What's going on with Nick?"

Jolted from her happy thoughts, Dani asked herself the same question. What was going on with her and Nick? He was always around, always willing to help. He'd done most of the demolition for the café himself, and had borrowed Seth to knock out the added construction. *That* had been a fraught weekend. Stella had come by just to watch. Testosterone bouncing off the walls, inside jokes and teasing between the two army buddies, sweaty t-shirts sticking to shoulders bunching with the effort of building a new frame and seating island, had all combined to leave Dani...itchy. Her dreams had been filled with large capable hands building *her* up to an explosive release.

Even though she'd stipulated that friendship was the only possibility for their future, her stubborn hormones hadn't gotten the message. They still flashed her to red alert whenever he passed into her personal space. It felt like he was always under foot, opening doors, a casual hand on the waist or the shoulder when he entered her space. She doubted he noticed how she tensed up whenever his hand came to a rest on her nape, sending tingling goose bumps chasing down her spine. Though he was driving her crazy, she couldn't complain. He'd been a helpful friend, and nothing more, as promised.

In his every word and action, he projected the caring friendship they were working towards. She continued to crave his touch, his attention, his kisses, his... well, her naughty voice had many opinions on the subject. The guilt and shame ate at her. Why couldn't she just accept that this man wanted nothing more than to be her friend? Why did she have to ruin things by wanting more?

It took a conscious effort on her part to not hijack their interactions and take it to a primal level. When he was on his back under the counter, installing her new sink and plumbing out the disposal, she'd pictured herself straddling those taut hips and riding him to completion. When his tool belt tugged the waistband of his well-worn blue jeans low enough to reveal the chiseled indent of his abs disappearing lower, she had to silence the voice that urged her to kneel down and lick him. Right. There. At the end of a long day at the stove, he would stand behind her and rub the knots in her shoulder with his firm fingers and warm palms, releasing the tensions she'd stored in there throughout the day. Dani ordered herself to relax and accept the gesture of friendship as it was intended, but the tension merely shifted from her shoulders to the pit of her stomach as she willed herself not to turn around and kiss him senseless.

Adding to the load of guilt weighing heavily on her mind, Dani felt disloyal. Here she was lusting after one man who still held a place in her heart, while flirting with another online. Was it cheating if you wanted two men at the same time? Well, not literally at the same time, but they both took up space in her heart and she was having a hard time reconciling her own feelings on that. True, she hadn't actually met Captain America, but they had regular "dates" scheduled to chat online, and she really felt like she'd made a solid connection there. He was funny, insightful, and charming. She found herself looking forward to their online interactions as much as she would a physical date. They had even begun to get a little more risqué in their exchanges. She needed to give the Captain a real chance. She had her shot with Nick, and blew it. He wasn't interested in trying again. She needed to move on as well. She should be ecstatic that she'd found someone else to talk to so easily.

Still, she hesitated to meet him face to face. What if something went wrong and changed the dynamic? What if he was another Felix? OK, there was no way he was a Felix, but what if she disappointed him and he pulled away? She was relying heavily on him for support as she tried to ignore her urges for Nick and get her restaurant up and running. She didn't think she could bear it if she lost his support now.

Pulling herself from her thoughts, she answered Mrs. Grady.

"What's going on with Nick? He's doing great. He's in a really good place, considering everything that's happened. He hasn't had an episode in weeks. But we are just friends. That's what we agreed on, and that's what he's been. I don't think he's interested in anything more."

"Piffle! I don't buy that for a minute, but we'll leave it for now. If not Nick, who's got you blushing at your phone?"

Feeling her ears go warm, betrayed by her blush yet again, Dani giggled. Giggled, for God's sake, like a sixth grader who just got passed a note from the boy she liked. She supposed, in a way, that's exactly what had happened.

"Just this guy I met online. We haven't even talked in person, but I feel like we've been friends for years. There's something compelling about him. He's funny, and sweet, and supportive when I need a boost. He always seems to know just what to say."

"Well, he certainly puts a smile on your face."

"That he does, Patty. That he does... I'm so excited. Are you sure that no one minds coming down here for Wednesday dinner? I know it's a bit of an inconvenience to get everyone out of the building..."

"Are you kidding? Sunny, we've all been dying to get into this place! We want to support you, and you need to practice in this kitchen. I can't tell you how grateful I've been that you've been keeping my freezer stocked for the dinners on top of getting all of this up and running. Believe me, we are honored to be your first guests."

"OK, OK, I'll stop worrying! I'm just so nervous and excited. I can't believe that the grand opening is next week!"

"You are ready. This place already shines, and I know you've got that kitchen organized to the last inch. Helen would be so proud." Dani looked over at the picture of her aunt featured prominently on the "Memory Wall." The young woman smiling at the camera, dressed in her Navy dress blue uniform radiated excitement and confidence. Dani had always marveled at the resemblance. As she turned from putting the lasagna in the oven and came to the island to give Patty a tight hug.

"What you're doing here is special, Dani. I'm proud of you, too."

"Oh, now I'm going to cry!" Dani laughed through the tears choking her throat. "Go round everybody up. I'll see you in an hour. And thanks Mrs. Grady, for more than you know."

Dani turned back to look at Aunt Helen's picture in pride of place on the wall, and whispered, "Here goes nothing! Wish me luck."

Promptly at 6 o'clock, the regular Wednesday crew arrived for dinner, with a few extra welcome faces. Patty Grady led the charge, followed by Jack and Joe. The Colonel escorted Mrs. Betancourt in and got her seated at the long table. Jimmy held the door for everyone, and then followed them in and headed back to the kitchen. Dani firmly turned him around and pushed him back out front.

"Tonight, you are a guest. I want your honest opinion. So, go sit and mingle. Meet my friends. Relax and enjoy! I don't want to catch you hiding in the kitchen tonight!"

"Yes, ma'am." Jimmy laughed as he found himself seated between the intimidating Mrs. Grady and the Colonel, who leaned over to whisper, "Her bark is worse than her bite."

"Which one?" Jimmy replied.

The bell on the door jingled, as Nick, Whiskey, and Seth came in to join the group. Bella followed them in and settled behind Nick's chair.

"I hope we're not late!" he called back to her in the kitchen, as they took their seats at the table.

"Nope, you're right on time." Dani came from the back carrying a tray of garlic rubbed bruschetta topped with fresh tomatoes, basil, salt, and olive oil. She set it down in the middle of the table. "We are still waiting on the girls."

"I'm here! I'm not late!" Stella swirled into the room, enveloping Dani in a cloud of perfume and a massive hug. "And I'm starving! This looks divine!" She reached for a piece of toasted bread before taking her seat. Olivia and Jamie followed her in, and took two of the remaining seats, after each giving Dani a quick hug and kiss. Dani was ecstatic that her friends from different areas of her life had all formed a tight bond so quickly.

"We all drove over together, and we actually left on time! But I swear we hit every single light on the way over here! I hope we didn't hold you up."

"Not at all, you're just in time. Sit and enjoy! I'll be back in a few with drinks and the salad."

Dani made introductions around the table, and everyone settled into easy conversation. Stella still refused to talk to Nick, pointedly avoiding any conversation with the man sitting across from her. On the whole, though, everyone was comfortable. Dani swirled back into the kitchen to finish prepping. They were sharing jokes and funny stories by the time she came back bearing the small glasses of ginger ale.

Raising her own glass, Dani cleared her throat.

"Thank you, everyone, for coming tonight. It means a lot to me that the first meal I serve in this restaurant will be to my nearest and dearest friends. I also want to thank you for the support each of you has graciously given me as I've worked to get this place up and running. I couldn't have done it without you." Getting choked up by the love she saw reflected back at her around the table, she finished quickly. "To Aunt Helen and The Sunshine Café. May we bring a little sunshine into your day!"

"Here, here," chorused around the table.

The Sunshine Café was officially open for business.

"So, Nick, how's everything going at the apartment?" Jack Delano asked from the end of the table.

"All good. I got the drywall fixed like you showed me."

"It's easier to do once you've seen it done. And when you've got that many holes to patch, sometimes it's just easier to replace the whole panel."

"Why were there holes in your walls?" Olivia asked. Her face showed an innocent interest.

Dani watched Nick turn in on himself. An awkward silence fell over the table. She knew he'd had rages before he left for therapy. He'd had significant repairs to make, but all of that was behind him now. He was doing so much better. She hated to see him hurting like this, so she dove into the gap to change the subject. She'd protect him if she could.

"So, Olivia, have you tried the San Jose Singles site yet?"

"I set up a profile, but I swear there aren't any guys on there for me." Olivia followed the conversation away from the treacherous edge. "I think you found the only keeper. Ugh!"

"What do you mean Dani found a keeper?" Mrs. B. perked up across the table. All eyes turned to Dani, expecting her to elaborate. Well, she'd opened the door. She might as well step through it. This would be her first solid step to put her feelings for Nick behind her.

"I met a guy online and he's pretty terrific." She glanced at Nick to see how he was taking this news, but he seemed remarkably calm. Was he smiling? She couldn't tell for sure because he was keeping his head down. Was he happy for her or was he laughing at her? If she'd needed any more confirmation that he didn't care about her as more than a friend, she'd just gotten it. If he still wanted her, no way would he be grinning that she'd moved on. Unable to explain why that truth hurt, Dani embraced it and moved through it.

"His name is Captain America, and he is really funny and sweet and kind. He's been such a big support as I've been getting this place opened."

"Why didn't you invite him tonight?"

"No offense, but meeting the whole family at once isn't my idea of a great first date."

"First date? You mean you haven't met the guy?" Seth asked and then grunted. Did Nick just elbow him in the ribs?

"No, I haven't, but we've been dating regularly online for a few weeks now. I wanted to get the opening of the café behind me before I added anything else on my plate. But I'll meet him soon. I really like the guy." This last she said directly to Nick, but he wasn't even paying attention. He was reaching behind his chair for something.

"Dani, can you come with me into the kitchen for a minute?" Nick held a large wrapped rectangle in his hands. What was that all about?

"Sure. You can help me bring out the salad and lasagna." She followed him back behind the counter. The open concept afforded little privacy, but at least the distance made it harder to hear exactly what they were saying.

"Listen, Nick, about this dating thing..." He put a finger on her lips and the words died in her throat. How did he do that? How did he scramble her wits with a single touch? It wasn't fair.

"Dani, I'm happy you've found somebody who can give you what you need." He let his finger drag down her chin before letting it fall again. It wasn't her imagination that he stared at her lips a second longer than he needed to. "I didn't call you back here for that. I wanted to give you this."

He laid the large rectangle on the stainless silver prep table. She tore the wrapping paper away to reveal a two foot by two foot walnut cutting board with inlaid maple stripes. In one corner, the logo of the café had been burned into the surface. The smooth and well oiled wood felt like silk as she ran her hand over the surface.

"Where did you get this Nick? It's gorgeous."

"I made it."

"You made it? You made this gorgeous cutting board from scratch?"

"I wanted you to have something from me to say good luck."

"But Nick, you already helped me so much, the counter... the bar..." Her words were failing her in the face of her surprise.

"Dani, you have supported me through so much. I wanted to do the same for you. That's what friends do, right? Now, every day when you are chopping whatever needs chopping, you'll do it on the board I made you, and you'll remember that you've always got a friend in me."

She leaned in and gave him a hug, too overcome to reply. Damn him. How was she supposed to move on when he kept doing sweet things like this? She'd just have to set up a date with Captain America. Once she had someone else in her life, someone who could help her take care of some of these physical needs, she'd be able to keep her reactions to Nick in the friend box. Yes, that's just what she'd do. He had worked hard to get himself well enough to be her friend, the least she could do was hold up her end of the bargain. It would work. It had to, because this was a friendship she refused to lose.

TWENTY-SIX

Monday morning at 11 a.m., Dani opened her doors to the public. She had a freezer stocked with emergency meals. The one remaining cooler was packed with Olivia's freshly baked fruit pies and coffee cakes, and her own famous chocolate chip cookies. The backside of the island was open to shelves stacked neatly with napkins, plates, coffee mugs, and silverware. She had cooked her way through her nerves all weekend, and now all she could do was wait for someone to arrive. The shredded napkin on the counter top was a casualty of the panicky thoughts running rampant in her mind.

When Jimmy stepped up behind her and put a hand on her shoulder, she yelped and the napkin bits shot into the air like confetti.

"Don't worry, ma'am. People will come. You'll see."

"I know, Jimmy. I know. I just can't wait until they do. If this doesn't work, I'll start back over from nothing again. I don't know if I can do that."

"Did you hear what you said? You didn't say you'd be back down at nothing, but that you'd start over from nothing. That's the key. Of course, you can, ma'am. But I don't think that's going to be an issue." He pointed out the window.

There was Nick leading a procession of vets coming straight down from the VA. Dani began laughing and crying simultaneously. He came up to the counter as the twenty guys of varying ages found seats together around the large tables. Dani ran from behind the counter and threw her arms around his waist, squeezing tight.

"Thank you!"

Nick dipped his head just slightly and leaned into the hug. It took real effort to let go and keep it friendly. Damn. She had to get better at that. Maybe she should have a no touching rule.

"You'd be surprised how many guys are just hanging out over there. I invited everyone within hearing to go out to lunch on me, and the place emptied out!"

"You are an amazing friend! Thank you! I'd better get moving." She pulled out of his embrace reluctantly and hustled out to the tables to explain how the restaurant worked and take drink orders. She'd certainly have to think about new rules later. Right now she had work to do!

Nick took his seat next to one of his new buddies from the therapy group, when a hand clapped on his shoulder and a voice spoke quietly, quite close to his ear.

"If you hurt her, you won't be able to run far enough fast enough." Jimmy fixed him with a glare.

Nick had the grace to flush. The young man had clearly seen through his careful mask. Confident his meaning was clear, Jimmy hustled to the kitchen to get plates for everyone.

Adam reached over and shook his hand, then gestured to the table that was clearly a custom build.

"This the one you were talking about building?"

"Yep. I built the table, the counter, the seating bench, and the island in the back."

"You do nice work, man. Listen, I've got this shop over in Berkeley, and people are always asking me to do custom jobs. If you want, I could send them your way, maybe bring you in for consultations."

Surprised at the man's generosity, he focused on his hand as he smoothed it over the reclaimed pine he'd lovingly stained and sanded for Dani.

"Why would you take a risk like that on me?"

"Because we all need somebody on our side. Besides, these pieces are gorgeous. You'd be doing me a favor." Was he ready to risk himself? He looked around at the shop. Dani had risked it all and look how it had turned out. She was so damn brave. If he wanted to be worthy of her, he needed to find his own bravery again.

"It's a deal," Nick said, reaching out to shake the man's hand again. "Thanks."

Seth chimed in.

"Hey, if you're ready to start working more seriously, Dad's got a list a mile long. He keeps asking about you. Seems our higher end clients are loving your work in our portfolio. I'm sure I could work it out so you could do your freelance stuff in our workshop, too."

"You're a good friend, Seth. You tell your dad we can talk about it. I think it's about time." Nick's grin split his face. His future was beginning to look brighter for the first time in ages. He still had to get through the evening without touching Dani like he wanted to, but solid progress was worth celebrating.

By closing time, Nick had officially reached the end of his tether. Letting go of Dani's hug earlier had been difficult. But when she had collapsed onto one of the stools at the bar happily exhausted, and it had been nearly impossible not to bundle her up in his arms and carry her home. His protective streak was being put to the test with not interfering as she ran herself down getting the restaurant opened.

Enough. He had to make his move. He couldn't take her out on a date to help her relax, but Captain America could. As he settled on his couch with his laptop, he ticked off all the reasons that this was a good idea. Dani needed a fun night out. She said she really liked him. She deserved to know the truth. And it was all utter crap. This was about him being selfish and wanting to have her in his life with no restrictions. But he was going to do it anyway. He didn't think he could keep up the charade much longer. Something was going to slip.

He opened up his browser and logged into his profile. It was nearly their normal chat time. There was already a message waiting for him. She must have written to him from the café to share her day with him. Warmth spread through his chest. Seth was wrong. She already cared for him. This would work.

SunnyD: I did it! We opened the café today! I was so worried, but it was amazing! A ton of people dropped in just to see what we had done to the place, and more than half stayed for lunch or dessert and coffee. We had such positive feedback from everyone! My feet are killing me, but I've never been happier!

CaptAm: I'm so proud of you! That's fantastic news. I wish I was there, so I could rub your feet for you. :)

He sat back to wait for her to respond. It was the first time he'd ever expressed an interest in being near her. He wondered how she'd take it. Within minutes she logged in, her profile chiming as she checked her messages. He toggled back over from checking the baseball scores, to see what she'd say.

SunnyD: I wish you were, too. I would pay good money for a foot rub right now.
CaptAm: You sound happy, but tired, too. I know you've been working really hard on opening the restaurant. When's the last time you took some time out for yourself?
SunnyD: I have down time, like right now talking to you.
CaptAm: I meant, time out, like going for dinner. Maybe with a friend.

Nick waited as the silence stretched painfully. What was she thinking? Had he moved too fast? Was she even interested in meeting him? Blessedly, the three little blinking dots signaled that she was typing a response to put him out of his misery one way or another.

SunnyD: I go out with friends all the time.

She wasn't making this easy for him. He tried a more direct tack.

CaptAm: Maybe with me?
SunnyD: What are you suggesting? :)
CaptAm: I'm suggesting that you have dinner with me. I feel like I know you so well. I want to celebrate with you. How does Saturday night work?

SunnyD: Saturday would be fine, but I have a ton of prep to do for the café Sunday morning so it can't be a late night. Where do you want to meet up?
CaptAm: There's this great restaurant downtown, Rafaelli's. I could pick you up around 7?
SunnyD: Ooh, I've heard that place is fantastic! But let's meet there.
CaptAm: OK. 7 at Rafaelli's.
SunnyD: I guess you'll need to know who to look for. I have blond hair and blue eyes. I'll be wearing a coral colored dress. How will I know you?

Nick's mouth began to water remembering just how amazing she looked in that particular dress. Stoked that she'd responded so positively, he thought for a second before replying.

CaptAm: I'll be carrying a bouquet of flowers, to celebrate your success. I can't wait to meet you. Well, I should let you get some rest. I know you'll be up early to head to the restaurant. Sweet dreams.
SunnyD: Sleep tight, Captain.

Pleased that the final phase of his mission was in motion, Nick logged off and turned in for the night. He settled into his bed, and pictured Dani doing the same thing across the hall. She slipped into his bed with him as he drifted off to sleep. She often kept him company in his dreams, where he could play out any number of the fantasies that tortured him during his waking hours. But tonight was different. In his dream, Dani climbed into his bed, spooned in front of him, and fell asleep. He wrapped his arms around her, keeping her close to his heart, and fell asleep too. Incredibly, this dream was even more tempting than his sexual fantasies. He craved the right to just hold her close and show her his love. Victory was near. He could hardly wait to make his dreams his reality.

TWENTY-SEVEN

Friday night, Dani crossed to the door of the café and turned the lock with a sigh of relief. She turned to the Memory Wall and laid a hand on Aunt Helen's picture.

"We did it, Aunt Helen. We really did it. I had to scramble a bit. We ran out of coffee on Wednesday, and on Thursday I had to throw extra pans of mostaccioli straight from the freezer into the oven when a counseling session let out at 6:30, and everyone came on over for dinner. We packed the house that night."

She pushed in chairs as she continued to the back.

"But overall, I'd call us a success! I've got regulars, Aunt Helen!"

Dani did a little happy dance, thinking of all the faces that had come through her door that week, many more than once. Slowly but surely, Dani could see the community she had hoped to build coming together. She watched strangers sit down for a meal next to each other and share dessert as friends. Conversations flew fast and furious around her tables and warmed her heart.

"I've got to stock up the freezer again, and ask Jimmy to take on more of the baking, but today was a good day."

These were problems Dani was happy to have. Her legs were aching, and her shoulders were full of knots. But her soul was glowing, and her heart was happy. She had done it. With her aunt's meddling, she had pushed herself off the path and found her calling. Giving the frame a quick polish, she smiled. The crushing grief was no longer so unbearable. She had a part of Aunt Helen with her everyday, in the form of the café. That empty ache in her chest had been filled by the bustle of other people who needed her. Memories of her aunt still popped up at odd moments throughout the day, but they brought peace instead of sadness.

"I miss you, Aunt Helen. But I know that you're up there keeping an eye on me as always. Thanks for giving me a push. We really did something special here."

With a soft smile, she walked out the back door and locked up for the night. As Dani strolled the few blocks home, she turned her thoughts to her date. What would Captain America look like? An image began to take shape in her head. He'd be tall, like the hero in the movie, and have strong arms and hands that could hold the weight of the world's problems. Golden brown hair cut short and finely honed features encasing deep brown eyes flashed into the image before she could stop them, and she realized whose face had just entered her fantasy.

She wasn't even surprised by it. Her dreams had not subsided. In fact, they'd grown hotter and harder for her to ignore. Every innocent touch drove her overwrought system crazy. But he didn't want her. He had been very clear about that and even after weeks of working close together he hadn't so much as tried to kiss her. He was moving on. It was time she did, too.

She really hoped that Captain America lit a similar spark in her. It would make life so much easier if she could feel this attraction for someone else. She trusted Captain America, perhaps more than she should given that she'd never actually met him. Still, she knew him so well. He was sweet and funny and honest and supportive. She was ready to try for new relationship, maybe even a new love. She had found her purpose professionally, it was time to find someone special to share her heart.

SATURDAY EVENING ARRIVED TOO QUICKLY. Her baking had held her up at the restaurant longer than she'd expected. Thankfully, Nick had been absent, and she'd been able to concentrate fully on her recipes, but a bad batch of blueberries had slowed her down. She rushed home to shower and change, adding an extra fifteen minutes to her routine to attempt to blow-dry her curls with a diffuser. Date makeup took another ten, and walking in the sky-high pumps that made her ass look amazing in the clingy coral dress, slowed her down even more. She sent a message via the app and hoped he would check it before thinking she was standing him up.

By the time she parked at Rafaelli's, she was a solid twenty minutes late and hoped that Captain America hadn't given up on her.

She entered the restaurant and approached the hostess.

"Hi, I'm meeting someone special tonight. I'm running late though."

"What is the name on the reservation?"

"Um,..."

The hostess leaned closer and whispered. "Are you here for Captain America?"

Dani nodded and giggled.

"Well, Sunny D, you are a lucky woman. That man is...well,

let's just say if you hadn't shown up, he wouldn't have gone home alone." Dani had to laugh.

"Sorry to disappoint, but if he's going home with anyone, it's going to be me."

"Let me take you to his table. Right this way." Dani followed the hostess as they wove their way through the tables to the very back of the restaurant. She spotted a bouquet of sunflowers resting on the table, overhanging the edge of the booth. Dani rushed past the hostess in her eagerness to meet him. She could just see the top of his brown hair and the sleeve of his suit as she came up behind him. She slid into the spot across from him, fairly bouncing with excitement.

"Hi, I'm so sorry I'm late. I'm..." She trailed off into silence, her jaw having gone slack, as she looked up and saw Nick Gantry sitting at her table.

"Hi. You must be SunnyD. I'm Captain America, though it feels a little foolish to be saying that out loud." Nick took her hand in his, gave it a squeeze. "Please, don't panic. Give me a chance to explain."

"What are you doing here? How did you...?" As her voice returned, it rose higher and higher in disbelief. Dani was unable to complete any of the questions swirling through her head, and fell back gracelessly into the booth seat. Shoulders down, she shook her head, feeling completely stupid. Tears for her own foolishness and naive trust welled in her eyes.

"Dani, it's me. It's just me. Shit! Why didn't I listen to Seth and Whiskey? Dani, please don't cry. I'm sorry. I just..." Nick broke off.

"Is this supposed to be funny? Is this a joke to you?" Dani's initial shock was giving way to anger at his betrayal. "Did you sit in your apartment and laugh with Seth and Whiskey? 'Poor Dani can't even get a date online. Watch this.' You have all been lying to me! For weeks!"

Nick reached for hand, "No, Dani! Honestly, I..."

"Honestly? You can sit there and try to make me think you know the first thing about honesty. Well here is some honesty for you! I thought I was finally had chance to meet someone who might think I was special. But no. Instead it was you. Lying to my face all day while I poured my heart out to you online, and you just led me right along! What the hell kind of 'friend' does that? How can I trust a word coming out of your mouth?"

With that she turned and slowly walked away from him, head held high, in her too tight dress and murderous heels, every step pulling her heart further from her chest. She had to walk past all of the other tables, wondering if they'd heard her meltdown. But she made it out the door before the first tear fell.

Nick lowered his head to his arms on the white linen tablecloth in defeat. The other patrons, who had clearly heard every word out her mouth, tried not to look at him. Even the waiter had the decency not to approach the table to fill the water glass again.

She hadn't seen it. She hadn't seen that she was special to him, no matter what the hell his name was. She hadn't even given him a chance to explain. He was an idiot. God, Seth was right and he was never, never going to live that down. He'd tried to win by tricking her. It seemed so obvious now. He betrayed her trust. The trust that she gave so freely.

He had to fix this. His spine straightened as his resolve returned, lifting his head off the table. He wasn't about to scrap the whole project because of one bad cut. He'd take her measure again, and make sure he said the right things this time. He could fix this. He'd spent too much time building up her trust to just throw it all away. He'd leave his heart at her feet. Then she could decide if she wanted to stomp on it or pick it up. He pushed away from the table, leaving a generous tip for the waiter who'd let him sit there for half an hour without ordering, and hustled home to catch Dani before she went to sleep.

TWENTY-EIGHT

DANI CAREFULLY LOCKED the door behind her, hung up her bad news date dress in the very back of her closet, and pulled on her comfiest sweatpants and softest t-shirt. She tugged her hair back into a messy bun and scrubbed every trace of makeup from her face. Then she calmly walked into her living room, opened her laptop, and erased her dating profile. She was numb, moving in a bubble, where the outside world couldn't reach in to hurt her. Not yet. She closed her laptop and her eyes, curling into the protective comfort of her couch. She poked her thoughts where they hurt the most, willing more cleansing tears to come.

She was alone. Again. She wanted a hug from Aunt Helen to soothe her and make it all OK again, like it had when she was a girl. She wanted a cuddle from little Taco to make her smile. She just wanted to feel that she was special to someone. Was it too much to ask? Why had he tricked her? Tears continued to stream quietly down her face as her pity party reached full swing. She got up to get her favorite couch blanket and heard his footsteps in the hallway. She froze as his distinctive tread beat a warning down the hallway. She listened intently, waiting for a slamming door to signal that he'd gone inside.

Instead she heard a bump and slide that sounded like a very large man sliding down her door to sit on the floor in the hallway. Great, now I'm trapped. She heard a scratch and whine. He'd brought Bella into this? That was low. She was waiting with baited breath for his next move, when he cleared his throat and began to sing. His clear tenor filled her apartment. She had not seen that coming.

"You are my sunshine, my only sunshine. You make me happy, when skies are grey. You'll never know dear, how much I love you. Please don't take my sunshine away."

The sweet song pulled the tears back to her eyes and set her heart aching because she wanted it to be true. She leaned on her door and slid down to sit on the floor of her entryway. She tipped her head back and rested it against the door with her eyes closed. For just a moment, she let herself dream that it was all true. That this man refused to be pushed away. That he loved her and wanted her in his life. That everything he said online and everything he did in real life stemmed from respect and love.

SIGHING DEEPLY, and listening to her subconscious, she turned her thoughts to Nick and Captain America. Dani could still feel the sting of his words as he said, "There's no one special!" She deserved to be someone special! She couldn't settle for less. But when she looked at how he'd behaved since returning from rehab, she certainly felt special. He had gone out of his way to help her with the restaurant instead of finding work elsewhere. He'd spent several weekends building pieces for her. He had given her emotional support when she'd needed it, and yet he'd respected every boundary between them.

Her heart nearly burst with bittersweet happiness. That

was exactly what she had wanted: the man she loved, the man who turned her knees to jelly with a single glance, the man who made her laugh out loud in an empty room, the man who had just the right thing to say to help her get through a tough day, the man who knew her inside and out and loved her anyway. Two men rolled into one.

Was she projecting her own feelings onto the actions of a friend? Could she forgive the lies? Could she risk her heart again to find out? But the reality was that she didn't know how he felt. Lowering her head to her knees, she gave up trying to understand and just let the sound of his voice wash over her.

When the singing stopped, Dani picked up her head and tried to convince her body that it was time to get up from the floor. Nick's voice coming through her door halted her.

"Dani, I hope you can hear me. I'm sorry if my surprise hurt you. I'm sure you'd like to be alone right now, but I am not walking away from you. I can't." She heard the conviction in his voice. "How can I walk away from my heart? Dammit, Dani, can't you see it when you look at me? I meant what I sang. I love you, Dani." Dani gasped. Had she really just heard that? Nick voice became softer, "I wanted to say that to your face the first time. I know I broke your trust, but that's not what I meant to do. Quite the opposite. I was working for a second chance."

She heard Nick shift as his head tapped against the door. Dani held her breath as she waited to hear what he had to say. When he continued, his voice was stronger, "The whole month I was away, I worked hard every day. I laid myself bare in that counseling room. I pushed myself to face my fears and my memories because of you. For you. For us. You are so damned special. It scared me, because I knew I wasn't good enough for you. Hell, I'll never be good enough for you, but it turns out, I don't care. I can't let you go. That guy you fell for online? He's one hundred percent me. He could say the things that I wanted to say to you during the day and couldn't. You wanted us to be friends, and I needed that too. You're my best friend, Dani, and I would hate to lose that, but I need more. I need to be your lover, your protector, your confidante. I need your laughter and love. I need you. Dani, SunnyD, by any name, you are the light that makes the rest of my day shine. I love you."

DANI SAT STILL on the other side of the door. Her mind had caught on one salient point. Nick loved her. He thought she was special and wanted her in his life. Captain America, the guy she'd grown to like and admire through words, was the same as the man she'd fallen for physically. The irony of her earlier thoughts was not lost on her. She had the perfect package: a physical attraction, an intellectual equal, an emotional connection. Nick's actions paired with Captain America's words suddenly made all the sense in the world. All she had to do was be brave and trust that this love could be real. That was the sticking point. Could she risk it all one more time for love?

Nick was still rambling on the other side of the door. She was no longer paying attention, but it gave her time to think, knowing he was still there waiting for her to respond. She looked at her sideboard where she had family pictures on display. She saw the love her parents had shining in their faces on their wedding day. She saw her grandmother in a pair of shorts and a kerchief, sitting on her grandfather's knee, arm around his neck, in front of their porch back in the day. The confidence in her eyes showed that she knew she was exactly where she wanted to be. Her family had plenty of love stories to point to, but how could she be sure that this was the beginning of hers? She looked at Aunt Helen's picture, and whispered, "How can I be sure?"

As she sat there, she recalled Aunt Helen's stories of her husband, Alfred. They had only been together a few months before he was called to war and never came home. Aunt Helen had been crushed, but she'd never regretted marrying him for a second. Nothing in life was a sure bet. She couldn't be sure. But would she regret not taking a chance on him? Yes. Likely forever.

But the lie, the trust... She had trusted him with her body, and he'd pushed her aside. That had hurt her deeply even though she understood why. She was afraid to trust him with her heart in case something bad happened again. What if he had a PTSD relapse? What if he changed his mind? What would he do?

What had he done this time? He hit rock bottom, picked himself up and got the help he needed. He had chased after her as both friend and lover to convince her that he was worth loving. He hadn't given up on their relationship like she'd thought. He'd found a way to build it back stronger than ever.

Well, when you looked at it that way, it made a lot of sense. Did she value their relationship enough to fight for it, too? She tried to imagine her life without him in it, not as her lover or as her friend, and it was too painful to bear. Of course, she still loved him. It was her turn to take a risk and jump in. There were no guarantees in love, but it was worth the risk. Having someone in the world wanting to show you how special you are was worth the risk. And she did. She loved him. In the end, that was the only thing that mattered.

DANI TUNED BACK in to what Nick was saying on the other side of the door.

"I don't know why I said what I said. Maybe I was scared of

what you made me feel, or how out of control I was. Maybe I just didn't want to cheapen our story with my asshole friends, but it wasn't true. There's never been anyone more special than you."

Drawing in a deep breath for courage, Dani abruptly opened the door, and Nick fell backward knocking his head on her hardwood floor.

"Say it again."

"You're someone special," he groaned from his prone position, holding his head.

"No, not that part. The really important part. The part you wanted to say to my face."

Nick rolled to his knees and pulled her down to join him. He cupped her face gently in his hands, and said, "I love you, Dani Carmichael. I love you, and I need you, and I want you like crazy." He leaned over to kiss her, but she blocked his lips with her hand.

"Nick, you hurt me. But then you helped me, and held me, and healed me. I love you, too. I need you in my life. Sometimes I want you so badly it hurts. Is this real?"

"As real as it gets. God help me, if I ever give you reason to doubt me again." He kissed her forehead, her nose, and finally her lips. He drew her close and she lost herself in the sheer pleasure of kissing him slowly. She let out a low moan as he tortured her, melting her with his tenderness. Pulling back, he looked into her eyes. What did he see there?

"Marry me, Dani. Be the someone special in my life. Give me another chance."

Shock froze her mind for a minute. Nick mistook her silence for doubt.

"Shit, I'm doing this wrong again. We shouldn't be on the floor," he muttered as he pulled her up to her feet. "Hang on a minute." He spun away into his apartment, leaving Dani staring after him. He returned, holding a plate of lumpy, half-burnt oatmeal raisin cookies.

"Hi, I'm your new neighbor Nick, and I was wondering if we could start over." Dani laughed until tears ran down her face.

"Did you make those yourself?"

"I did. I had Mrs. Grady supervise." Dani sampled a cookie, and he took advantage of her silence.

"Marry me Dani. I love you. When I look at you, I see us married, having kids, growing up, and growing old. I see us together in twenty years with our kids going off to college, and in fifty years snuggled up on a porch swing. I see my future. I know I don't have a lot going for me right now, but that'll change. I..."

Dani halted his babble of raw emotion again with her soft fingers gently covering his mouth.

"Say that important part, just one more time."

"I love you, Dani Carmichael, and I always will."

"I don't think I'll ever get tired of hearing that." She moved into his arms. Bella swarmed the cookies that hit the floor, forgotten by her humans.

"Do you want to hear me say it in a church?"

"Yes, I do. I love you, Nick Gantry, and I want to start over with you as many times as we need to get it right."

EPILOGUE

THE LATE SUMMER heat was brutal. The sun beat down on the tar roof of the Sunshine Café, making it feel like the entire kitchen was an oven. Dani regretted having to turn the ovens on at all, but she needed to fill her freezers before she took off next weekend for a Girls' Night Out event. Nick and Jimmy had assured her that the place would not burn down without her. Given the current heat in the kitchen, she wasn't optimistic. She whisked the eggs with the cheddar cheese and milk, before adding cubed ham and broccoli. The massive bowl would fill two full trays. She'd already done 4 double batches. This was the last one. She poured the mixture into the two greased pans and popped them in the ovens with a groan as more heat blasted into the room.

She wiped the sweat from her forehead with her apron, and chugged water from a now lukewarm bottle of spring water. As soon as these crustless quiche were done, she could shut down the kitchen for a bit and put her feet up. Since they'd expanded their hours to weekend mornings, she'd been run off her feet. Jimmy was proving to be a godsend, but she didn't want to overload him. Once they'd worked out a tentative truce, he'd taken

Nick up on his offer to tag along to counseling sessions. He was a new man. Dani didn't want to do anything to threaten his hard won growth. She needed to hire more help, and soon. She made a note to ask Nick to ask around at the VA if anyone had kitchen experience.

Tugging her frizzing hair back into a fresh ponytail, she washed her hands and went out front to see what needed clearing. Something always needed clearing.

"Stella? Olivia? Jamie? What are you doing here? Did I get the weekend wrong? Oh my God! I'll run home and pack right now. I'm so sorry."

"No, no, Dani, relax. We just came by for a meal. Everything is set for next weekend. You're still coming, right?"

"Yes, Nick and Jimmy are kicking me out. Are you all going to be there?"

"Sadly, I can't make it. I got booked to do a series of 'real life' makeovers on Ellen and they need to film them as soon as possible." Jamie's shoulders dropped. "But you guys go and have a great time. I promise I'll make the next one."

"I'm already packed and ready to go." Olivia grinned from ear to ear.

"Of course you are. I will pack ten minutes before I have to leave and we will still get there on time." Stella teased her new friend. "Come on, let's go find a seat."

"I'll be right out to get your drink orders." Dani dashed back into the kitchen, to prep their plates, and ran into Nick, Seth, and Whiskey coming in the back door, with Bella hot on their heels.

"Hi guys!" She gave Nick a quick kiss hello. "This is quite a surprise. The girls are out front. If you're here for lunch, I'll get you set up in just a minute."

"We'll just go on out and grab seats." Whiskey took Seth by

the arm and Bella by the leash and pulled them both into the dining room.

"Hey. Did you drink enough water? You look flushed." Nick took her face in his hands, a move that never failed to make her heart stutter. "You need to take better care of the woman I love."

"I was just getting to that when everyone showed up. Will it make you happy if I take a lunch break and eat with our friends?"

"Dani, you make me happy. Period." He pulled her in for a kiss that made the warm kitchen behind her feel like the Arctic in comparison. When he stepped back, the room spun and Dani wondered if she was dehydrated or demented from the power of that kiss. "Why don't you go out front and sit down now? I can prep the plates." And with a push he nudged her back out towards the front of the café.

She looked up as she cleared the counter to see she had a full house! They were going to be slammed when the noon counseling meeting let out. Looking closer, she realized it was all family. Her friends and Nick's had taken one of the round tables. Mrs. B., the Colonel, Jack, Joe, and Patty had gathered around another, and were joined by Antonio and Eleanor Valenti. The biggest surprise was finding her mom and dad, sister and brother-in-law, and their three girls arranged around the long rectangle table! They'd come down from Seattle! It wasn't her birthday, was it?

"Come here, honey. Sit with us." Her mom patted the empty chair next to her and Dani automatically obeyed. How did moms do that?

"I can't believe you're really here. Welcome to the Sunshine Café."

"We're sorry we couldn't make it for your opening, but we are here now. It's lovely, Dani. We are so proud of you." Her dad pulled her into a hug, and she didn't even mind how sweaty she was. His bear hugs were one of the things she missed most, and she'd take as many as she could get while they were in town.

"Why is everyone here? What's going on?"

"We were invited." With a smirk, her sister Jen refused to say more. Brat.

Before she could pester her any further, Nick cleared his throat. He and Jimmy stood backs to the counter, with two huge trays of chocolate chip cookies.

"Dani, the last time I did this, I was rushed and ill prepared, not to mention terrified." Bella came and sat by his leg with a gentle lean, supporting him as his voice wavered. "I'm hoping I can do better." He moved forward to set the trays of cookies down for everyone to enjoy, removing one from the top before continuing. He held the cookie up to her.

"Dani, you stole my heart with your smile and your chocolate chip cookies. I am hoping I can do the same. You are the light in my life. When I was lost in the dark, when I couldn't see that I was worth fighting for, you showed me a reason to fight. You brought me into your life, and gave me more family than I ever expected to have. Everyone in this room has felt the shelter of your love and compassion. We are better people for knowing you. None more so than me. I love you Dani, and I'm going to spend the rest of my life proving that to you, in word and deed." He handed her the cookie. "Will you marry me?"

Dani looked down at the cookie, but couldn't see it through the tears in her eyes. She blinked frantically, and realized that pressed into the top of the cookie, was a diamond solitaire ring. She looked up at Nick, eyes wide. The poor man looked like he was about to burst from nerves, but she couldn't find her words. They were trapped in her chest beneath the heart that had swollen so suddenly from the unexpected outpouring of love. The best she could do was nod and leap into his arms. It was clear enough.

Everyone that she loved most in the world was in that room, cheering for their happily ever after. She couldn't believe he'd pulled this off.

Nick took the ring out of the cookie and slid it on her finger.

"It was my mom's. It took me awhile to get it out of storage." Dani admired the way it sparkled on her third finger, a symbol of their love and trust.

"I love it, and I love you, Nick. But the next time you want to surprise me in front of everyone we know, could you let me at least take off my apron? I'm a mess." His belly laugh filled her soul with happiness. She could spend a lifetime teasing that joy from him. In fact, that sounded like a pretty good plan.

"You're perfect, sexy dress, hot mess, just the way you are, Dani, apron and all." And he kissed her in front of their family to more applause. "Now, 'Get Lucky Cookies' for everyone."

She looked around the room again at all the loving faces surrounding her and felt very special indeed.

ACKNOWLEDGMENTS

Note: In this book Nick takes his rescue dog to a place called Operation Freedom Paws to train her as a PTSD service dog. This is a real organization in San Martin, CA, doing fantastic work for Bay Area veterans. If you are interested in their mission or feel the urge to help them out, you can find them here: http://operationfreedompaws.org/

This book has been true labor of love. Through many, many revisions I have been blessed to have an amazing team on my side. The Legends: Cheryl, Lorey, Ashley, and Lissa, thank you for being my unflagging cheerleaders, and partners in sarcasm. The Sassy Bitches: Layla, Victoria, & Allyson, thank you for write-ins and laughter and panicked deadline edits. To Sarah MacLean and Eloisa James, thank you for both taking the time to encourage a new writer who was out of her depth. To Cherry Adair, thank you for your mentoring, your Finish the Damn Book Contest, and the best advice ever: Butt in Chair, Hands on Keyboard. Thank you to the Old School Romance Book Club, for being my safe place to take a break from the drama of my story and real life. You have been waiting patiently. I hope you like it! A big thank you to my editor, Jennifer Graybeal, and my cover designer, Lee Hyat, for working under tight deadlines to help me make this the best book it could be. To my girlfriends, for giving me the friendships and foundations that give me strength, whether you are next door or on the other side of the world, thank you. There wouldn't have been a Girls' Night Out without your influence. To my mom and dad, for flying around the world to chase your grandchildren, for pushing me out the door so I could hit my word counts, and for all of the sacrifices you've made for me growing up and still today, thank you. I love you more than I can say, and I am sincerely sorry for the cranky teenager who crashed in my room from age fifteen to eighteen. Karmic payback is on its way. To my daughters, who celebrate my writing news with dance parties and ice cream cones, thank you for understanding why mommy leaves to work and panics when you mess with her laptop. You are my heart and the reason I write. To my husband, J.R., who has supported me in this, even when it was just a dream. You said, "If you're going to do it, you should really do it." Here I am, really doing it, babe, and I couldn't have gotten here without you. Thank you for being my partner in the incredible life we're building and for a shot at this dream.

Someone Special is Book 1 in the Girls' Night Out series. I hope you enjoyed it.

Girls Night Out Series:
Someone Special
Second Chances
Three Strikes
Forever Nights

If you'd like more information about upcoming release dates, purchasing options, or joining my newsletter, please visit my website www.4evamoore.com.

I also love to connect with my readers on Facebook. You can find me at www.facebook.com/4evamoore

Please consider leaving a short review on Amazon if you enjoyed this book. As an indie author, your support makes a huge difference. Thank you!

Made in the USA
San Bernardino, CA
16 March 2019